ECHO

ECHO

Alicia Wright Brewster

DRAGONFAIRY PRESS
ATLANTA

ECHO

This is a work of fiction. All characters, organizations, and events portrayed in this book are products of the imagination or are used fictitiously.

Cover design by Georgina Gibson
www.georginagibson.com

Published by Dragonfairy Press, Atlanta
www.dragonfairypress.com
Dragonfairy Press and the Dragonfairy Press logo are trademarks of Dragonfairy Press LLC.

First Publication, April 2013
Trade Paperback Edition, April 2013
Trade Paperback ISBN: 978-0-9850230-2-7

Published in the United States of America

Library of Congress Control Number: 2012951596

To my sister Kenya,
for inspiring me.

CHAPTER 1
COUNTDOWN: 10 DAYS

Has it started?

This was my first thought every morning for the past nine months—ever since they'd told the public about the Vision, and about their plan. My pulse pounded in my ears. Red numerals blinked from the handheld communicator on my bedside table.

10:04:21

Ten days, four hours, twenty-one minutes until the end of all things we knew—or so the Vision said. The Council had warned us they'd cut it close. They would make every second count. And after all the seconds had been used up, they would rewind time and give it another shot.

I hoped the rewinds had started. They'd probably waited too long. It would be too late to change things.

A red alert light blinked on the communicator. My heart stopped beating and dropped into my stomach. I accepted the incoming message and watched text scroll up the screen:

"Ashara Vinn: We are now in the fifth timeline, after having performed four time rewinds. Based on your performance in the last timeline, you have been assigned to the Ethereal task force. Please report to the Council building immediately."

The *fifth* timeline?

They'd said I wouldn't remember what happened—only the elders would remember everything—but I hadn't expected this. I'd gone to bed yesterday in the original timeline, and now it was the fifth. That meant I'd experienced these last ten days four times already. And apparently, the Council had failed to avoid the end of the world each time, or else the rewinds would have ended.

I tapped the communicator against the table and checked it again. *Damn thing must be malfunctioning.* The Ethereal task force, it said—as in, a task force of ether manipulators. But I *wasn't* an ether manipulator. I scanned the message a second time to make sure I hadn't imagined it.

The red light blinked again as a new message arrived. It displayed on the screen: *"Immediately."*

I leapt out of bed and froze in front of my dresser. What did people wear to the Council building? It would have helped if I knew exactly what I'd be doing there. I didn't think I had any business clothing or dresses, at least none that I could locate. Perhaps casual would be more appropriate anyway. More versatile. Plus, it was burning up outside.

I yanked a sleeveless top and lightweight shorts from the dresser. I belted the waist and hooked my comm unit to the belt. Before leaving my shared bedroom, I kissed my six-year-old sister, Sona, on the forehead.

The soft sounds of my parents' snoring floated into the small hallway. Mom would have wanted me to wake them, but I couldn't bear to. She'd had so much trouble sleeping in the past nine months.

The Vision had hit her harder than anyone. Sometimes I caught her muttering curses about the Council, especially the head elder. And then my brother, Pace, died . . . If Mom was sleeping now, I wouldn't wake her.

On the way out, I grabbed a brush from the bathroom and ran it through my dark hair a few times before tying the unruly curls into a ponytail.

At the doorway, I breathed in the smell of fresh air and flowers. The two suns had broken above the horizon, bathing the sky in red and yellow streaks.

I broke into a jog and raced through my home cluster. The wooden houses sat close together, separated by lawns and the occasional tree. Dirt walkways meandered through the grass, most leading nowhere in particular. I ignored them and made a straight path toward the edge of the cluster.

I dodged small children being ushered from their homes. Many of them yawned or rubbed their eyes with tiny fists. If their parents had assignments, these kids would be headed toward the community recreation center. My chest ached knowing they wouldn't be with their parents during these last ten days—just like I wouldn't be with mine now that I was going to the Council.

Most people in Vallara weren't assigned anywhere. The Council had claimed they wanted us all to relax and spend time with our loved ones. With some exceptions, most adults with assignments were scientists, fighters, sociologists, and all kinds of doctors. The others had nothing but free time now. School had shut down. Manufacturing had shut down. And now my family and others spent their days together without school or work commitments.

I hadn't been assigned before now. I was supposed to spend these last days with Sona and my parents, who had also made the "unskilled" list.

Now I was off that list and on the Ethereal task force.

I tore my eyes from the kids and steeled myself against the ache in my chest. We all had to make sacrifices for the good of the whole. The Council always stressed this.

It took me only a couple minutes to reach the widest dirt walkway inside the cluster and, from there, only a minute more to reach the low wooden fence marking the edge of our community.

A sleek black transport idled just outside, directly in my path. Its capsule-shaped body hovered several inches above the ground, emanating a steady hum. Beyond the tinted windows, a silhouette reclined in the backseat.

I moved to detour around the vehicle. The driver-side window slid down, and an impassive gentleman with hair graying at the temples peered out at me.

"Ashara Vinn?"

I slowed but didn't stop. "Yes. That's me."

"Get in." The vehicle door slid open. "I'm your Council transport."

When I hesitated, he repeated his command, this time louder. "*Get in.*" He pointed upward to the sky. "We have no time to waste."

I resisted the urge to look where he pointed. Numbers representing the countdown had been continuously projected in the sky for the past nine months—as if we needed a constant reminder other than our comm units.

The weight on my chest lifted a bit when I saw who was in the backseat—my distant cousin and best friend, Rey. We'd grown up together, since our mothers were so close and gave birth to us only two months apart.

"It's okay, Ash. Get in." As usual, Rey's sleek dark hair was pulled back into a ponytail. His olive-skinned face shone with excitement.

"The trip is forty miles," the driver said. "Eight minutes. We should arrive at the Council just in time for the morning briefing."

Rey scooted to the other side of the vehicle, and I slipped in next to him. I tackled him into a tight hug and squeezed, letting his familiar arms comfort me. The door whirred as it closed, and the transport shot off toward the Council. Despite the dirt road in this region, the ride was smooth as the vehicle skimmed above the ground.

I finally released Rey from my hug. He chuckled and patted me on the back. His brow furrowed. "You're going to the Council?"

"Looks like it." I searched the inside of the door for a window control, but no switches marred the smooth metal surface. I raised my voice and called to the driver, "Will you put the window down please?"

I couldn't help feeling excited to ride in a Council vehicle. I'd read about them at the University, a school for anyone over the age of twelve. But being unskilled according to Council standards, I never expected to ride in one.

The window glided down. I leaned away from it, expecting the wind to batter me at this speed. But the interior of the vehicle remained just as still as it had with the window up. I inched my head outside and felt little more than a soft breeze.

I peered downward. The vehicle's flat, wheelless bottom flew just above the ground. A Breather transport. The driver, a Breather, was an air manipulator displacing the air to move us this fast. Twelve years ago, when Rey had first discovered *he* was a Breather, he spent a month chattering nonstop about getting one—as if he could afford a piece of equipment like this.

Rey had applied for a position at the Council once a year since the age of thirteen, but they hardly ever accepted unknown recruits. Most Council members belonged to families that had been involved with the Council when it formed, almost two centuries prior. The Vision apparently changed that, because the Council publicly asked all elemental practitioners—people who could manipulate the elements—to register their abilities. Rey had been the first one in line to do so, and he'd been recruited along with the few other practitioners I knew.

Rey shouldered me to the side and stuck his head out the window along with mine. "It's amazing, isn't it?" He leaned his body farther outside.

"Hey!" I grabbed him around the waist and anchored him to the seat. "Could you not do that? You're going to give me a heart attack." He pulled his torso back inside. "And you know you have a window on your side too."

"Yeah, but I can't annoy you from over there." He flashed me his lopsided grin. My mouth twitched though I tried not to return the smile. That trademark grin of his, along with the shining dark hair, had proved a winner with the ladies in the past few years. He was like a brother to me, but even I couldn't resist a smile when he gave me that grin.

My stomach lurched as I caught sight of the trees rushing past us beside the road. I'd never moved this fast before. My insides didn't appreciate it.

I pulled my head inside the vehicle. Rey and I leaned back in our seats, and the window slid up into place. For a few minutes, we sat in silence in the backseat. I twisted my fingers in my lap as Rey mutely examined the interior—which was odd for him since I usually had to beg him to shut his mouth.

Our driver stared straight ahead, his back stiff. I wondered if everyone at the Council was like that. Cold and detached. They'd always claimed there was nothing hush-hush going on behind their doors. They worked for the people, protected the people. They also set rules for elemental practitioners. Those rules had never concerned me since I *wasn't* a practitioner.

But the way the Vision was announced—after the Council's plans to deal with it were already under way—I now wondered how much I really knew about this allegedly benevolent body of practitioners and scientists.

"So you're going to the Council?" Rey asked again. "I thought only elemental practitioners were supposed to be there today."

My pulse sped up again, just when I'd gotten it under control. "I'm on the Ethereal task force."

"You're an *ether* manipulator?" His mouth dropped open. "Wow, okay. How come you're just now telling me this?"

"First of all, we don't know that. It's probably a mistake. And second, I got the message just fifteen minutes ago, on my comm."

"You've been in this transport for almost five minutes. 'Ethereal task force' should have been the first words out of your mouth. This is how the conversation should have gone: 'Hi, Rey. You look remarkably handsome today. Guess what. I'm on the Ethereal task force.' Just like that."

"I have a lot on my mind."

"Like being an Ethereal?"

"I don't think so. I'm probably just helping with their organization or something."

"Oh, that must be it. They pulled your school records, and based on your numerous courses that have absolutely nothing to do with politics or leadership, they decided that *your* organizational skills were unmatched."

I scowled at him. "Sarcasm is not nice."

He snatched my comm from my belt and hit the recall button twice until the message I'd received first thing this morning scrolled across the screen. "Based on your performance in the last timeline? What does that even mean—you displayed Ethereal ability?"

I shrugged. "Or I demonstrated some kind of leadership skill that would be useful to the group."

He raised a skeptical eyebrow. "You're eighteen. They have elders and experienced practitioners to handle leadership roles. The only reason you'd be assigned to that task force is if you're an Ethereal."

I kept my face blank and pretended not to agree with him, but I'd been thinking the same thing. Either I was an Ethereal, or someone high up at the Council thought I was. My entire body felt light, like this was a dream.

Elemental practice didn't run in my blood. Rey inherited it from his father, the side of his family I didn't share blood with. I wasn't supposed to be anything, let alone an Ethereal. I hadn't been trained. I didn't even have a working understanding of the science behind it. Rey, on the other hand, had been practicing and basking in the semi-fame that came with his Breather ability for the past twelve years.

I hung my head between my knees for the remainder of the trip, concentrating on breathing evenly, and definitely *not* panicking.

CHAPTER 2

Our transport coasted into High City, the most urban area in the province of Vallara—although nowhere near so populous as what our ancestors had left on Earth-One. We passed several multistory buildings of concrete, metal, and glass. A few other structures were wooden, but larger than anything in my home cluster. Here, the wooden exteriors had been stripped and stained, while most of the houses in my cluster still wore the bark of the trees that had made them.

People milled through the streets; some on foot, a few in wheeled black vehicles. We whizzed past so quickly that I didn't have time to study them. It had been years since I'd been inside a city. We had few of them on Earth-Two, and no others as big as this.

We entered a green oasis, surrounded by a circle of manicured trees isolating the space from the rest of High City. A paved road led up to the Council building, cutting through concentric circles of gardens. The building sat by itself in the middle of the oasis.

The transport slowed and stopped. Outside was the stark-white rectangular structure that headquartered the Council.

I stared up at the three-story building. My fingers curled around the armrest. At a knock on the window, I jumped in my seat. Rey stared at me from outside the transport, his hand poised to rap on the window a second time. I loosened my white-knuckle grip and slid the door open.

Despite the warmth of the two suns shining just above the horizon, I shivered in the shadow of the Council. A light breeze lifted my ponytail off my neck. Rey nudged me from behind, and I realized I was dragging my feet. As much as I wanted to run screaming in the opposite direction, I pushed forward.

A crowd of around fifty people clustered in front of the steel fence that circled the building. From their clothing, I could tell they were Believers. They wore their full ceremonial garb, some in red robes and some in yellow. The robes represented the red sun Ra and the bright yellow Solaris, which they worshiped as gods.

Believers didn't spend much time in High City, since it represented everything they found wrong with Nonbelievers. If there was any place in the world that rejected their gods more, or relied more completely on technology, it was High City. Mostly, we Nonbelievers stayed in our towns, and they stayed elsewhere in theirs.

It didn't take long to figure out what the Believers were doing here. Most of them held signs: "Let the Gods Decide," "We Welcome the End," "Know Your Place."

A redheaded teenager, probably only a couple years younger than Rey and me, held a sign that read, "Leave Our Planet." I shook my head at that one. This was almost as much our planet as it was theirs. The Believers' ancestors had been the first to leave Earth-One for Earth-Two. They'd been the immensely rich few who were willing to give up their earthly possessions for an interplanetary adventure. Upon arrival, they'd immediately adopted the two suns as their gods.

The ancestors I shared with Rey had followed only fifty years later, in the group that had won the lottery to come here. Fifty years hardly gave the Believers full rights to an entire planet.

Besides, they were the ones ready to abandon Earth-Two to whatever was threatening it. Let the gods decide? And if the alleged gods decided to kill us all, we should just happily go on to the afterlife—if there was one? Leaving all this up to some imaginary gods didn't seem like the logical choice.

Rey shoved people aside and muscled us through the crowd to the gate. I thought he might have pushed the redheaded teenager a little harder than necessary. The kid stumbled out of our way as we pressed forward. I wrapped my hands around the vertical rungs of the gate and peered inside. The crowd of Believers closed in behind us.

The double glass doors to the Council building opened. A tall man with dirty-blond hair stepped out. From twenty yards away, his eyes met mine.

Loken.

For only about the hundredth time that day, I fought to maintain control of my emotions. Loken's lips pressed into a tight line as he approached, stern as usual. Instinctively, I stepped backward, crushing the toes of a small woman standing behind me.

"No respect for anything, you people," she shot at me with a glare.

I glared right back at her.

"You know," the woman grumbled, crossing her arms over her chest, "the whole point of coming to this planet was to get away from all the unnecessary tech on Earth-One. All the smog. All the fumes. Get back to nature." Her voice rose to a shout. "But you people care nothing about the gods or the land! You destroy. You control. You . . ."

She continued her rant, but I tuned her out.

When Loken reached the gate, the latch popped open. The gate rolled to the left, leaving just enough room for one person at a time to enter. I slipped through, followed by Rey. The volume of the Believers' mutters and occasional shouts increased. But many of them shuffled backward under Loken's hard stare.

"Rey. Good to see you," Loken said, his voice flat.

He and Rey shook hands and exchanged grim-looking smiles.

He turned his attention to me. It had been nine months since Loken had broken up with me after almost a year of dating. His duties came first, he'd said at the time. His hair had grown since then. It fell to the nape of his neck now and was shaggier than he used to keep it. I liked it.

For the most part, Loken's face looked the same now as it had when we'd dated. Same defined cheekbones, same wide-set gray eyes, same full mouth. He used to smile with that mouth a lot, but not now.

"Hello, Ashara," he said.

I grunted instead of responding. It stung to hear him call me by my formal name, instead of "Ash" or "Asha."

"I didn't expect things to go this way," he added, shaking his head.

"What way?"

Loken waved for Rey and I to follow him toward the building. "I expected you to be out of danger during this whole thing. It kind of defeats the purpose of . . . other choices we made."

"You mean choices *you* made."

Sunlight glinted off something on the right side of Loken's face. I looked closer. A thread of metal, a couple millimeters wide, made a swirl design at his temple. The metal tattoo inched down the side of his face and neck and disappeared into his shirt collar.

I grabbed his arm to hold him in place, and touched the side of his face. My light-brown skin contrasted with the soft tan of his. His cool skin chilled my fingertips—even cooler than I remembered.

"What have you done to yourself?" I asked.

He removed my hand from his face. As he did, light reflected off his forearm. I grabbed his wrist before he could pull it back. Turning the forearm over in my hands, I traced the metal tattoo with my fingertips. It swirled and twisted over his arms after emerging from his shirtsleeves. On the back of his hands, it matched the lines of his most prominent veins. On the front, it followed the creases in his palms.

Loken was a Bender, a metal-manipulator, and he felt more whole with metal nearby. He'd told me so a hundred times. I knew he took his practice seriously, but this seemed a bit extreme.

He let me examine him at first, just stared at me with gray eyes that were like the sky during a storm. Something fluttered in my chest. Loken yanked his arm back and resumed his walk toward the front of the building, this time at a faster pace.

"It was necessary," he said.

When we reached the door, he held it open for me. "I'm going to lead your task force, Ashara. The others will be led by elders, but Elder Ethereal is otherwise occupied. The elders thought it would be best if I took an active role in your training, since I have some knowledge of how you think and what learning styles might work for you."

"They couldn't find an Ethereal to lead the group?"

"All members of the Bender task force are well trained, since they came into their abilities when they were kids. They don't need me for training, and they have Elder Bender to lead them. You, on the other hand, need the best trainer the Council can give you." He gave me a pointed look and then led us down a long hall, around a corner, and toward a back corner of the building.

I squinted until my eyes adjusted to the glaring white lights overhead. My nose wrinkled at the overpowering smell of cleaning supplies in the hallway. Not a scuff marred the white walls. I made a point to walk down the dead center of the hall, careful not to touch anything in this eerily clean building.

In soft tones, a female voice emanated from the walls, barely audible: *"Please stay calm. Remain calm. Please stay calm. Remain calm."* I suspected it was meant to be reassuring, but it made me want to bolt back to my home cluster. People only ever told me stay calm when there was a legitimate reason *not* to be.

"So I'm an Ethereal?" I dreaded the answer in the pit of my stomach.

"Why else would you be here?"

"I told you," Rey whispered.

"Shh." I jabbed him with my elbow. "How is that possible? The ability would have manifested by now. And none of my ancestors were practitioners."

"Maybe some were, and they just didn't know," Loken said. "If one or two generations never showed an elemental ability, the knowledge that you had practitioners in your bloodline might have gotten lost."

"Or it was your biological father," Rey suggested. "Was he a practitioner?"

I shrugged. "I wouldn't know. So what will I be doing in this task force?"

"I don't have all the details yet." Loken's mouth twisted to the side in a look that shouted disapproval. "So far, all I've heard is that I'm to retrieve you from the gate and be your team leader."

"What happened last timeline? What—"

“Here we are,” Loken said, pushing open a door at the end of the hall. I hesitated. Rey shoved me into the room.

CHAPTER 3

Over a hundred people were already packed inside, crammed together in tight rows. No one spoke louder than a whisper. Every eye was trained on a low stage in front, where seven individuals stood apart from everyone else.

"What's going on?" I whispered to Loken out of the corner of my mouth.

He jerked his head toward the rows of people and joined the seven others on the stage. Rey grabbed my arm and pulled me toward the back of the room. At over six feet tall, Rey had no trouble seeing over the crowd. At five foot four, I had to stand on tiptoes and still couldn't see much.

With a sharp clap of hands from someone in front, everyone went silent.

"Welcome back," said a solemn female voice. I couldn't locate the speaker through the crowd of people. "You all know the rewinds have begun. This is the fifth timeline." The voice paused as whispers raced through the crowd. "The weight is great on the shoulders of all elemental practitioners—on all of you. I appreciate those who registered for this duty when we asked you to come forward and volunteer. Thanks to you, we now number over two hundred. We believe we've given you the best and broadest range of training available in the last few months."

She cleared her throat. The next words came out in a rush. "But things have gone a little differently than we expected in the previous timelines. We'll need to give you all additional . . . more *focused* training."

As the woman spoke, I inched my way between two people who blocked my view, trying to see her face. The voice belonged to a woman in all black. Her dark-brown hair was twisted back into a tight bun. From the fine lines on her forehead and around her mouth, and her confident tone, I guessed she was elder.

A glance at her waist showed a miniature flame-thrower hooked to her belt. That would make her a Burner, a fire manipulator. The flame-thrower was just for convenience, of course. If she was an elder, she'd be able to generate fire from heat in the air.

The woman continued. "In the original timeline, we suspected the cause of the world's end would be experiments conducted by our own scientists or scientists abroad. Specifically, we suspected that efforts to simulate the Big Bang would be at fault. Although we were able to stop these dangerous experiments, Elder Seer and his associates assured us that we were still on our way toward the end."

She paused and scanned the room, letting her words sink in. A low murmur grew into confused questions, indecipherable with so many people chattering at once.

The speaker waited for the noise to quiet down. "So we performed our first ever rewind ritual. We used all the power we could gather, but we were only able to send us back ten days. And we could only preserve the consciousnesses and memories of the eight elders—the six elder practitioner specialists, Elder Kohler, and Elder Seer. If you have any questions about specific events in prior timelines, please come to one of us. Time travel can have interesting results . . ."

As the woman covered the nuances of time travel, I let my gaze wander, taking in these people I'd work with for the next ten days.

A gangly man next to the female speaker carried several vials of water attached to loops on his belt. A Flooder, no doubt. Behind him stood a petite blonde who also had vials on her belt, except they were filled with dirt. That would make her a Mover, someone who controlled earth. I'd love to be a Mover—to control the ground beneath our feet. That was something I could understand.

As usual, Loken wore his weapons belt slung around his waist. It carried a shortsword on one side and a dagger on the other. The belt was standard issue for a Bender.

As the woman at center stage spoke, Loken unsheathed his dagger. He turned it over and over in his hands. The blade repeatedly lengthened and shortened, and lengthened again. I'd seen him manipulate metal before, but this looked like a nervous habit. Loken didn't watch his hands as he toyed with the weapon; his eyes stayed pinned on the speaker.

Next to Loken stood another Bender, a tall, bulky man whose small eyes stared straight ahead. Like Loken, he too had a weapons belt slung across his hips.

Three people on the stage carried no tools representing their elements. One of them I identified as Elder Seer. The traditional black Seer hood hung over his forehead, hiding his face and expression. Although they carried the elemental practice gene, Seers weren't technically practitioners.

I guessed another man on the stage was a Breather. An air-manipulator wouldn't need any tools, since his element floated all around us. Unlike the others, his face carried a soft, reassuring smile. Rey would be lucky if this man was his task force leader.

Occupying a back corner of the stage, and scanning the room with narrowed eyes, stood Elder Kohler, head of all the Council. I couldn't remember what his element was. His thick gray hair held only a sprinkle of remaining dark strands. It gave him more of a distinguished look than he had several years ago, when he first became the head elder. He'd been in the public eye a lot lately, ever since publicity of the Vision had started.

I couldn't figure out why my mother despised Elder Kohler so much. He seemed polite enough when he spoke to the press. But she couldn't hear his name without scowling or stomping from the room in a huff. My stepfather, Talin, wasn't much better. He went quiet whenever Rey brought him up in conversation.

I wondered if Elder Kohler was an Ethereal, and what tools of the trade Ethereals carried with them. What would someone need to manipulate *ether*? I wasn't entirely sure what ether even was—yet somehow I was on the task force.

When the woman's speech on time travel ended, I focused on her words again.

"In the second timeline," she said, "fights broke out among the practitioners in our ranks. As you all know, we originally planned to have the elders advise the task forces but not be a part of them. In theory, this left the elders free for management duties."

I glanced around the room, trying to determine if anyone else looked as confused as I felt. They all stared straight ahead, nodding along with the speaker's words. How could the practitioners have fought with one another in the second timeline but not the first? They should have behaved exactly as they had before. Right?

"But the task forces needed strong leadership. We assigned the elders to be their leaders halfway through the second timeline. That calmed the infighting. Unfortunately, by the time we had everything under control, it was too late to search out the cause of the end. In the third timeline, we spent the entire ten days researching possible end-of-the-world scenarios."

The woman speaking mopped her forehead with a handkerchief before proceeding. "In the fourth timeline, the elders disagreed about what threatened us most. As a result, we were disorganized, split into factions. It was only toward the end of the fourth timeline that we noticed the Mage migration."

The tension in the room shot upward. Hardly anyone remained still. Feet tapped nervously on the bare white floor. Fingers threaded and unthreaded together. Hands raked through hair. Whispers skittered through the crowd.

I gulped down the lump in my throat. When Rey's arm snaked around my waist, I leaned my head back against his chest and let his familiar smell—like fresh air and soap—comfort me. Still, fear clawed at my insides, threatening to consume me.

The woman gestured toward Elder Kohler and stepped back to let him take center stage. At seeing his impeccable posture, I couldn't help but straighten up and lift my head from Rey's chest.

"As most of you know already, I am Elder Kohler." The head elder's voice came out raspy, thanks to an accident that had burned his neck, right shoulder, and arm years ago. His throat bore a path of scarred skin that dipped into his collar. A miniature microphone clipped to his shirt amplified his gruff voice through the room.

I moved my attention from his throat back to his face. Elder Kohler was staring at something in my direction. I turned to see who stood behind me—a middle-aged man who leaned forward slightly on his toes, anticipating Kohler's next words. I turned back to Elder Kohler. Our eyes met and held.

I dropped my gaze to the back of the person in front of me, but couldn't shake the feeling of being watched.

"As we've discussed over the past months," Elder Kohler continued, "you'll be on the front lines when it comes to avoiding this . . . thing."

I itched to raise my hand and ask a question—a hundred questions. But everyone else, including Rey, nodded quietly. They seemed to understand what he was talking about. I, on the other hand, hadn't a clue what had been discussed over the past months.

Elder Kohler pressed a coin-sized device between his fingers, and the wall to our left dissolved into an image of a list. "Here's how the next ten days will go." A red line underscored the first item on the wall, which read, "Break into groups."

"We'll break out into our individual task forces, led by these fine people." He gestured to the people with him onstage. "Besides me and Elder Seer, each elder will lead the task force associated with his element. With one exception." His gaze shifted to me for a split second, and then went back to sweeping the room. I squirmed. "The Ethereals will no longer be led by Elder Ethereal. Loken will be their task force leader."

The red line on the wall moved downward to the second item on the list: "Training."

Elder Kohler said, "For the next few days, we will be training."

"We've *been* training," Rey muttered at my side.

"I haven't," I hissed. "So shush."

"The training we've done so far," Elder Kohler continued, "has been pretty basic compared to the crash course you'll receive over the next few days. Ever since the Vision, we've planned for many potential circumstances." His face went grave. "We did not, however, plan for your having to fight Mages. You'll all need to learn some new skills."

Mages.

He said more words after that, but their meaning didn't register. The walls crept in around me. My eyes darted about the room, searching for an escape route. My chest felt empty except for the rapid breaths vibrating through it.

I squeezed my eyes shut, but the images invaded my thoughts anyway. For my brother Pace's twelfth birthday, I'd taken him to the community garden just east of town. He loved to play in the fountains, where the water spurted in shapes of birds and geometric patterns. That was the only time in my life I'd seen a Mage.

Tears pooled inside my eyelids. I clenched my eyes shut tighter, refusing to let them fall. Mom and my stepfather chose to cremate Pace. There hadn't been much left to bury.

Rey patted my hand, which was clutched around his arm. I jerked it back. It left white marks where my fingers had pressed into his skin. I swatted him away when he tried to put an arm around me; I didn't want his pity.

I'd had seven months of pity from my teachers and friends already, as they'd tiptoed around poor, traumatized Ashara, who couldn't save her little brother. Poor Ashara, who was unconscious while Council officials dispatched the Mage. Poor Ashara, who was sleeping on the job while her brother was murdered. I hadn't even seen him die.

The Mage had been a Mover, an earth manipulator. Like human practitioners, Mages specialized in particular elements—just like they had when they *were* human, before they lost control of their energy and became monsters. The ground had rumbled beneath our feet as Pace and I ran through the market, trying to escape. Other people scattered around us, but the Mage stayed locked on Pace and me. I stumbled, slammed my head, and everything went black. When I awoke, my brother was gone.

I gritted my teeth and forced my eyes back toward the front of the room. My fingernails grated against my palms inside clenched fists. The pain helped me focus on the present.

"Depending on how you do during training," said Elder Kohler, "you will be regrouped into action teams, each consisting of practitioners with different elemental abilities. Despite the regrouping, you will continue to answer to your task force leaders." He gestured at Loken and the others standing around him. "They will continue to train you and will assign you to certain action teams as necessary. In your action teams, you'll most likely be securing areas where Mage activity is suspected, or you'll track down and kill Mages."

Words tumbled out of my mouth before I could stop them. "We're going to *hunt* Mages?" My voice squeaked at the last word. Warmth flushed over my cheeks. I was just as eager as the next guy—more eager, really—to have all Mages extinguished from our planet. But that didn't mean I was fit to hunt them. I pressed my fingernails harder into my palms to keep my hands from trembling.

Elder Kohler glared at me. For a moment, I thought he would ignore the question. Then he answered, "Yes. Mages are dangerous, energy-hungry beasts. If they come out in public, and we leave them to their own devices, they will slaughter people in the streets. I'm sure *you* understand this." He paused, then added, "If too many of them gather in one place, we have no idea what will happen. Does that answer your question, or would you like to waste more of our time?"

Two hundred faces turned to look at me.

"Yes," I squeaked. "I mean no. I mean . . . that answered it." My voice trailed off to a whisper.

Elder Kohler continued, without sparing me another glance, "We must keep the Mages from converging here in Vallara. We have too many practitioners and too much technology at the Council and at the nearby University. If the Mages were to tap into that energy, the result could indeed change the world we know."

He paused and peered around the room, as if waiting for his words to sink in. "We have some idea of the routes the Mages will take, based on their movements in the prior timeline. Unfortunately, those routes will likely vary from the previous timeline, so we'll have to stay vigilant. Listen to your leaders. Do as they ask."

The practitioners nodded their heads, their faces serious.

Elder Kohler gestured toward the only other man, besides himself and Elder Seer, without an obvious elemental tool on his person. "Elder Breather will lead the Breather task force. Breathers, please follow him out when I dismiss you." Elder Kohler pointed at the others on stage, one-by-one as he introduced them. "Elder Mover, Elder Burner, Elder Bender, and Elder Flooder will lead their respective task forces."

Last, he waved Loken forward. "For those of you who don't know him, this is Loken. He will replace Elder Ethereal as leader of the Ethereal task force." The whispers rose up again. Elder Kohler held up a hand to quiet them. "If you're in that group, Loken will explain the new . . . developments."

Developments? Am I a new development?

"Remember, anything we do here is for the greater good."

Every person in the room, except me, joined together and repeated, "For the greater good."

Elder Kohler nodded. "Dismissed."

CHAPTER 4

My head swam as I trudged after Loken. He led the Ethereal task force around a corner and out the back door. There were five of us other than Loken. Three guys, a girl about my age, and me.

Manicured grass covered the space between the Council building and the back of the surrounding security fence. In the hour since I'd left home this morning, the suns had traveled higher into the sky. I raised a hand to shield myself from their glare.

Loken sat cross-legged on the ground, and the rest of us joined him in a circle. The grass tickled my legs as I folded them in front of me. Somehow, I ended up sitting next to Loken. Our knees brushed together, shooting a warm thrill through my body. I inched closer to the dark-haired man on my other side.

After everyone was settled on the ground, Loken folded his hands in his lap and scanned the group. He examined each of the other members one at a time. I averted my gaze and tried to ignore the flip-flop in my belly when he looked at me.

His eyes had been the first thing I'd noticed about him when we'd met over a year before. A gray that couldn't decide, from one moment to the next, whether they wanted to be dove soft or cold steel. The day we'd met, laughter danced behind those eyes.

He'd taught an *Advanced Elemental Practice Class* at the University. Of course, I hadn't been in attendance. Rey signed up as soon as he had the prerequisites. He and Loken became fast friends, and Rey introduced us when I stopped by after class one time. Loken refused to budge from my side until I agreed to a date.

He broke up with me a year later, which I now knew was around the time the Vision occurred—although it was a secret back then. Pace died a couple months later. Loken tried to be there to help me through it, but I refused to see him. While my world continued to spiral out of control, the Council added to my troubles by announcing the Vision.

Things had been a lot simpler on the day Loken and I met. Pace was alive and well, Loken wasn't obsessed with saving the world, and I wasn't a Mage-hunter.

If we were going to work together, I'd have to grow a tougher skin—stay focused. There were too many memories to sort through. But I couldn't do this job if I was going to fall apart every time I looked at him.

I steeled myself and looked straight into Loken's face. Most of my team members wore smiles, but every single one looked forced. Mine felt painted on my face. Inside, my stomach churned.

"As I'm sure you've noticed, you've gained a couple new people on your team, including me." He touched his own chest and jerked his head toward me. "So let's do some introductions."

"Introductions?" said the stocky middle-aged man across from me. His deep brown skin looked unblemished except for the fine smile lines around his mouth. Dark curly hair was cropped close to his head. "We were all here just yesterday. Except that was what?" He mouthed numbers, silently counting. "Forty days ago?"

That prompted a giggle from a slender girl on Loken's other side. She looked about my age. "Sorry." The girl shrugged. "I laugh when I'm nervous."

Her short, stylishly mussed hair blew around her head in the light breeze, framing almond-shaped eyes. Her skin had a golden undertone that suggested partial Earth-One Asian ancestry. The girl puffed up her cheeks and blew a breath to flip an unruly lock of blue-black hair out of her eyes.

It was nice to see that the rewinds screwed with other people's heads the same way they screwed with mine. Technically, since this was the fifth timeline, the day we thought of as "yesterday" had ended long ago. We'd lost forty days.

Actually, we hadn't lost them. We'd been awake and active, going about our business. I'd been spending time with my family, while the Ethereal task force had been doing . . . whatever it was Ethereals did. We just couldn't remember it. It was like the whole world had amnesia, and we needed the elders to tell us what had happened.

The part-Asian girl wiggled her fingers at me. "Hi. I'm Krin. You are?"

I opened my mouth to talk, but Loken beat me to it. "This is Ashara," he said. I glared at him. If he noticed, he ignored it. "She's been assigned to this group after displaying Ethereal ability in the last timeline."

My eyes strayed to a camera propped on the back of the Council building. If everything had gone as planned, it and other cameras had been recording for the last forty days. The elders, whose consciousnesses had been preserved, would have watched as many of those recordings as possible before the last rewind—recordings that might include me, doing stuff I didn't remember doing, stuff that made these people think I was an Ethereal. It was all too surreal.

"Do we really have time for this introduction thing?" said a blond boy. He looked only a few years older than me, around Loken's age. His fair hair was slicked back off his forehead. He glanced at me and frowned. "We need to get to work. We can't spend our time coddling this little girl. I vote we continue on without her. *As planned.*"

The boy looked around the group, his eyes wide and expectant. From the upward tilt of his chin, I guessed he was used to getting his way. The others averted their eyes. They didn't agree with him openly, but none of them spoke in my favor either.

"That's out of the question," Loken said.

The blond boy opened his mouth to speak again, but Loken's glare shut him up.

"Introductions," Loken repeated, still looking at him.

The blond boy huffed a loud, exaggerated sigh. "Okay, if we have to do this. I'm Elis. Elemental practice has never skipped a generation in my family." He stuck his chin out and stared down his nose at the rest of us. "I discovered my gift when I was three, and I've been practicing ever since."

Krin rolled her eyes skyward. "It sounds like you're very important."

Elis's lips pursed, but he said nothing more.

"I'm Jin," said the dark-skinned guy who'd remarked about yesterday being over forty days ago. He smiled, showing off a deep dimple in one cheek. "Both my brother and I are Ethereals."

Elis's eyes widened and he nodded, impressed. "I didn't know that."

"Is that rare?" I asked.

"Very," said the man next to me, the only other person in the bunch who hadn't spoken yet. He looked to be in his late twenties. Almost as dark as Krin's, his hair was cut short and out of the way, contrasting with shockingly blue eyes. Even in the Dutem season, when both suns graced the sky, he'd somehow managed to keep his clothes unwrinkled and sweat-less. "Less than three percent of practitioners are Ethereals," he continued. "It's rare enough to have two practitioners within a single generation. Two *Ethereals* in a single generation is remarkable. Why isn't your brother on our task force?"

"He didn't register. He's just fourteen and our sister wouldn't let him."

The blue-eyed man rested his elbows on his knees and rocked forward, examining Jin more closely. "I'd be interested in researching your family tree. How many . . ." His voice trailed off and he chuckled softly. "Sorry. Just stop me next time I get carried away with my curiosities. I'm Mauryn, by the way."

I waved in greeting. Mauryn waved back, showing off a red strip of cloth tied around his wrist. Odd, since red was one of the colors the Believers were so fond of. I wondered what it signified on Mauryn's wrist.

All eyes fell on me. I glanced at Loken for a hint as to what I was expected to do, but his expression was as blank as everyone else's.

"Okay." I sucked in a deep breath. "I'm Ashara."

"Ashara *Vinn*?" Elis asked. The disdain had melted from his tone.

"Do I know you?"

Elis shook his head.

Mauryn leaned forward again, the way he had a moment ago when examining Jin. "Most practitioners have heard of you."

I glanced at Loken for confirmation, but his expression remained unreadable. Facing Mauryn again, I quirked an eyebrow upward. "Why?"

"It's not every day that a Mage just shows up in public and attacks children. You must have a strong history of elemental practice in your family. When did your ability first manifest?"

A warm flush crept over my cheeks. Did *everyone* know my story? And what did elemental practice in my family have to do with Pace's death? I hesitated before saying, "I, um, just found out I'm an Ethereal."

"Are you adopted?" Krin asked.

"No. But I never knew my father. I'm guessing he had practitioners in his family." *Or this is all a big mistake, and I have no business being here.* Later, I'd have to press Loken about what I'd allegedly done in the prior timeline that had prompted this new assignment. I nudged Loken's leg with my knee, "Now that we're done with the introductions, do we have something planned for the day?"

Loken cleared his throat and swiped a hand through his hair. "Absolutely. I'm going to give you guys a crash course in Mage-combat."

My vision filled with the sight of my mother. Tears fell, dragging her dark eye makeup in streaks down her cheeks. That's how she looked whenever I went with her to visit Pace's grave. Only this time, in my mind's eye, the name chiseled into the gravestone was my own.

My eyes darted around the yard, first to the fence separating me from the world outside the Council grounds. Unlike the front side of the fence, this side had no opening. The pattern of ten-feet-high silver-colored bars traveled across the backyard and around to the front of building, with no way past except over the top.

I turned the other direction toward the back of the Council building. A woman with a long blond braid over her shoulder leaned against the door to the building. Lean muscle stood out on the arms she crossed over her chest.

"Who's that woman?" I inclined my head toward her.

Loken answered without turning to look. "Elder Ethereal is watching over us today to make sure the transition goes smoothly."

"Why aren't you leading us?" Elis called across the yard to the elder.

Elder Ethereal pressed her lips tighter together. "It's not my job." Her voice came out low, and perhaps with a hint of annoyance. She stayed stock still against the door, but her gaze shifted to Loken.

"Like I said, Elder Ethereal is just observing. You're to address any questions to me."

"Why isn't Elder Ethereal leading us?" Elis asked. "The elder elemental specialists are leading all the other groups."

Krin's lips twisted to the side, like she'd just finished sucking on something sour. "Do you ever just *stop* talking?" She turned to Loken. "With all due respect, sir, can we know why we aren't being led by Elder Ethereal?"

"That's fair enough," Loken said. "The Elders believe that, as a group, you have enough basic training that you don't need an Ethereal to train you. I have as much knowledge as anyone about Ethereal abilities, and I have more experience with new recruits than any of the elders even."

"Has she been reassigned?" Krin asked.

"Yes, of course." A muscle in Loken's jaw twitched.

"Was she reassigned because you were assigned here?" I asked. "Or were you assigned here because she was reassigned?"

The jaw muscle twitched again, and I knew I'd asked the right question. Loken answered through gritted teeth. "She was reassigned because I was assigned here."

Despite months of intense training and discipline, everyone started talking at once.

"Why?"

"What happened?"

"This wasn't the plan."

I'd been involved with the Council for no more than a couple hours, and already I was getting a little sick of these people and their *plans.* I'd much preferred the plan where I spent my last few days with my family, and no one expected me to help save the world. The plan where my mother wouldn't have to cry over another of her children's graves. And I wouldn't have to be *in* that grave.

Loken raised a hand and waited for the group to quiet down. At the same time, he flashed me a cold stare. "Elder Kohler assigned me to this task force because—on top of my education in elemental theory and training—the elders believe I'm best suited to integrate Ashara into the group."

All eyes locked on me, and I tried to shrink into the ground. Sadly, beneath the soft grass, the hard dirt would not give.

"Loken!" snapped a voice behind me, from the back door of the Council building.

Loken turned to meet Elder Ethereal's frown. His lips pursed and unpursed in silent conversation with the elder. His expression slackened, and I figured he'd lost the argument. He turned back to the interior of our circle. "Let's move on to defense."

CHAPTER 5

Loken hopped to his feet. "Pair up."

I caught Krin's attention as we stood. She and I moved in the same direction to partner.

"I'm with Ashara," Loken added.

I stifled a groan.

Mauryn and Jin stepped to the side and faced each other. Krin and Elis eyed each other. She dragged her feet over to his direction, flashing me a wide-eyed look of mock horror.

As soon as we were separated into twos, Elis shot a ball-shaped pulse of light toward Krin. It sparkled in the sunlight, like a cross between a liquid and a gas. The white-blue shape zipped across the space between them. Krin shrieked and threw her arms up to block her face. The ether ball sizzled as it struck her forearm, leaving a dark ash mark.

Krin peeked out from behind her hands and slowly lowered them to her sides. Her face reddened.

Elis cocked his head back and laughed. He laughed so hard that he had to suck in deep, steadying breaths. Just as his laughter began to subside, he glanced at Krin, whose fists were balled. He clutched his side, and the laughter started anew.

"You okay?" I asked her.

Krin shot forward and reached Elis before he could straighten from his fit of laughter. She swung her hand back and then rammed her fist into his face. The laughter stopped abruptly.

"My eye!" He clutched the left side of his face. "My eye! Loken, she hit me."

Krin flipped her hair off her forehead and sneered. "He deserved it."

"This is defensive training." Loken grabbed Elis's face, pushed Elis's hands away, and stared at the eye. "Where was your defense?" I might have imagined it, but I thought the right side of Loken's mouth twitched upward, almost into a smile. The expression was gone before I could be sure.

"She hit me with her *fist*." Elis pointed to his eye, now surrounded by reddened skin. His dark-blond eyebrow was split open with a fresh cut. Blood dripped down his face. That would be an awful bruise tomorrow.

"That's what happens when you don't defend yourself. You think the Mages will fight fair?" Loken tilted Elis's face upward, so he could examine the eye more closely. "You're fine. Krin, take him inside to get cleaned up. We need him to be able to see."

Krin yanked Elis toward the door. "Come on. And don't bleed on my clothes. I like this shirt."

With a last pleading look at Loken, Elis followed Krin inside.

"Back to work, everyone. Any form of attack is acceptable, but defense must be ether-based." Loken gestured to Mauryn and Jin to pay attention to each other.

A shimmering blue sphere appeared around Mauryn. It pulsed, flashing from white to blue and back again each second. A low thrumming sound emanated from it and vibrated around it. Light winked off its exterior, like it was thousands of white-and-blue gems.

My mouth dropped open.

Jin circled Mauryn's ether shield and raised his hands in front of him. That same white-blue light floated around Jin's hands as he stalked Mauryn from outside the shield.

"Hey." Loken snapped his fingers in front of my face.

I dragged my attention away from Jin and Mauryn and back to Loken.

"How much do you know about what you are?" he asked.

"I'm the same person I was yesterday." I knew my answer would irritate him. It was small of me, but I was still a little bitter about the way we'd left things. I was prepared to learn my lessons and kick some Mage butt. But I wasn't in the mood to make this easy for him.

He narrowed his eyes. "How much do you know about being an *Ethereal*? You know what I meant."

"I'm not convinced I am one."

"You think the records are inaccurate? We've spent the last nine months setting up a system of preserving data through the timelines, but we got it wrong? Is that it?" His volume increased with each word. I fought the urge to smile.

I didn't answer and painted a blank mask on my face.

"Are you saying we actually *didn't* catch you on video frying a Mage with an ether bolt? And that the elders didn't watch this video in the previous timeline?"

"I did *what*?" I tried to imagine myself with streams of light shooting from my hands like miniature lightning, the way I'd seen an Ethereal do once during a festival exhibition. Tingles of excitement raced across my skin. I was an *Ethereal*. An Ethereal! Maybe being assigned to this task force wouldn't be so bad. I had some vengeance to exact, after all.

"I don't really know anything about what I am. I mean, I know I can manipulate ether. But I'm not entirely sure what that is or how I'm supposed to control it."

"Then we'll start at the beginning, with an element that's easier to understand." Loken unsheathed his sword and held it up between us. As per custom in Vallara, its blade was a foot and half long. He gripped the naked hilt—Bender swords had no leather grips—and held it up for me to examine.

"It's metal," I said. "I know you can manipulate it. I've seen you do this before, Loken."

"But you've never heard me explain it from one practitioner to another, so just listen." I opened my mouth to speak again but thought better of it. I snapped it shut. He continued, "I command metal in direct or indirect contact with my body. More accurately, I share a consciousness with metal. I am stronger when more of it is nearby. It is stronger when I am nearby. Do you understand?"

No. But I nodded.

The sword thinned and lengthened in his hand. The blade became longer and narrower. I'd seen him perform this little trick before, so I wasn't impressed. The sword then grew thicker, staying at the longer length. That part I hadn't seen before.

"What's the difference between this sword and the one I held a minute ago?" he asked.

"It's longer."

"What else?"

"It's just as wide. So it has more metal in it than it did before. Right?"

"Exactly. And where did that metal come from?"

"You created it?"

The edges of his lips tugged downward. "You know better than that. Elementary physics, Ashara. I can't create matter."

"You pulled it from the air?"

"That's a good thought. An elder Bender could do that, and there was a time when I could do it with serious concentration."

"But you can't anymore?" I asked.

He shook his head. "We're all weaker in these new timelines. We were strongest in the before, when we were our original selves. Elder Kohler likes to say that, in these new timelines, we're just echoes of ourselves. Our abilities are weakened. We have to adapt."

"So how did you add metal to the sword?"

He inclined his head toward his arms. The metal tattoos that had traced his right forearm had disappeared, leaving tanned, metal-less skin. The sword shrank back to its normal size. As it did, the excess metal bled from the handle up Loken's arm, writhing into the shape of the tattoos I'd seen there earlier.

"You cheated!" I said.

"No. I adapted."

"Can I tattoo ether into my skin like that?"

"You don't need to. You're more like a Breather than a Bender, except you're even better. Ether is everywhere. It's the stuff that connects all the other stuff together. There is no place you will ever be that is without ether."

At a flash in the corner of my eye, I spun toward Mauryn and Jin. The bubble of light still encircled Mauryn. Jin threw progressively larger ether balls at the shield. Brilliant blue balls of light, growing in size. As each one hit, it generated a new flash of vivid blue.

A sharp pain stung my backside. I squealed and whipped back around to Loken. He was swinging the flat side of his sword toward me again. I jumped out of the way.

"Ra's teeth, Loken! What was that for?"

"You're not paying attention," he said in a flat voice.

He was right, of course. I hadn't been paying attention. But he'd just hit me with a sword. Not exactly gentleman-like. "The next time you hit me, I *will* hit you back."

"Or you could practice some actual defense. I find that the best way to tap into your potential is instinct."

I didn't like the sound of that. "So . . . you're going to attack me until I defend myself with ether?"

"That's the general idea, yes."

He spaced his legs into a ready stance. I stared at his chest, where I had a view of his limbs in my peripheral vision. I was ready—well, as ready as I could hope to be seeing as how I had no idea what I was doing.

Loken raised his hands, palms facing outward. He touched his right thumb and middle finger together. The tension in my muscles relaxed against my will as I waited for him to do something. I willed myself to stay alert.

A small, metal bead formed where his fingers met. "Ready?" Loken asked.

Doubting my readiness but seeing no other option, I waved him forward. He brushed his finger outward from his thumb in a flicking motion. Before I had time to react, the metal bead struck my collarbone.

I squealed and slapped a hand over where it hit, like I'd just received a tiny, *painful* bug bite. I rubbed the spot and scowled at him. "Ra's crooked teeth!"

A gasp sounded from my right. Jin stood there, frozen and open-mouthed. Mauryn's shield dropped and a frown creased his forehead.

"What?" I whipped my head around, right to left, searching for whatever had prompted that reaction from Jin, and that disapproving look I was getting from Mauryn. "What?" I asked again.

"Could you please not use the gods' names as curses?" Jin asked. His body remained stiff and unmoving.

"Why?"

Loken whispered in my ear, "Jin is a Believer."

"Really? Then why is he helping us?" I turned back to Jin. "Why are you helping the Council? Aren't you guys opposed to stopping the end, and to using all the high technology the Council loves so much? Let the gods decide? Nature first, or something?"

Jin's face reddened. "Gods or no, I'm just as nervous as you guys about what comes next. About what comes when everything ends. I'd rather stick with the world I know."

I could relate to his mixed feelings. Before Pace died, I'd never given the alleged gods a second thought. Now I wondered. I liked to think Pace had moved on to a better place. It helped me sleep at night to imagine him up in the sky with the gods, playing and laughing and watching over me.

But that was all just fantasy. If there were gods, they wouldn't have taken my brother from me in the first place.

I'd have to be more careful about cursing with Jin in the group. After centuries on this planet, our cultures still hadn't learned to accept each other. At least I could try to coexist peacefully with my other task force members.

"I'm sorry," I said. "I'll work on the cursing thing."

"That's fine," he said, but his expression remained tense.

He shifted back toward Mauryn, angling his back toward me. I'd have to make amends for that slip of the tongue later. For now though, back to work.

I braced myself toward Loken, holding both arms up in front of me and bouncing on flexed legs. I could protect myself from a little bead. It was just a scrap of metal. A tiny thing.

Loken flicked another speck of metal, and I jumped to the side. He aimed the next one at my stomach. I flung myself at the ground to avoid it. The next piece was bigger, probably half an inch in diameter and moving fast toward my prone form. I threw my arms up to protect my head. Pain shot through my forearm as I took the hit.

I picked myself up and rubbed a welt that was forming on my arm. My lip stuck out in an unattractive pout. That *hurt.*

Loken raised his hand again. I narrowed my eyes and bounced from side to side, this time hiding my throbbing and soon-to-be-bruised left arm behind me. Instead of attacking again, Loken frowned.

"What?" I said, still bouncing.

"You can't fight me like that."

"But I can get out of the way. Run."

"Yes, you could run." He grunted and held up one hand in a stop sign. "Would you please stop that?"

I stopped moving but kept my knees flexed just in case he decided to play dirty. He'd already warned us that Mages wouldn't play fair.

"You should run," he said. "But right now, I'm trying to teach you what to do when running is not an option." He paused for effect. "I'm sure this is something you understand."

My legs locked beneath me as I abandoned my concentration. That was a low blow. I understood better than anyone that there were situations when I couldn't run. I couldn't run away when that Mage had attacked Pace. That would have meant leaving my brother there unprotected. Not that I'd been able to do much to protect him anyway. I locked my jaw and willed away the tears that threatened to spill.

"You have no right," I said in a low voice.

Loken's stern expression relaxed. He stepped toward me and reached for my shoulder. I ducked away from his touch. My gaze dropped to my open-toed sandals and stayed there.

"Hey, Asha." He reached for my shoulder again. This time, I let him fold me into a hug. My muscles relaxed as soon as my face pressed into his chest. With his arms wrapped around me, my world couldn't collapse. "I'm sorry. That was too far."

He stepped back from me, tilting my face up to look at him. "I'm sorry," he said again. "I know how much you loved

Pace. We all did." His fingertips crept around to the back of my neck and massaged. "I miss him most when it rains."

I managed a wistful smile. "He loved to jump in the puddles. He always came back inside soaked to the bone and squeezed me until he'd soaked my clothes too."

Loken nodded. His fingers stopped massaging but rested gently on my skin.

My insides felt ripped to shreds, yanked into despair at being reminded repeatedly of exactly how Pace had died, and at the same time, elated at the betraying tingles that ripped up and down my spine from Loken's touch.

I shrugged his hand off. "I don't need the reminder."

"I'm just trying to keep you alive."

"I *know*," I said, more forcefully than necessary. There were way too many emotions skittering around inside me, colliding with one another, tearing up my insides. I had to stay focused on this job. There was no time to shatter to pieces. "Let's get back to work." I shooed him away, back to his spot across from me.

"Right." His face returned to its usual implacable expression. "Close your eyes."

Reluctantly, I allowed my eyelids to drift shut. Loken stayed silent, and the seconds stretched into minutes. Sweat trickled down my brow. My eyelids fluttered to keep it from seeping into my eyes. I imagined the other team members staring at me as I stood there sweating. My discomfort grew as each moment passed.

Finally, Loken spoke again. His voice surrounded me as if echoing from far away. "Like all power, your elemental ability comes from the suns. Try to imagine suns powering your inner energy. They are allowing you to transform the ether around you. Think about the ether in the wind. Feel it against your skin. Know that it is connected to you."

The softness of his rich tenor lulled me into relaxation. My knees weakened, but my weightless body didn't fall. I scrunched my eyelids tighter together and concentrated on the wind sliding across my skin.

Loken's voice floated around me. "Think about what would protect you. An ether shield perhaps. Or a bolt directed at my metal attack. Do you feel it?"

"I feel the wind." The breeze brushed against me.

"Good," he said. "Now push on the space around you. Transform it into something that will protect you."

I imagined the wind rushing outward from me, shoving Loken's annoying metal beads away. But even as I tensed all my muscles, willing it into existence, I felt only air and frustration. My eyes snapped open.

"Why would I just stand here and let you attack me?" The whole situation was illogical, unrealistic. "Let's say I'm not in a position to run. Then I would attack *you*. I won't stand here waiting for you to kill me. And if I'm lucky, I'll have a weapon."

"Would you like a weapon?" he asked, his voice suspiciously emotionless.

I searched his face for a sign of his meaning. "Yes . . . please."

He withdrew the dagger from his belt, flipped it around in his hand so he held the blade, and offered me its handle. Like the sword, the knife had no leather grip, so Loken could manipulate it without having to work around a nonmetal material.

I wrapped my fingers around the naked handle. I hadn't expected him to agree so easily. Of course, I would have preferred the sword, but I could work with this.

"Try not to hurt yourself." Loken released the blade into my hand.

Three metal beads hit my forearm in quick succession, the same arm he'd already injured. He inclined his head toward the dagger. "Are you planning to do something with that?"

I lunged, knife pointed forward. I aimed for his stomach, expecting him to move out of the way. Best-case scenario, I would graze his arm or the side of his waist as he moved, and he would be too distracted to shoot at me.

As I leapt forward, he sidestepped. The next bit of metal hit me square in the forehead. I barreled past Loken, off-balance. He shoved me to the ground with a palm in the small of my back.

The dagger slipped from my hand and clattered to the earth. Loken swept it up, leaned over me and pressed the blade to my neck. "Now what have you learned?"

That you're a creep. "I don't know."

He held the knife up. "This is not your weapon. You don't know how to use it. You don't know how to manipulate it. Ether is your weapon. It's the only weapon you need." He slipped the dagger back into its sheath at his waist. "And no one can steal it from you."

CHAPTER 6

Muscles I'd never noticed before screamed at me as I slid into the transport next to Rey. The suns had set a few minutes earlier. Loken had dismissed us to spend the short darkness hours with our families.

Elis objected to not training all night. Ashara needs it, he'd said. But Loken insisted all of us needed sleep and time to unwind if we were to perform at our best.

I was really beginning to dislike Elis.

Rey flashed me his trademark lopsided grin. "So how was your first day as an Ethereal?"

I considered flinging an ether ball at his smug face. Sadly, I had no idea how to do that. So instead, I leaned back into the vehicle cushion. The leather sighed as it accepted my weight. "I'm the worst Ethereal ever." The exhaustion that had chased me most of the day finally caught up. I let my eyes drift shut.

"But you *are* an Ethereal?" Excitement rang in his voice.

"That's what they tell me."

The smooth motion of the vehicle lulled me into something that resembled relaxation. It was hard to be completely at ease with my comm pressed against my waist. Its countdown clock ticked closer and closer to the end with each second that passed.

Rey shook me so hard I thought my brain would smash into my skull.

"What?" My eyes flew open and I shoved him away.

"Why aren't you excited about this?"

"It's not that I'm not excited." I yawned and stretched my arms. The yawn went on longer than expected, and Rey stared at me with raised brows as he waited.

"Are you done?"

"Maybe. It's just that I'm more tired than I am excited. Did you know you have to channel your own energy into elemental manipulations?"

He gave me a blank expression.

"Right, of course. You knew that. You've been a practitioner most of your life." My gaze scanned up and down his body; his excited expression, the nervous drumming of his fingertips against the armrest. "How come you're not exhausted?"

"You get used to it."

Rey left me in peace when I shut my eyes this time. I awoke to find his face leaning over me, two inches from my nose.

"Hey!"

"We're home." Again, he flashed me that crooked smile. It was hard to be mad.

"You don't have to look so cheery about it," I muttered as I stumbled out of the vehicle. He grabbed my arm to keep me upright.

Rey practically flew through the wooden fence that surrounded our home cluster, while I trudged behind him. I waved goodbye and turned toward my house, expecting Rey to head toward the opposite side of the cluster. Instead, he fell into step beside me and slung an arm over my shoulders.

"You and your mom are coming over for dinner again?"

He nodded, adding a little skip to his step. I suspected he was taunting me with his boundless energy and continuous smiling. I didn't appreciate it.

"She's probably already at your place," he said. "Mom's really into the whole family-time thing lately."

"Can you blame her?"

"Not at all."

We walked the short trip to my house. Despite Rey's annoyingly cheery demeanor, I allowed his arm to remain slung over my shoulder. And I resisted the urge to slap the happy expression off his face. After a few minutes, I caught myself smiling along with him. The boy was tough to resist.

I breathed in deeply when we turned onto the walkway to my front door. The house always smelled divine when Rey and his mother, Reesa, joined us for dinner. The scent of freshly baked bread floated out the front door, thanks to Reesa's baking prowess. It mingled with the aroma of cooked meat, which my mother was fixing.

"Hey, you two." My stepfather, Talin, sat in a rocking chair on the front lawn. His usual spot.

"Hi." I kissed his forehead. He and Rey shook hands and patted each other on the back.

Sona leapt up from where she sat playing on the ground. She kissed me on the cheek and then propelled herself at Rey's legs. "Rey!" He lifted her up. She threw her gangly arms around his neck and squeezed.

"Hey, Sonie." Rey bounced her up and down until she squealed.

"Hello to you too," I said.

"Hi, Asha." She grinned at me, showing me the gap where her front two baby teeth had recently fallen out. "I just saw you last night. It's been two whole days since I've seen Rey." She turned to Rey again. "I like your hair."

"It's the same as it always is, Sona." I hid my laughter behind my hand. Sona's ongoing crush on him had gotten worse in the past few weeks.

She pulled the end of his ponytail forward so she could play with it. "I still like it."

"So what's for dinner?" Rey asked her.

She giggled and hid her face against his neck. "I didn't cook."

"You didn't? But I'm hungry." He tucked a stray lock of her blond hair behind her ear.

"Mom cooked! And your mom too."

Leaving them to their love-fest, I made my way into the house. The smells of meat and bread overwhelmed my senses. My mouth watered.

My mother, Nesstra, stirred whatever was inside a large pot on the stove. Reesa sat at the kitchen table with Barte, her youngest son, Rey's little brother. She chattered away at Mom. Her face lit up as she recapped the wonderful time she, Mom, Sona, and Barte had at the lake earlier today.

"Asha!" Reesa stood and gave me a hug. As usual, she smelled of bread and pies. I hoped she was cooking pie for dessert. It was the end of the world, after all. If any event called for pie, it was this.

One of the few things I liked about this whole end-of-the-world thing was that the number of hugs I got on a daily basis had increased dramatically since the Vision was announced. We appreciated one another more than we did before. If we all came out of this alive, we might be better for this crisis.

After the day I'd had, I appreciated the affection even more than I had yesterday. I squeezed Reesa tightly before releasing her.

Rey came inside and kissed both women on the cheek. He tore off a piece of the fresh bread sitting on the countertop. Reesa swiped her hand at him. He sidestepped it and stuffed the bread into his mouth, filling his cheeks with it. "Good bread, Mom." Bits of food sprayed from his mouth. "I'll help with the table." He picked up two food platters and carried them to the outdoor dining area.

I pulled plates from the cupboard and followed Rey out.

My family and Rey's ate a dinner of meat stew, fried fish, salad, vegetables, and bread. Sona spent most of the meal batting her eyelashes at Rey; never mind that he was her distant cousin and twelve years her senior. Most of the food had disappeared before the expected questions came.

"So, Asha," said my mother, too loudly, so I knew she was faking casualness. "I haven't seen you since last night. I thought we were going to spend the day together."

"Uh-huh." I stuffed a piece of bread into my mouth and made a show of chewing it.

"You didn't tell her about your new assignment?" Rey asked.

I kicked him under the table. Everyone else stared at me expectantly. I chewed slowly. I didn't want to answer questions about what I allegedly was. I didn't have any of the answers. But I did have some questions on a related topic. So I forged ahead.

"I'm assigned to the Ethereal task force."

"To the *what*?" Talin was up so fast that I flinched away from him, startled. "You're not trained for that. What in the names of the gods are they thinking?"

Part of me wanted to tell him not to worry, but the other part agreed with his concerns. And he didn't even know about the Mages yet. "Talin, please calm down. They're training me. It's perfectly safe," I lied.

He ripped his comm from his pocket and pressed a few buttons.

"Who are you calling?" I asked, feeling like a small child whose parent was complaining to her teacher.

"Loken."

"What? No!" I snatched at the comm, but Talin stepped smoothly away from me. The comm issued a beep as the call connected. In hindsight, I probably should have erased Loken's contact information from Talin's and Mom's comms when we broke up.

"Loken, what in darkness and light is Ashara doing with the Ethereals?" Talin barked into the device. There was a pause before he spoke again. "And are you actually going to be able to protect her? . . . What? Don't you hang up on me. Loken!" he shouted.

After a moment of tense silence, Talin slumped back into his seat. "I never liked that boy."

"You loved him when we were dating," I joked. Talin glared at me, and my grin withered.

"That was before I knew he would always put his job above his lady. Those Council members—you can never trust them."

Mom shot Talin a pointed look. He clamped his mouth shut.

I couldn't deny that Loken valued his job over me. I hadn't known the real reason he broke up with me until the Vision was publicized three months ago. Then it became clear. The Council had waited to tell the public about the Vision, but Elder Seer had seen it all nine months ago. Loken broke up with me nine months ago. Not a coincidence.

Talin muttered to himself for several seconds, too quietly for me to make out his words. Tension thickened around the table. I caught myself twisting the edge of the tablecloth in my lap.

Reesa excused herself from the table and beckoned for Rey and Barte to do the same. Barte followed, shooting glances back over his shoulder. Rey averted his eyes and pretended he didn't notice his mother's less-than-subtle instruction to leave us alone.

"The Council's not so bad," Rey said. "My grandfather had friends who worked there—good, kind, ethical friends. They just want to make the world better."

No one responded. Rey shrugged and left the table to join his mother and brother.

"Ness, we could just take the girls somewhere," Talin said. He looked to my mother.

Throughout Talin's outburst, she'd been pushing her remaining food around her plate, peeking at me occasionally. She gave up pretending she was eating and tossed the fork onto her plate. "You think the Council would let us leave? They have to think about the *greater good*." Those last two words sounded bitter coming from her mouth.

"I don't care about the greater good!" Talin shouted.

Mom sneaked another peek at me.

It was time to ask one of the many questions that had hung on my mind all day. "How is it even possible that I'm an Ethereal? Was my father a practitioner?"

Talin's mouth snapped shut.

I wished I could call the words back. I'd asked about my father once before, when I was twelve. Mom told me she'd tell me all about him when I was older. But I hadn't asked again, even though I thought about him. My family was more important than my curiosity. And Talin was my father in all the ways that mattered.

"Sorry," I said. "Just . . . maybe it's time we talked about him."

Mom stared at her plate. The seconds ticked by.

"Forget it," I said. When no one spoke, I turned to Sona. "Doesn't Rey's hair look nice?"

When I awoke, the world was still dark outside my window, which meant I hadn't slept for long. During the Dutem season, nighttime was much shorter than in other seasons. I rolled toward the wall and prepared to go back to sleep. Sona's soft whisper stopped me.

"Asha."

"I'm sleeping," I mumbled into my bedcovers.

"I can't sleep. Tell me a story."

With a sigh, I dragged myself out of bed and crawled into Sona's. She sat up so I could squeeze between her small body and the headboard.

"You know I'm no good with stories." I stroked her blond hair. "You want to hear about the journey from Earth-One again?"

"Gods, no. You've told me that one too many times already."

My lips scrunched into a pout. "It's the only good one I know."

She didn't speak for a while, and then said, "Are you going to die, Asha?"

"No," I said, immediately. My chest tightened as the words flew out. I had no way of knowing if that were really true. But I also couldn't sit here and let my sister worry about that when I could comfort her.

"Because I don't want you to."

"That's not going to happen."

"Pace didn't think he was going to die either." Her voice was so soft; I had to lean over and put my ear by her mouth to hear it. "Promise me."

I tilted my head back against the headboard and stared upward. Shadows danced across the ceiling in the dim lights of the lamps on either side of the room. "I promise I'll do my best to stay alive." It was the best I could do as far as promises went.

She twisted around to look at me. Her eyes searched my face. She was too smart not to notice how carefully I'd worded my promise.

"Your *very* best?" she insisted.

I nodded. "My very best."

CHAPTER 7
COUNTDOWN: 9 DAYS

The next morning, with Ra teasing the horizon and Solaris right behind it, Rey and I stepped out of the transport in front of the Council building. The crowd of Believers outside the gate was twice as big today, with signs twice as large. When we approached, a low buzz hummed through them.

"Let the gods decide!" a man yelled, accompanied by shouts of agreement from his companions.

Rey grabbed my arm and pulled me through the crowd to the gate. Some of the Believers refused to make way. A woman shoved me out of Rey's grasp. Numerous hands and shoulders pushed me back, until Rey yanked me in the right direction.

Rey placed his hand to a metal sensor plate to the side of the latch. The panel beeped, and the word AUTHORIZED scrolled horizontally across its top. The gate popped open a foot. Rey and I squeezed through, and it whirred shut behind us.

Despite my mother's numerous childhood warnings that I shouldn't look directly at the suns, I peeked upward for a partial second.

I'd always felt a connection with Ra, even though I knew it was just a sun—no different from the sun our ancestors had left on Earth-One. Still, it was a little romantic to think of Ra and Solaris as gods watching over us. On the other hand, if they were up there, they'd proven themselves pretty useless over the past nine months.

"You coming?" asked Rey from the door of the building.

"Right behind you." With my chin held high, I strode through the front door behind Rey, feigning the same confidence he exuded. I wouldn't want to keep the murderous Mages waiting.

Unlike the day before, the various groups of practitioners wouldn't all be starting the day in the same room. "See you later." Rey waved, leapt over the metal railing of the staircase, and took the steps to the second floor two at a time.

"Yeah, later."

This morning's message on my comm unit instructed me to meet the rest of my task force in the basement training room. I took the stairs downward at about half the pace Rey had taken them in the opposite direction.

The steps ended in a brightly lit room with a thick mat covering most of the floor. The smell of sweat and leather hit my nostrils. It almost drowned out the scent of cleaning supplies that clung to every surface inside this pristine building.

Bladed weapons of all shapes and sizes lined the far wall. The sight of them slowed my footfalls. Leather armor and padding hung on hooks along the wall to my right. On my left, foam weapons and other nonlethal devices lay piled against the wall.

A circle was drawn on the mat toward the center of the room. I sank to the floor at the edge of the circle and waited for the others. According to my comm, I was a few minutes early. I tapped my fingertips against my knee.

My breath caught at the sight of Loken at the bottom of the steps. I ignored the feeling.

"Are you just going to stand there?"

His eyes darted around the otherwise empty room, as if searching for an escape route. "No one else is here?"

I made a show of scanning the room, first examining the blades, then the padding, then the pile of foam weapons. "Hmm. Doesn't look like it."

He turned over his shoulder to look at the staircase. It was still empty.

"I don't bite," I said. "Mostly."

Loken sat on the other side of the circle, as far away as possible. I chewed the inside of my cheek to stop myself from telling him what a coward he was. He'd take on the world but wouldn't sit within six feet of me.

"So," I said, "how are you doing with the whole end-of-the-world thing?" I tried to ease the tension a bit with a smile, but his gaze remained fixed on something over my head.

"We don't have to talk if you don't want to, Ashara."

"And what if I want to?"

He didn't answer, so I gave up on the conversation. I didn't want to let him off the hook too easily though, so I continued to stare at him, letting my gaze drift downward to examine his posture; stiff shoulders, hands clasped together in his lap. I pressed my lips together to keep from smiling.

I liked that I made him so uncomfortable. In these times, I'd take my little joys where I found them.

"So," I tried again, "what have you been up to these past nine months?"

He stared at me for a moment before answering, perhaps trying to decide whether to answer at all. "Recruiting mostly. A lot of it overseas."

It was some consolation that I'd been dumped for a cause as important as this one. But I didn't see why recruiting required him to be single. I waited for him to explain, but he didn't. And since I didn't want to look like I cared, I opted not to ask.

A silver-and-gold chain peeked out from the collar of his shirt. Although I couldn't see the chain's details from where I sat, I knew a thin gold wire snaked around the mostly-silver chain in an intricate pattern. When I'd bought it for him, I knew he'd love something so beautiful that was made of metal.

"You still wear it?" I asked, touching my collarbone to indicate the necklace.

His face stayed blank. "It never hurts to keep extra bits of metal around."

The smile I'd been fighting a moment ago turned to a scowl. "Nice, Loken." Sarcasm dripped from my voice. "Do you think you could maybe *try* to be polite?"

His eyes finally dropped down to meet mine. "The world is ending in nine days. It's not my job to be polite. It's my job to keep you alive."

I mumbled something Jin wouldn't appreciate.

Krin stormed down the stairs and skidded to a halt several steps inside the training room. "Oh good." She doubled over, panting. "I thought I was late."

"No. Loken and I were just having a lovely conversation about how much of a jerk he is."

She looked back and forth between the two of us, shrugged, and plopped down on the floor next to me. "It's none of my business if you two want to ignore the serious sexual tension in the room. But since we have work to do, I suggest you just take it to the bedroom and get it out of your systems."

I tried to think of a witty response, but Krin was talking again before I came up with something brilliant. She scooted around the circle to sit next to Loken. "So, what are we doing today?"

"Offense," Loken said.

Krin punched him in the shoulder. He looked down at the spot she'd hit like he didn't quite believe it.

"So we're going to learn how to kill Mages today?" She giggled and punched him in the shoulder again.

"Yes." He glanced again down at his arm. Annoyance plastered his face.

"And what am I going to do while they fling ether at each other all morning?" I asked. "Since all I've done so far is run and duck."

"Offense," he said again, standing as the remainder of the group entered the room together. "But first a field trip."

Loken moved toward the door and gestured for the team to follow. He led us back up the staircase and down the main hallway. I inhaled a deep breath of air after emerging from the sweat stench of the training room.

Like yesterday, that not-at-all-reassuring female voice droned its pleasantries through unseen speakers in the hallway: *"Remain calm. Please stay calm. Remain calm."* Wonderful. Because with the world ending, and me about to hunt killer-Mages after only a day of training, it was just so realistic for me to *stay calm*. I wished there was a way to shut that woman up.

We hooked a right near the back door, entering a hallway I had yet to explore. A bright-silver metal door at the end of the hall drew my attention as I turned the corner behind the rest of the team. Every other interior door I'd seen on this floor was white. This one contrasted against the stark-white walls that covered the inside of the building. Its smooth, fingerprint-free surface reflected the lights shining overhead.

A metal plate occupied the wall to the right of the door. Loken pressed his hand to it. The door slid away and disappeared into the left side of the doorway. Loken stepped through and down the stairs on the other side. His footsteps clanged against the metal steps as he descended.

Unlike in the overly bright training room on the other side of the building, dim lights filled this room with shadows. The team clustered at the bottom of the steps, blocking my view. As they shuffled slowly out of the way, I caught sight of what had stopped everyone else in their tracks.

A glass wall separated us from what looked like a large cell. The only entry point into the cell was another thick metal door with a security pad next to it. Behind the glass, three people stood as far away from one another as they could possibly get within the enclosed space: a hugely tall man, a woman with blond hair that hung past her waist, and a smaller man. All three were nude.

They looked human but . . . wrong somehow. Despite their lack of clothing, they made no effort to cover themselves. The larger man's muscles bulged in odd places. While the woman wasn't as massive, her body was more toned than any woman I'd ever met, more so than even Elder Ethereal.

From across the room, their black eyes cut through the darkness. A chill raced up and down my back like icy fingertips.

I stared at the smaller man. His eyes bore through me. I wondered if he saw me at all, or if he just happened to be looking where I was standing. At first glance, I'd thought him to be relatively slight. Although the other man dwarfed him, his thin arms were as tight as a predator's, coiled to strike. The sharp planes of his face only emphasized the eerie black of his eyes, sunken into their sockets.

Loken's voice startled me from the man's hypnotic gaze. "In case you haven't guessed it, these three are—"

"Mages," I whispered.

"Yes. Two Breathers and an Ethereal."

Mauryn, Jin, Elis, and Krin had the good sense to cluster against the wall opposite the glass cell, as far away from the

Mages as they could get without bolting back up the stairs. For some reason I couldn't explain, I was standing in the middle of the room. I must have wandered here when I'd locked gazes with the smaller male.

Gently, Loken peeled my fingers from his arm, where I'd clutched him without meaning to. A red outline on his skin remained where my fingers had pressed. He patted my hand and placed it back by my side.

Loken strode toward the glass wall and pointed at the Mages one by one. First the smaller male, then the female, then the largest one. "This is what happens as Mages age. Immediately after the transition from human practitioner to Mage, immediately after their energy consumes them to initiate that transition, they're very much like us. Except that they no longer feel obliged to wear clothing."

Krin giggled. Her hand flew to her mouth to cover it.

"Most of the energy a Mage takes in, he transforms into another form of energy and outputs. The energy he doesn't expel gets incorporated into his mass. They grow taller." He pointed at the largest Mage, who was taller than any one of us by at least a foot. "And bigger, less human."

As Loken paced in front of the glass wall, the largest Mage turned to follow Loken's path. When presented with his profile, I saw the fist-sized bulge toward the left side of his forehead. The Mage's eyes momentarily fell on me, and I flinched. Krin shuffled closer to me. I glanced her way to find her trembling and staring at me wide-eyed.

I felt exactly the way Krin looked—terrified, ready to bolt up the stairs and all the way back home. But I also itched to learn everything I could about these creatures. If I could help exterminate them, I would do just that. My hands curled into fists.

Krin took another step closer to me.

"I thought you guys have been training already," I hissed at her. "Why is everyone acting like they've never seen a Mage before?"

"We've been training," she whispered, "but not to fight Mages. Mostly drills to help us with our control and focus. Basic Ethereal stuff, like shields and energy balls. Then defensive skills. Anything to get us ready for some kind of natural disasters or manmade weapon." The pitch of her voice increased steadily. "And Mauryn was able to project himself across a room once. But never—"

"How'd he do that?"

"Who?" Her fingers dug into my arm until I had to pry them loose.

"Mauryn? Which one is he again?"

"The guy with the short dark hair. Pale skin. Likes to ramble on about all the stuff he knows, even though I rarely know what he's talking about."

"Right. How'd he project himself across a room?"

"Something about separating your body into energy and moving it through the ether in the air. But that's not the point. We were never trained to fight Mages! We're supposed to be preventing wars and dismantling science experiments."

"At the end of the day," Loken continued, "a Mage will always be attracted to the most powerful thing in the area. So why do you care how old a Mage is when you fight him?" Loken asked the group. His gaze swept the room and landed on Jin.

"Young Mages are less predictable," said Jin. "Out of control. Many of them die before they can mature because they draw energy without moderation. Often they implode from the overload. Older Mages have survived as long as they have because they've adapted. They draw energy only in selective situations—when they need it. And only from specific, powerful targets."

“What does that mean for us?” Loken asked him.

“A young Mage is more likely to kill you just for being in his vicinity. Expect an attack. With an older Mage, you may be able to avoid confrontation by staying out of his way. One way to do that is by spreading out, dispersing the energy of the people around you. But that can backfire if the Mage ends up attacking you when you’re on your own.”

Loken turned to me. “What do you do when you see an old Mage?” He pointed again to the monstrously large one behind the glass.

Before I could answer, clanging sounded from the stairway. We all turned as Elder Ethereal entered the room. Today, she wore a Bender-style weapons belt around her waist. Her blond braid trailed behind her.

“If we’re done with the chitchat, perhaps we can move on to some offense,” she said.

CHAPTER 8

Loken spared Elder Ethereal a quick, blank look and then clapped his hands. "Line up! Let's do some offense."

I fell to the back of the line. I expected Loken to face the person in front. Instead, he stepped aside and let Elder Ethereal face the group.

At the front of the line, Krin stumbled back a step, stepping on Elis's toes. He grunted and shoved her forward, back toward the elder.

"You want me to attack an elder?" Krin asked when she'd halfway recovered. Her voice came out in a petrified squeak.

"That's the idea, yes," Loken said.

"Is she . . . is she going to attack me back?"

We all looked at Elder Ethereal for an answer, but she just waved Krin forward.

Loken asked, "Is there ever a time in the real world when you are fighting but your opponent is not?"

"I guess not," Krin whispered. Color drained from her face.

With trembling fingers, she raised her hands and pointed them toward the elder, whose pale eyes glared at her. A thin line of light crackled from Krin's fingertips. Elder Ethereal sidestepped, and the light flew past her left shoulder. As she moved, she waved a hand toward Krin. From the elder's hand, a small spark of ether—a miniature blue light—flew at Krin and hit her square in the forehead. It sizzled into a tiny puff of smoke.

Krin scrunched her forehead and rubbed the dark spot of ash just below her hairline. "That stung," she muttered. She dragged her feet to the back of the line. I patted her on the shoulder as she stepped behind me to await her next turn.

Loken joined us at the end of the line. "You're lucky it only stung. You could be dead. Next time, remember there is no offense without defense. Every time you attack, expect a counterattack."

"Next time, you should just punch her in the face," I whispered. That got a small smile out of Krin.

With a cocky grin, Elis stepped forward and flung three blue ether balls at Elder Ethereal in quick succession, all chest height; one to the left, one straight in front of himself, and one to the right.

Elder Ethereal's body became a blur as she dodged all three and returned to her original position. Somehow, while maneuvering, she'd managed to wage her own attack. The small spark hit Elis in the face just as it had Krin.

My mouth dropped open as I watched her. I'd expect a Breather to move that fast, but an Ethereal? I needed to learn to move like that!

Next up, Mauryn approached. He examined the elder for a moment, and raked a hand through his already impeccable dark hair. Elder Ethereal looked him up and down and nodded approvingly.

Mauryn leapt into motion. He fired a streak of ether across the room, directly at the elder. Elder Ethereal darted out of the way and counterattacked with the same miniature spark of light she'd used with the others. A white-blue sphere flashed around Mauryn as he threw up an ether shield for a split second. The spark sizzled against the sphere and disappeared.

As soon as he dropped the shield, Mauryn spun to one side, just as another spark flew toward him. His body blurred as he moved, just like the elder's had a moment ago. Her jaw clenched as she tossed four more sparks in his direction.

Mauryn held his arms wide open and released a blaze of ether in a sweeping arc. Elder Ethereal's sparks died in the blaze. I raised a hand to shield my eyes against the shimmering light. It pulsed on the elder's side of the room. Mauryn's body trembled more and more the longer he kept it going. A drip of sweat popped out by his temple and rolled down his cheek.

With a long gasp, he collapsed to the ground. The light blinked out, leaving a clear view of Elder Ethereal. She stood exactly where she had been before, surrounded by her own small sphere of light.

She dropped her shield, strode forward, and tapped Mauryn on the forehead. "Now you're dead. Next time, don't use all your energy at once."

Loken hooked his hands under Mauryn's armpits, hauled him to his feet, and supported him to the back of the line.

For his turn, Jin bolted around the room, zigzagging. By normal standards, I'd think Jin was pretty fast. But after the prior display, Jin's feet seemed to slog along as he ran. Elder Ethereal spun a slow circle in place and waited.

For a whole minute, Jin ran around the room, flinging ether. Elder Ethereal dodged each attack easily, with a sidestep or a quick shuffle forward or backward. Eventually, Jin's steps slowed, and the wheezing began.

Jin stumbled to a stop just in front of the glass wall. Elder Ethereal flung a small spark at him. Jin leapt out of the way, still wheezing. The spark missed him and sizzled against the glass.

Elder Ethereal grunted and attacked again, this time with a bolt, like a flash of blue-tinted lightning. Jin rolled to the side. The bolt flew past him and banged against the sensor panel next to the metal door of the Mage cell.

The impact vibrated the glass. Three pairs of inky-black Mage eyes locked on the elder.

"Whoa! Whoa!" Loken rushed forward to stand between Elder Ethereal and Jin.

The elder strode forward until she was nose to nose with Loken. While Loken was broader through the shoulders, they were about the same height. She stared at him until he took a step backward, his head bowed.

"My apologies, Elder. I'm just concerned about the glass."

"That glass is shatterproof. It's been tested against every element. You think I'm an idiot?"

"No, ma'am. Not at all." But he stayed in front of Jin, shielding him from the elder. "Will you go to the back of the line please, Jin?"

Jin scrambled to his feet and jogged away, shooting Loken a grateful smile.

"How do you win?" I asked Elder Ethereal as I stepped forward for my turn. She didn't answer, so I turned toward Loken. "Any attack, any defense, it's all useless." I gestured toward Jin. "Is that the best we can hope for? Run, hide, pray?"

Loken started, "You—"

"How do you think you win?" asked Elder Ethereal, interrupting Loken.

"If I have a choice, I never get into this situation." I pointed a finger back and forth between me and the elder. "One on one with a Mage. Even as an Ethereal, I'm less powerful than the Mage. His energy has taken control, and he's more powerful in his element than I am in mine."

"So how do you think you win?" the elder asked again, her voice tinged with annoyance. She flipped her blond ponytail over her shoulder and crossed her arms over her chest.

I threw up my hands. "I don't know. Maybe I can't!"

"You can. But you have to be smarter than you're being right now."

I grimaced at her words, but held my tongue.

"As any *seasoned* practitioner will tell you, Mages are pure instinct," the elder continued. Her lips pulled back in distaste as she eyed me. "That's what distinguishes them from humans. An older Mage will always go to the greatest energy draw in the area. A younger Mage will move toward the largest energy draw but may also attack anything else along the way."

"So either can be distracted by the right source?"

She nodded. "Generally, we hunt in teams, so we distract or immobilize while one of us goes in for the kill."

"And how do you—" Her words struck me after I'd started speaking. "Wait, you *hunt* them on a regular basis?" Terror iced up my back. I felt as if all my limbs were frozen in place. Behind me, Krin clutched my arm again.

"Sometimes, yes," said Elder Ethereal. "Most of them are no trouble at all. They hide away near volcanoes, at the bottom of the ocean, or wherever else they can be surrounded by their elements. Every once in a while, though, one will cause trouble near humans. Then we'll hunt it down." She cocked a single eyebrow and added, "Do you think you can do that?"

She took two large steps back and beckoned me forward for my turn. I guessed her question was meant to be rhetorical.

"Now quit stalling," she said.

The room went quiet except for the steady thrum of energy emanating through the glass. I hoped I wouldn't make a total fool of myself. If I died nine days from now, I'd like it to be with my dignity intact.

I extended my arms straight out in front of me the way I'd seen Krin do. A muffled laugh sounded from the line behind me. It probably came from Elis.

Just as Loken had taught me, I concentrated on feeling the world against my skin. But all I felt was air, same as always. No ether. Still, I commanded power into my fingertips and imagined bolts of ether streaming from them toward the elder.

Nothing happened. Another chuckle came from my right. This time, it wasn't muffled.

I dropped my arms to my sides. "I can't do it."

"Elder," said Loken. "Would you counterattack please?"

What?

I squealed, ducked, and threw my arms over my head. A bright light flashed. The world slowed. Twinkling lights winked between me and the elder. Everything outside a three-foot space around me went fuzzy.

Elder Ethereal charged forward, sparkling like a bright blue statue. She hit a barrier and flinched backward. A low growl emanated from deep in her throat.

My vision focused outward. I was enclosed inside a brilliant white-blue bubble. *Yes! I created a shield. How awesome am I?*

I smiled so widely that my cheeks hurt. All these trained Ethereals standing around, and I was the one who wouldn't get hit. I puffed up my chest and smiled inside my little blue bubble. I hoped they could see me inside here, safe as could be. If I were a good dancer, I'd have done a little dance to celebrate.

Elder Ethereal drew the sword from her weapons belt and stalked to the shield. At first, she tapped it with the blade. My smile faltered but stayed put. Ether was the strongest element; that's what people kept telling me. That little sword was no threat.

She swung the sword forward. Metal clashed against the shield, throwing blue sparks outward. A sharp ringing grated against my eardrums. I pressed my hands to my ears, trying to block out the ringing. The sword struck again, and the world vibrated. I stepped backward away from the elder, taking the shield with me, until I pressed against the wall by the stairs.

With each strike, the world teetered around me. The sharp screeching-ringing attacked my ears. My teeth clattered together. Brightly colored spots danced in front of me. Red, blue, yellow, red, green, red.

Suddenly, it all stopped. The world stilled again. The only motion I felt was the banging of my heart against my chest. I lifted my face to find Loken standing between Elder Ethereal and me. His hand gripped the elder's sword arm. Her top lip was pulled back in a snarl.

I dropped the shield. Krin bent down and cradled my cheek in her hand. "You're bleeding, honey."

"Am I?" My tongue was a cotton ball in my mouth. I could barely push the words out.

"Your nose," she said. "Let's get you cleaned up."

With the colored spots still dancing before my eyes, I let Krin lead me up the stairs and out of the basement.

CHAPTER 9

Sitting on the edge of a sink in the restroom, I tilted my head back and pinched the bridge of my nose with a tissue. The blood flow had finally started to slow. My breathing still came in long rattling gasps. I felt light-headed, and the colored spots continued to bounce around my vision.

I shook my head hard to clear it. That chased away most of the spots.

Krin handed me a fresh tissue. I snatched it from her and tossed the old, bloody one in the trash.

"What just happened?" she asked.

Blood slipped down from my nasal cavity into my throat. I spat it into the sink before resuming my position with my head tilted back. "How am I supposed to know?" My voice came out nasally. "You're the expert. Everyone's an expert except me, remember?"

I couldn't keep the bitterness out of my voice. I thought I was finally making progress, that I would earn some respect among the group. It was tough to do that when I was bleeding from my nose. I spat more blood into the sink.

Krin blinked more times than necessary before answering, like she was restraining herself from saying what she really wanted to say. "You want me to leave?"

I knew I wasn't being nice, but I was handling a lot right now. We all were. The difference was that I'd been prepared to relax for these last days. Now I was on the front lines, learning how to destroy super beings.

"No." I banged my head against the mirror. Not hard enough to hurt myself; just enough expel some of my frustrations. "I appreciate how friendly you've been to me, despite my being a complete jerk."

She grinned. "I know. I'm awesome."

"You're okay." I smiled back, hopped down from the sink, and checked my nostrils in the mirror. No more bleeding. I wet a tissue in the sink and started cleaning the crusting blood away.

"So . . . what just happened?" Krin repeated.

I replayed the scene in my head. Elder Ethereal had attacked my shield, and then *what*? No idea. But there was one thing I did know. "I threw an ether shield!"

"Yes, but you're an Ethereal. We tend to do that. Ether shields. Bolts. Balls. The interesting part is that Elder Ethereal couldn't get through it."

I felt my eyebrows draw together. "Is that not normal?"

"Not for your first shield ever. And even for an experienced Ethereal, it wouldn't hold for long against an elder or a Mage. That was amazing!"

I frowned as the rest of the memory replayed in my head. Elder Ethereal had struck the shield at least four times, probably more. Only it had felt like she was pounding against my head. A pulsing started by my right temple, the beginnings of a headache.

I raised a finger to touch the aching side of my face. "But it hurt like my head was about to explode. Still does."

Krin waved my concerns away. "You're not used to the power yet. It'll grow on you."

The pulsing in my head grew more insistent. "Ow! Well, I hope it grows on me fast because . . . *Ow!*"

"I know, honey. Let's see if we can get you some drugs for the pain." She pulled me toward the door. "Back to work?"

We'd dawdled for too long. I missed the times back at the University when I'd go into the restroom and chat with friends about teachers, classmates, and boys. Now, classes were canceled indefinitely, and it took bleeding from my face to steal a few minutes away. And what did we talk about? Fighting Mages and the end of the world. I missed the simple days.

"Do we have to?" I asked, even though I knew the answer.

As she pushed the restroom door open, Krin asked, "What's the deal with you and Lo—"

Before she could finish, rapid beeping emitted from both of our comms. I grabbed mine and watched the red lettering scroll across the screen. I almost let out a breath of relief at not having to answer the question she had been about to ask, but the words on my comm stopped me. The same words played aloud through hidden speakers:

"Elemental practitioners, report to the briefing room. Non-practitioners, evacuate the building and return home immediately. Please stay calm. Remain calm."

On instinct, I made for the front of the building. Krin grabbed the back of my shirt and hauled me toward the briefing room where we'd met the morning before. I stumbled over my feet as she dragged me.

Right. I'm a practitioner. That was still growing on me. *I get to kill Mages.* That part I liked—if I could figure how to do it without dying horribly and breaking my poor mother's heart.

We collided with a throng of other people packed tight into the hallway. A few of them pushed against us, heading toward the front doors. Krin steered me through the gaps in the crowd, until we finally shoved our way into the briefing room.

Elder Kohler and Elder Ethereal stood close together at the front of the room, whispering in hushed, frantic tones. The other elders clustered around them. Loken stood a couple feet away, craning his neck toward them. I guessed he was attempting, not so subtly, to eavesdrop on their conversation.

The eavesdropping must have been unsuccessful because Loken began pacing the front of the room. His mouth moved, and his arms gestured in jerky motions. But he didn't seem to be speaking to anyone in particular.

I pushed my way to the front of the room and placed a hand on Loken's shoulder. He jerked away, his eyes wild. His shoulders relaxed a bit when he focused in on me. Then he returned to his pacing.

"Hey," I said. He ignored me. "Hey." I stepped into his path.

Loken searched my face. His gray eyes seemed darker than usual, like a storm brewed behind them. He bent over and crushed me in a tight hug. At first I tensed, but then allowed myself to settle into his chest. His shirt smelled of metal and something sweet—cinnamon maybe. When he pulled away from me, I itched to push the lock of blond hair off his forehead.

The moment passed too quickly. Loken opened his mouth to say something, shook his head, then turned away from me. He went back to pacing and muttering to himself. Nervousness roiled in my chest. If ever-steady Loken was agitated, I had good reason to worry.

I located Krin toward the back of the room and joined her. My attention was drawn back to the front as Elder Kohler's artificially amplified voice filled the room.

"We have a bit of a situation on our hands." Whispers scattered throughout the room, and Kohler cleared his throat. The noise didn't die down. "Quiet!" he shouted.

I jumped at the sound of his raised voice. His voice grew barely louder when he shouted, given the permanent damage his long-ago accident had caused to his vocal cords. But the gravelly rasp in it became even rougher. A harsh sound.

Elder Kohler scanned the crowd with a glare fixed on his face. His gaze landed on me, paused, and then moved on.

He opened his mouth again. Before words could escape, the door to the briefing room burst open. A loud crunching sound reverberated through the space, as the door lefts its hinges and flew across the room.

Practitioners scattered from the doorway, pressing closer together. Two people were too slow. The door slammed into them and threw them across the room, crushing them into the far wall. I tore my eyes from the blood beginning to leak underneath the now-detached door—blood that used to belong to the two people trapped between it and the wall.

I spun back toward the doorway. There stood a familiar-looking man. He looked larger now that there was no glass wall separating us. Dark hair, dead eyes, completely nude. The smallest Mage from downstairs.

I shrank farther away from him. But the only doorway was behind him. Panic tore into my chest, collapsing my lungs so I could hardly breathe.

Two loud bangs exploded through the room, and two holes opened up in the Mage's bare chest. He jerked backward at each of the two impacts. Blood leaked from the holes. I whirled around to find the source of the shots. A male practitioner held his arm extended forward, trembling. In his hand, a metal-looking weapon pointed toward the Mage.

Is that a gun? I'd seen them in history books, but they'd been outlawed by the first colonists on this planet. Too many accidental and unlawful deaths on Earth-One, they'd said.

The Mage zeroed in on the shooter. The bullet holes shrank, and the flesh on his chest knitted back together. The holes sealed up, closing the bullets inside. The Mage rushed toward the shooter, so quickly that he seemed to disappear and then reappear in front of him.

Another shot fired. The Mage's body jerked. His face twisted into a snarl. He ripped the gun from the shooter's arm with one hand and, with the other, gripped the shooter around the neck. The shooter's eyes bulged. He clawed at the Mage's hand.

Elder Kohler, Loken, and Elder Ethereal leapt into action, positioning themselves around the Mage and his prey. Loken drew his sword and circled. He searched for a place to strike. Elder Kohler shot a stream of fire from his palms at the Mage. The flames hit him in the back. My nostrils filled with the stench of burnt flesh. My stomach lurched, threatening to expel its contents.

The Mage kept his grip on the shooter, whose face drained of color. Soft whimpers issued from the shooter's mouth. Elder Kohler's fire continued to burn at the Mage's back, but the bare skin healed almost as quickly as the fire destroyed it. The flesh melted and reformed again and again.

Loken charged. Elder Ethereal shot a bolt of light. But a brilliant blue shield closed around the Mage and his victim. Loken's sword clashed against the shield but couldn't break through.

The shooter's face went sheet white. His mouth dropped open in a silent scream. His skin transitioned from white to gray and continued to darken. Gray bits of flesh flaked off his face and fluttered to the ground. His skin darkened further.

My hand flew to my face to cover my eyes, but I peeked through my fingertips. As much as I knew I shouldn't, as much as I knew I'd never be able to wipe this scene from my memory, I couldn't look away.

In the Mage's grasp, the shooter's skin darkened to black. Like a pile of ash, his body collapsed into pieces and scattered across the floor. Some flakes of it floated in the air and slowly drifted downward.

The Mage's shield fell and he spun around, searching for new prey. Loken ran forward, drew back his sword, and severed the Mage's head. The body dropped to the floor on top of the pile of black flakes and dust that had been the shooter. As the head rolled clear, all practitioners in its path scrambled out of the way.

The room was deadly silent for a moment. Too long. I wanted someone to say something, needed someone to reassure me that I wouldn't end up like that man. Shallow breaths tore through my lungs.

Everyone started talking at once. Krin's voice chattered beside me. I couldn't make out the words over the screaming inside my head.

"So, as I was saying." Elder Kohler's amplified rasp rang out louder than the din in the room, breaking through the fog in my head. "We had a bit of a . . . um . . . mishap with the caged Mages in the basement."

He lowered his voice as conversations around the room quieted. "They escaped. You should also be aware that attacking a Mage will almost always make you a target. So don't do it until you're ready."

Elder Kohler stared down at the pile of black ash. His shoulders slumped. "And don't use an archaic weapon when you do it. That's why we're training you on your elements."

CHAPTER 10

Before I had time to sort out everything that had just happened, Loken was stuffing me into a transport. I locked my arms against the doorframe and planted my feet. He'd have to forcibly move me to get me into that vehicle. I was going nowhere.

Did I want to end up an ashy pile on the floor? Gods, no. On the inside, I was screaming so loudly that the sound nearly blocked out everything else. But I'd had enough. These Mages had to die, and I could help that happen. In theory.

"I'm staying." I fixed Loken with my best glare; eyes narrowed, lips pulled tight. This was difficult to do while bracing my arms against the transport's doorframe.

"You're going." He stared right back at me. His hand didn't move from my back.

I pushed harder against the transport to keep myself out. "You need Ethereals to help you dispatch the Mages."

"Actually, if you'd been paying attention, you'd know that we don't. We need Breathers, Flooders, Burners—practitioners who can slow them down. Then we need Benders to dispatch them. Sword removes head. That's how it works. Of the twenty-three Mages I've helped dispatch in the past five years, only four of those kills included the help of an Ethereal." He raised four fingers to emphasize his point. "Four." He looked too smug. I wanted to wipe that irksome smirk off his face.

I ducked beneath his arm, released the doorframe, and spun to face him, close enough that I could feel the chill of his body against mine. We were sharing the same space, with nothing but electricity and stubbornness between us. Lots and lots of stubbornness—mostly his. Okay, maybe fifty-fifty.

"If you let me stay, I promise to be better tomorrow." I held my breath and waited.

The muscles in his neck tensed. I counted five whole seconds before he spoke again. His voice sounded strangled by his throat. "You'll take this seriously and stop questioning everything?"

Internally, I flinched at his words. I *was* taking this seriously. That's why I asked so many questions. Just because I stank at manipulating ether didn't mean I wasn't trying. But I brushed off the barb and concentrated on my end game—staying at the Council to hunt the escaped Mages.

I laid a hand on his right arm, which he'd crossed over his chest along with the other. He yanked his arms down to his sides. I took my opportunity to sidestep away from the vehicle, which meant closer to him. His neck bent toward me. I molded myself to the length of his body, instinctively. My nose filled with the sweet metallic scent that was so unique to him.

His arms came back up and wrapped around my waist. "Asha, please go," he whispered.

The hammering in my chest increased its pace. Even after months apart, being together was still so natural. Like gravity. I concentrated on breathing normally even though I felt breathless.

He jerked away from me. His arms left my back like I was on fire. His face flushed red. "Go, Ashara," he growled. My stomach dropped at the sound of my full name. I liked it when he called me Asha. He gave me a harder shove than necessary toward the vehicle door. "Get. In. The. Transport."

"Why am I on the gods-damned team if I'm not meant to do the fighting?" I shouted. "This is my fight. *Mine.*" Exhilaration raced through my veins. These creatures had to be stopped. I'd been too weak in the past, but now I could change that. I *needed* to be here, watching the last one of them die in pain.

"You're not trained. The team will be better off without you. And you'll be alive. If I have to send you home in an urn, it'll break your mother's heart."

"If they're better off without me, why was I even added to the task force? Why not leave me out of it? Somebody thought I was worth the trouble."

He opened his mouth, shut it again, and finally made some words. "Please, just go home." His eyes pleaded with me, and I wanted so much to give him whatever he wanted. "I don't want to have to worry about you when I should be worrying about everyone else. So get in the gods-damned transport and go home. Go be with Sona."

I wavered. I did want to spend as much time as possible with my sister and my parents. But I also wanted to fight—and I wanted to win this argument.

My desire to be near Sona won out. I glared at him as I tucked myself into the vehicle. He'd played the little sister card; I hated that he knew me so well.

But I loved that I still affected him like he affected me.

I spent the first half of the ride home pouting. My face pressed against the back window as I tried to keep the Council building in view. My thoughts turned to Sona and my parents. Excitement at seeing them, at actually spending time with them, stirred inside me. I tapped my foot in an impatient rhythm on the transport floor.

When the vehicle slowed in front of my cluster, I slid the door open and leapt out before it came to a full stop.

"Thanks for the ride," I shouted to the driver as I took off toward home.

I raced around the final corner that brought my house into view, and a wave of disappointment crashed over me. The front yard was vacant, which most likely meant no one was home. Even at the height of the Dutem season, we spent most of our downtime outside. After all, our ancestors had left Earth-One partially to get away from an overpopulated land where people spent way too much time avoiding one another.

Even though I suspected no one was home, I stepped under the archway into the house. Inside, the temperature was only slightly cooler. I did a quick sweep of the bedrooms and confirmed that the place was empty. Then I scampered back outside.

Talin's old rocking chair swayed in the soft breeze, creaking with each sway. It rarely stood empty when Talin was home. I slumped down into the chair and propped my heels on the tree stump in front of it. Some of the tension eased from my muscles. I tilted my head back and enjoyed the soft wind brushing across my face. I could almost taste the grass on the tip of my tongue, as it bowed in the soft breeze.

Sona's tinkling laugh split through the air. "Asha!" she squealed as she turned the corner and came into view. She ran toward me and propelled herself into my lap.

Mom and Talin followed behind her. Like Sona's, Mom's face lit up when she saw me. "What are you doing home?" Hope flickered across her face. "Are you out of that task force?"

"No." The edges of my mouth tugged downward. "At least, I hope not."

She wrung her hands together. Talin, on the other hand, eyed me with quiet understanding.

"There was an incident," I said. Mom's eyes went wide. I continued in a rush to stop her from speaking again. "It's fine though!" I lied. "But some of us were sent home early to get us out of the way."

"Just *some* of you?" asked Talin, in his soothing voice.

I knew I shouldn't tell them what was going on. Or more precisely, I shouldn't tell Mom. She'd just fret and stress me out. But the understanding and patience etched on Talin's face made me talk.

"Actually, I think it was just me. All the practitioners were called back to the briefing room. But Loken"—I toyed with the idea of calling him a bad name, but restrained myself because of Sona's presence—"sent me home. I should burn his balls off with an ether blast. Or explode him. Is that something I can do, explode him?"

"I don't think so." Talin patted my shoulder.

Mom clasped her hands over Sona's ears and scolded me.

"Sorry," I muttered.

She released Sona's ears. "Be nice, Asha. I always liked that boy, despite his working at the Council. And I like him even more right now. You should invite him and his mother over for dinner. I haven't seen her in forever."

I released the band around my ponytail and scrubbed a hand through my hair. It eased my headache a bit. Of course, a few of my fingers got snagged in the mass of curls. I tugged them loose. Sona wrapped her arms around my neck, and I buried my face in her soft hair.

"Why are you upset?" Talin asked. "Do you really want to be on this task force?"

"I do." My voice was partially muffled by Sona's head. "I wasn't sure I belonged at first. I thought it was all a mistake. But it's not."

"Really?" Talin lifted my feet from the tree stump and sat down on it to face me. "So then, something happened? To convince you that you belong?"

"Yes." I lifted my face from Sona's hair, so I could speak more clearly. "I created a shield."

"Well, that's great!"

"I don't know . . . It's good, but it's not going to kill any Mages." My hand flew to my mouth as soon as the words came out.

Mom's face crumpled. Talin stood and wrapped his arms around her.

"Ra's yellow toenails," I muttered under my breath.

"You're going to be fighting Mages?" Mom's voice reached a squeaky pitch. "I can't . . . you can't . . ." Talin pulled one of her hands into his and patted it. "But yesterday, you said . . . *Mages*?"

Talin held up a finger toward me, indicating I should wait, and led Mom just out of my earshot. He sat her down on one of the outdoor dining chairs and whispered something I couldn't hear. Mom stared at me with eyes wide, shaking her head over and over at whatever Talin was saying.

With my mother on the edge of panic, I hadn't noticed Sona staring up at me. Her blue eyes watered. "I don't want you to fight Mages, Asha."

I ruffled her hair, mussing the fine blond strands. "I know, sweetie."

"I don't want you to die."

Mom and Talin rejoined us at the tail end of Sona's sentence. I sucked in a breath and held it.

Talin lifted Sona from my lap, passed her to Mom, and shooed them both away. When they disappeared into the house, he gestured after them. "Your mother, and Sona too apparently—they're afraid to lose you in the exact same way we lost Pace."

So we were actually going to talk about this. That was a change from the norm. Usually we all just sat around in silence whenever Pace came up, no one willing to recognize that we were all thinking the same thing. No one voicing that he'd died at the hands of a Mage. On my watch.

Unshed tears stung my eyes. I refused to let them fall. "That was a one-in-a-million chance, Talin. Mages don't just wander around in the open and attack little children."

"You know that's not how it happened. That Mage went after the two of you. He ignored everyone else in the town center and went after *you*."

"I did everything I could!" I shouted, even though I didn't believe it. I'd gone over the scene a hundred times in the past year, looking for a missed opportunity, a way I could have saved him. There was nothing. There was no scenario I could come up with that allowed me to save Pace. Still, I couldn't help feeling the guilt. Just because I didn't see a way to save him, that didn't mean there hadn't been one. I just wasn't strong enough or smart enough to spot it.

"I know." Talin sat down on the tree stump again. "There was nothing you could have done."

I dropped my gaze to my hands.

"Asha." He lifted my chin so I'd have to look at him. "There was *nothing* you could have done. That's not why I'm bringing this up."

"Then what are you getting at?"

His lips pressed together. "Your mother is afraid she's going to lose you too."

I wasn't suicidal or anything. I just needed to make up for that one time when I hadn't been strong enough. And I needed my vengeance.

"I'm not going to die. They're training me very well." After a pause, I added, "And as you can see, Loken is determined to keep me away from any real danger."

Talin held his palms open, pleading with me. "All I'm saying is, be smart. If you're in over your head, tell someone."

I nodded. "Don't worry. I've got everything under control."

CHAPTER 11
COUNTDOWN: 8 DAYS

I awoke before my alarm, after a fitful night of half-sleep. Through the window, darkness still blanketed my home cluster. Bright pinpoints of light were scattered across the sky.

I stared at the numbers on my comm unit, which continued to count down to who-knew-what. Despite the darkness, my body refused to go back to sleep. I shut my eyes and counted backward from a hundred. By the time I reached one, I was still awake.

My mind was too busy for sleep. There was no doubt I was an Ethereal—a pretty decent one, judging from the strength of my shield. And, apparently, everyone at the Council knew who I was. I shouldn't have been surprised really. I'd never heard of something like what happened to Pace occurring before. The news had been bound to spread.

And for some reason, Elder Kohler and Elder Ethereal didn't seem particularly fond of me, although it must have been the elders who decided to add me to the Ethereal task force. They were the ones who had knowledge of the prior timelines. No one else could have made that decision.

I needed to talk to someone—preferably an elder—about why no one was being straight with me about my placement on the task force.

I crawled out of bed and tripped to the floor as my foot caught in the sheet. Sona mumbled something unintelligible and rolled toward the wall. She cocooned herself deeper into the blankets, tucking them all around her.

I tiptoed around the room, gathering my clothing and toiletry items before heading out into the hallway and to the bathroom.

Steam curled around me in the shower. I flinched at first as it hit my aching muscles. Yesterday had been tougher on my body than I'd realized, and now I was paying the price. My back, arms, and legs stung as the steam loosened them. Like needles pricking deep into my skin. I leaned my head against the shower wall and groaned. The tightness in my muscles released.

After dressing and attempting to tame my hair, I stood outside Mom and Talin's room and pressed my ear to the door. Their dual snores vibrated through the wall, so I decided not to bother them. I blew a kiss at their door and at my own bedroom, where Sona still lay sleeping.

Eerie quiet pierced my ears as I stepped out of the house, broken only by scattered chirps of night birds and the sound of the wind rustling the leaves. I wondered where the two remaining escaped Mages had gone, and whether the Council had located them. I whipped my head from left to right and back again as I walked, sure a Mage hid behind the tree up ahead, or around that corner, or right behind me.

I slowed as I reached the fence surrounding my home cluster. Instinctively, my face turned upward and to the north—to the numbers of the countdown clock that glowed above, stark white over the sky's deep blue. I was too early for my morning transport. It wouldn't be here for another hour, if it was coming at all—if I was still welcome on the Ethereal task force.

I needed a ride to the Council *now*. Making the trip on foot was impossible; it was way too far. If I were a Breather, I could get there in no time . . . Luckily, I *knew* a Breather.

I unclasped the comm unit from my waistband and raised the speaker to my lips. "Contact Rey."

"Command confirmed," came a pleasant female voice in response. After several more seconds, it added, "Rey is not available."

"Try him again!"

"Command confirmed."

Several more seconds and then Rey's sluggish voice came through the speaker. "Ash? What's wrong? Where are you?"

"I'm at the cluster fence. I need a ride to the Council."

He paused. I imagined him checking the time on his comm. "You're an hour early. The transport will be there in plenty of time to get us to training."

"I don't want to wait for the transport."

No answer.

"Rey!"

"What, *what*?"

"Wake up. I need to leave now." Then it occurred to me that, unlike me, Rey probably hadn't been sent packing when the Mages escaped yesterday. "Hey, do you know what happened to the escapees?"

"We couldn't find the other two." The panic that had tinged his voice when he first answered had subsided. Most likely, he'd determined that whatever I needed wasn't urgent after all.

"What do you mean you couldn't find them?" I asked.

"Weren't you there?"

"No." My jaw tightened. "Loken sent me home."

He muffled a chuckle—poorly. "That's what you get for having your boyfriend as a group leader."

"He's not my boyfriend."

"The way you two make eyes at each other whenever the other one's not looking, I'm not sure why you bothered breaking up."

"It wasn't my choice, remember? Your friend is a stubborn, irrational jackass who thinks he can't do his all-important job if he has actual emotions. You know what he did yesterday? He made me—"

"Do I really need to hear this? Don't you have any girlfriends you can rant to?"

"They're all still asleep."

"So am I," he growled.

"You sound awake. Will you take me to the Council?"

"What am I—your personal transport?"

"Yes, please." I caught myself smiling into the phone. It was nice to relax and have a conversation about things that weren't life and death.

"What do I get out of it?"

"The pleasure of my company."

"Hmm, not interested. What else have you got?"

All I had on my person was my comm unit, and Rey had his own. But I knew one thing that always piqued Rey's interest. "There's a cute girl on my task force. I'll put in a good word for you."

"How does that do me any good when we're all going to die in eight days?"

"I bet she'd like you. And she has great legs."

"You think I'm that superficial?"

"She seems rather spirited."

"Give me a few minutes to get dressed," he said. The communication line went dead. In two minutes, Rey stood in front of me. I almost stumbled over my feet when he appeared, as if out of nowhere. I hadn't seen or heard him approach. He grinned at me, his mouth fixed in that lopsided smile.

"Exactly how fast are you?" I asked.

"I've never clocked myself. But . . . pretty fast. I'm moving the air around me more than I'm moving myself, so in theory, there's no physical limit to my speed." Grinning, he added, "So how do want to do this? Shall I toss you over my shoulder, caveman style?"

"How about piggyback?"

He turned around to show me his back. I hopped up and secured myself by wrapping my arms around his neck. He hooked his arms under my knees.

"Ready?" he asked.

We took off. I squeezed my eyes shut and tightened my grip, expecting the wind to batter me as he ran. Amazingly, I felt no more than a light breeze.

The trees on both sides of us whipped past so quickly that I had to avert my eyes to avoid dry-heaving. Luckily, I hadn't eaten, so I was in no danger of losing my breakfast. I pressed my forehead to the top of his head and tried to ignore the world blurring past me.

Rey's feet fell softly as we flew over the land to our destination. Through his back, his heartbeat created a steady rhythm against my chest. It amazed me that he wasn't panting, and his heart wasn't racing.

A cloud of dizziness fell over me as we slowed in front of the building. The world tilted. All I saw was the green of the surrounding gardens and the dark silver of the Council fence. My legs trembled as I leapt to the ground off Rey's back.

"My gods. That was . . ."

Rey smoothed the front of his ponytail into place from where I'd mussed it. "Magnificent. I know."

When things around me stopped spinning, my gaze landed on the fence around the Council building. The gate was closed—really closed. In place of the bars that usually encircled the property, now stood a steel wall blocking all view of the building. The fence had morphed into something impenetrable. It stood close to fifteen feet tall, a circular barrier in the middle of the gardens.

I approached and slid my hand along the metal surface. So smooth and perfect that it felt like glass under my fingertips. The metal formed one unified piece, as if it had come out of a mold looking that way. I pounded my fist against it. Solid.

"Loken," Rey said.

I spun to look at him. My eyes narrowed. "What about him?"

"Well, him or another Bender. Someone changed the fence to keep us out."

"Why would they keep us out?"

Before Rey could answer, a shout sounded from inside the wall. "Stop him! Don't let him out."

"Or to keep something else in," Rey added.

The volume of activity increased on the other side of the wall. More shouts. And a drawn-out screech that sent my heart plummeting down into my stomach.

Gods. The escaped Mages!

I jerked backward away from the wall. Rey grabbed my arm to keep me from tripping over my own feet. I yanked away, trying to escape, trying to get as far as possible from the wall. Or maybe I wanted to get *inside*. I wasn't sure. My self-preservation instinct warred with my desire to kill those miserable creatures.

"We need to help!" Rey shouted. He raced around the entire circle of the wall, leaving on my right side and returning on my left only a few seconds later. "There's no way in."

My eyes scanned the wall, searching for a foothold, something to help me climb over it. But there was nothing. Just smooth, uninterrupted metal.

In a whoosh of air, a huge nude body flew over the left side of the wall from inside. It landed soundlessly on the ground. I focused on it, and froze.

The largest escaped Mage.

My mouth hung open. I stood less than twenty feet from the creature. My legs wouldn't work; I couldn't run. My chest tightened. My lungs stopped breathing for me.

Before I could react, Rey lifted me and whisked me farther away. The Mage raced forward to where I'd stood a second before.

An opening appeared in the metal wall as a portion of it melted away to create a path. Loken darted through. Several people I didn't recognize followed.

Stormy gray eyes landed on me and then went wide. "Get out of here!" Loken shouted. His face twisted in horror, or anger. I wasn't sure which.

The four people behind him converged around the Mage. Loken ran toward us, lifted me from the ground, and dropped me back in Rey's arms. My legs kicked as I fought against them. It was up to *me* to choose whether I wanted to join this fight. *Me*. My choice.

"Get out of here," Loken said to Rey, his voice low. When Rey opened his mouth to speak, Loken shoved him back the way we'd come. "Go now, Rey. Or I swear I'll kill you next time I see you."

Rey moved. And then we were out of range to see or hear anything.

CHAPTER 12

For almost an hour, I paced back and forth under a tree, as Rey relaxed in its shade. I knew how long it was because I checked my comm unit, or the numbers glowing in the sky, every few minutes.

"Why hasn't Loken contacted me to say he's okay?" I said for about the tenth time since Rey had forcibly removed me from the Council.

My chest ached. Loken had to be okay. If we got through this, if there was still a world for us to live in eight days from now, maybe we could work out our differences. I'd be less of a wreck than I'd been since Pace had died. He'd be less of a zealot. We could get back to salvaging something of a life.

At five minutes before the scheduled morning meeting for my task force, I stood before Rey with my hands on my hips. "Time to go," I said.

Rey glanced down at his own comm. "They haven't called us."

"Right. They haven't asked us not to show. So I think it's fair that we go to the morning meets."

"When did you get so bossy?"

"I've always been this bossy."

He grinned. "True. And I've missed it these past months." He leapt to his feet and brushed the grass and dirt from his clothing. "Let's go."

I climbed onto his back, and he raced us back to the Council building. Fortunately, I remembered right away to squeeze my eyes shut, so the world rushing by wouldn't make me ill.

"Wow," he said after a minute, tapping the side of my leg.

My eyes flew open. I braced myself for the worst. I tried to recall everything I'd felt and thought the day before, when I'd created that ether shield. I'd need that shield ready—and preferably some offense too—if we had to fight.

I scanned the Council building. All was back as it should have been. The wall had returned to its normal state—a fence with vertical bars. Clustered around the gate was a large group of Believers, but smaller than the groups that had been there the two days prior. Their red and yellow robes stood out in stark contrast to the bright white and chrome of the Council building.

As we pushed our way through the crowd, my nose filled with their scents—earth and wind and sunlight. I'd never noticed how they smelled before, like they had a oneness with the world. I wondered if they all smelled that way.

"Come on." Rey pulled me the rest of the way through the crowd. He activated the gate by swiping his hand across the biometric security plate near the latch. The gate whirred open just enough to let us squeeze through.

Inside the property, I left Rey on the lawn and raced downstairs to the training room where the Ethereals had met the day before. I was a few minutes later than our scheduled meet time, thanks to Rey's arguing with me about whether we should come or wait for a summons.

All faces turned toward me as I entered.

"You're late," said Loken, his expression flat.

"And you're obnoxious." I headed for the space on the floor beside him, the only remaining place in their circle, and tried not to breathe heavily after my run through the building. Loken's slitted gaze followed me as I flounced onto the floor next to him. I hoped I looked cool and confident—instead of desperate to hear what in Solaris's name was going on here.

He turned his attention back to the others. "As I was saying when we were interrupted"—he shot me a pointed glance—"two of the escaped Mages are still on the loose. Before dawn, we found one of them in a generator room on the third floor. We attempted to secure the property." Another piercing look in my direction. "But he escaped. We assume the other left the area sometime yesterday."

"Any more casualties?" Jin asked. The whites of his eyes were redder today than they'd been the day before.

I'd only known the man for two days. In those days, I'd found him to be confident and passionate, enough to go against his people's ways and join us. But this man—with the slumped shoulders and a trace of stubble on his chin—was like a different person.

I shot a questioning glance at Krin and inclined my head toward Jin. She shrugged.

"Of the two injured during the briefing yesterday, Palis didn't make it through the night. Coron should be fine, but he's out of commission for at least a few days."

"What about civilians?" Jin asked.

"We got a call ten minutes ago that one of our Mages did some damage about fifty miles north of here. There's a body count."

"How many?" Jin's jaw tightened as he squeezed out the words. I imagined guilt eating at his insides, chewing at his very being, turning his soul into something that could not be mended.

I knew the feeling.

"It wasn't your fault, Jin," I said.

"Wasn't it? I damaged the security panel with my little running-around-the-room stunt yesterday. Would they have escaped if the cell hadn't been damaged?"

"It's hard to say," Loken said.

"Did they escape during any of the previous timelines?"

No response from Loken.

Jin's shoulders slumped even further. "So it wasn't inevitable. It was just my recklessness."

I jumped to his rescue. "But lots of things have changed since the prior timelines, right?" I looked to Loken for confirmation. He nodded. "You may have played a teeny-tiny role in this change, but it's a combination of factors. My guess is that there was no—or very little—Mage-combat training in the other timelines. You can blame the escape on that just as much as on anything else that's changed."

Jin's frown deepened. "So you're telling me I would have helped the Mages escape last time too, if I'd only been given the opportunity?"

"No," I said. "I'm saying that all of us played a role. Everyone involved. The Council for deciding on the training. Loken for bringing us downstairs." Loken glared at me. "Elder Ethereal for attacking you."

Loken flinched when I mentioned the elder. "Elder Ethereal was helping us train."

"That's not helping Jin," I muttered softly, so that only he could hear.

Jin didn't speak. His shoulders rode just a little bit higher.

"So what now?" I asked Loken.

"Now we go get those bastards. Unfortunately, that means your training has to be cut short, but we have to deal with this crisis."

Loken led us to the elevator off the main hallway. Just like with the door to the basement, a metal panel occupied a rectangle of wall space next to the door. Loken pressed his hand to it. His hand twitched and then a small light above the panel flipped from red to green. With a hiss, the elevator doors slid open.

"Did that thing just prick your finger?" I pointed at the metal panel.

Loken nodded and stepped into the elevator, beckoning for the rest of us to follow him.

"Is that the way the door to the basement works too?" The elevator doors closed us inside. "That can't be sanitary—the same needle pricking everyone who comes through here."

"There's no better way. It checks my DNA and my handprint. In the past, the security panels used to scrape our fingertips for the DNA. But that system was too easily fooled with someone else's dead skin cells, nail filings, or hair." He took in my appalled expression. "Don't worry; it's self-sanitizing." He wriggled his fingers at me. I scooted to the other side of the elevator so he couldn't touch me. "I've never been cleaner."

"Did you just make a joke?" I asked as the elevator doors opened.

Loken tilted his head to the side, as if contemplating this. "Hmm, no, doesn't sound likely."

He grinned and strode from the elevator toward one of several dozen transports. Every single one of them rested flat on the ground. No wheels. They were all Breather transports.

I wished Rey were here so I could see him drool over this.

The elevator dinged behind me, accompanied by voices and movement. People spilled past me into the room. A door banged open, and more people trampled out from the stairwell.

"Gods." Rey's voice echoed from behind me. He stood just to the side of the elevator, staring at the vehicles arranged in neat rows throughout the room.

He wrapped his arms around me and lifted me into the air, jumping up and down like an excited little boy. "I get to drive one!"

"Really?"

"Yes! Yesterday they stuck me down here all day on emergency transport duty—in case any non-Breather needed to get somewhere in a hurry. No one did." He scowled. "But today, someone else gets that dull job, and I get to drive."

Rey beamed at me. He was practically glowing, and as usual, his cheer was infectious. I laughed as he lifted me in the air once more and then set me down on my feet.

"I tried to get assigned to your transport," he whispered, "but Elder Breather thinks I'm too close to you and Loken already." His gaze swept beyond me to Krin's svelte form, all legs and cheekbones, climbing into the transport closer to us.

I shoved him away and laughed. "You just want to ride with Krin."

"Have you talked to her about me yet?"

"You mean since I saw you thirty minutes ago? No, not yet."

"Well, what's the holdup?" he shouted over his shoulder as he made his way to the transport next to ours.

I climbed into the vehicle where my team was assigned. Loken climbed in next to me. The driver's door opened, and a lanky brown-haired boy folded himself into the front seat.

"I'm Yashor." He turned and waved at us. His fair skin had a smooth, red-cheeked complexion that suggested he was young, but perhaps a year or two older than me. "I'll be your driver today. The trip will be relatively short, about fifteen minutes."

Rey's transport rose several inches into the air and floated to the far side of the room. A feeling of weightlessness came over me for an instant, and then our vehicle followed his. Additional vehicles lifted from the floor behind us.

When Rey's transport reached the wall, a piece of ceiling opened up twenty feet above, leaving a hole just larger than the vehicle. Rey's vehicle shot upward and through the ceiling.

Our transport floated forward into the space Rey's had just occupied. We shot upward, and my stomach felt as though it had dropped into my shoes.

And then we were above the ground and gliding north at an unreasonable speed. It was like running with Rey except, this time, I was enclosed along with six other people. I squeezed my eyes shut and relaxed my head against the headrest.

"Feeling sick?" whispered Krin from my left.

I nodded.

After a pause, she added, "My eyes are closed, so if you were making a gesture or something to answer me, I didn't see it."

I released the breath I'd been holding. "I'm good, I think. My eyes are closed too."

"I think I'm gonna be sick," said Elis's voice.

"There's really no reason for you to feel ill," Mauryn offered. "Yashor, our kind vehicle operator, is repositioning the air all around us. The pressure on your body is drastically reduced. In fact, if you close your eyes, it feels like you're not moving at all."

"I think I can tell when I'm going to be sick," Elis said, his voice tight.

"Mauryn," I said, "remember when you told me to stop you when you get carried away?"

A soft chuckle and then, "Sorry. I'm done now."

I wondered what Jin was up to since, besides Loken, he was the only team member who hadn't spoken since we entered the vehicle. I opened one eyelid just a crack to peer at him. Jin's eyes remained open but pinned on the floor. Poor guy.

If he was lucky, if we were all lucky, we'd catch up with these escaped Mages and put them back where they belonged—in a cage or in the afterlife.

CHAPTER 13

"Stay put for now," Loken said as he hopped out of the vehicle just outside a small city.

Rey's transport idled just ahead. I was pleased our two teams hadn't split up. Rey was turning out to be the one familiar and comfortable thing in the midst of this madness.

"Hey." I tapped Yashor, our driver, on the shoulder. "Where did the others go?"

"There were other reports of Mage sightings besides this one." He turned around to face me. "We don't know which are legitimate, so we have to investigate all of them."

"If we were all going to split up, shouldn't we have separated the task forces, so that there's an Ethereal, a Breather, a Flooder—and so forth—in each group?"

"I just do what I'm told." Yashor shrugged and turned back to the front of the vehicle.

A heavyset man, with sweat dripping from his face and pooling around his collar, jogged over to Loken. They met several yards away from our vehicle.

The man dabbed his forehead with a handkerchief before puffing out, "It was definitely a Mage. So tall." He raised a hand to indicate about a foot higher than the top of his head. "A woman! With hair down to her butt. And those eyes. As black as hell, I tell you. Those things aren't human. I can't believe they were ever human." He bent over and clutched his knees. His breaths wheezed from his lungs.

"Where did she go?" Loken asked.

"Back the way you came," the man said. "We lost her trail. Too fast. The way she moved, it was like the wind—"

Loken cut him off. "How did the city fare?"

"The joint temple is destroyed. Priests were lost."

"Show me."

The heavyset man scrambled into the vehicle, and Loken folded his long limbs inside after him. I scooted across the seat to make room. The man's arms brushed against mine in the crowded space. I cringed as his sweat slicked my shoulder and forearm. Our new arrival directed the driver through the streets, pointing and shouting instructions. Yashor nodded and obeyed.

My face pressed against the glass. Although I'd heard of this place—Masgar, it was called—I'd never seen anything like it. Unlike most civilized cities on Earth-Two, this one mixed Believers and Nonbelievers. As a result, the city got little financial support from its neighbors. I'd heard that some nearby townspeople refused even to sell their wares or offer services to those living inside Masgar.

As we coasted through the city, I recognized some Believers by the red and yellow of their accessories. Wristbands, headbands, earrings, necklaces. I'd have been thrilled to see such different people living together, if it weren't that so many of them wore faded and fraying clothing.

On the outskirts, the homes resembled those in Vallara, except with smaller yards and smaller structures. Mismatched and splintered, their external wooden walls looked unkempt. Color chipped from the few that were painted.

The city center was little better with its pitted dirt roads and undecorated stone buildings. People wore mostly drab clothing, except for the occasional flashes of red and yellow. They mingled together as they stopped and chatted.

I remembered what I'd wanted to ask Loken while he was outside. "Loken," I said, "why didn't we divide up the task forces?"

"We'll do that for future outings. At this point, the task force members don't have enough training to fly solo without the support of their teams and team leaders." He jabbed a finger at my face. "And you, stay close to me. You would have stayed back at the Council if I'd had my way."

I made a rude sign with my hand when he turned away.

After several minutes, we'd seen no sign that a Mage had been here. Although run down, the place seemed safe enough. As far as I could tell, the Mage hadn't destroyed anything or killed anyone. No dead bodies spotted the ground. No destroyed buildings lined the road.

My anticipation rose as we drifted farther south, toward what the city was most known for. Once we made it over this last hill, we should see the joint temple. I craned my neck, searching for the famous Temple of Masgar.

This structure represented over a century of cooperation in Masgar to find commonality between its two peoples. The officials of Masgar had dedicated this temple to the people, to worship whichever gods they chose. According to my social studies books, it was a place to worship Ra, Solaris, and any other "god" the citizens chose to follow.

My mouth hung open as the tall structure came into view. Light glanced off the building, reflecting rays directly at us. Even through the tinted windows of the transport, I had to shield my eyes to get a better view—a shining beacon in the midst of an unkempt town.

Our transport and Rey's slowed to a stop in front of the temple. I stepped out, filled with awe. Rey came over and stood beside me, also staring up at the magnificent structure, glistening red and gold in the dual sunlight. What remained of the crumbling walls consisted of reddish and gold-colored stones.

My gaze finally strayed from the top of the temple and swept the entire structure, or what was left of it anyway. The right side had collapsed into itself, the red and gold stones broken and scattered along the right side of the lawn. My stomach knotted in mourning for this beautiful thing that had been destroyed.

Mauryn stepped closer to the temple and pressed his palms to the red rock. "In the names of the gods," he muttered as he slid his hands over the stone. "This temple is just the first step. Someday, we're all going to live as one people, worshiping as we like, believing what we like. No more separation based on religion and over-reliance on technology."

He pressed his face against the exterior. His eyes drifted shut as if he were listening for a heartbeat in the stone. He stayed there in silence long enough that I felt like an intruder for staring.

"Um, Mauryn. Are you okay?"

When he opened his eyes, tears glistened under his eyelids. "Wonderful. I don't think the people in this city truly appreciate what this temple means to our world." He fingered the red strip of cloth tied around his wrist. "It's the beginning of so much more. If we can merge religion and science, we can be—"

"You're rambling." Elis's voice was flat, bored.

I narrowed my eyes in his direction.

"What?" Elis said. "Mauryn said we should tell him when he gets carried away." He shrugged and strode toward the remainder of our team, clustered with the group from the other transport.

"How was the ride?" I asked Rey, who like me, continued to examine the temple. "And what task force is that?" I waved toward the group of people I didn't recognize, who had ridden with Rey.

"They're from the Flooder task force. The transport—it was like flying! And so simple. Just a little propulsion from the bottom, and it's just like I'm running inside the vehicle. When we're done with this Mage thing, I *have* to get a job at the Council."

"You do realize we may *never* be done with this?"

"You know, you can be pretty negative sometimes. All the time, really."

I showed him the same hand gesture I'd given Loken in the transport.

"Ra's calloused feet! What's in there?" Loken's shouts jerked me from our conversation.

Loken was leaning over the short, heavyset man who'd led us to the temple. The man cowered beneath him.

"Wh-what's where?" the man stuttered.

"In the temple?" Loken jerked his arms toward the partially crushed red-and-gold structure. "There's a reason it's the only thing in the city that this Mage targeted." Loken fisted a handful of the man's shirtfront. "What in the bright sky is inside that temple?"

"Th-they were doing some experimentation inside. Some of the Nonbelieving p-practitioners."

Loken pulled the man so close that their noses almost touched. "There are unregistered practitioners in this city?"

"Y-yes."

Mauryn spoke up. "Not everyone believes what the Council believes. Not everyone was on board with your little registration program or believes that the end of the world is nigh." I thought there might have been a drop of sarcasm in that last part. It was hard to tell.

Loken ignored Mauryn's comment and continued to interrogate the man who'd led us here. "Do you also ignore our mandate that practitioners are not to gather together without notifying the Council in advance?" The words rumbled upward from Loken's throat, more of a growl than typical speech.

"I-I don't know. I don't know!" the man shouted, tugging to escape Loken's grasp.

Loken threw him to the ground and tossed him a disgusted look. He took in the Ethereals and Flooders staring at him. He fixed his face back into his normal, controlled expression.

"You." Loken pointed to Krin, Jin, Elis, and several of the Flooders. "Go inside the temple and get a count of the bodies. And see if you can identify how many were practitioners."

They nodded and scampered off. Elder Flooder—whom I'd seen briefly at the first meeting a couple days earlier—followed. The elder led the group through the front door of the temple.

Three priests, two in red robes and one in yellow, lay prostrate in front of the temple. At first I thought them all dead. But muffled chants rose from them. The others and I kept our distance from them.

Loken, on the other hand, strode forward and tapped the yellow-robed Solaris priest on the shoulder. The priest startled at his touch and sat up, frowning.

"What happened here?" Loken asked.

"Could this wait until I finish praying?" The priest's forehead creased as his frown deepened.

"No." Loken knelt in the grass, putting his face at the priest's level.

After making a disapproving *tsk-tsk* sound, the priest said, "A Mage." His voice trembled. Red, puffy lids rimmed his eyes.

Loken's voice softened as he caught a good look at the priest's face. "What did you see?"

"I was inside, leading a prayer—"

Loken cut him off. "You pray inside? I thought all you Believers prayed in sunlight."

"The temple has . . . *had* a glass ceiling. On the side of the building that . . . that . . ." His voice caught in his throat.

Loken nodded and gestured for the man to continue.

"There was no warning. The temple shook. Paintings fell from the walls. The holy sculpture of the gods crashed to the floor. Some people ran for the doors. A few stayed; maybe they were in shock. I pushed as many as I could toward the doors."

He inhaled a deep, shaky breath before continuing. "The ceiling cracked. I ran. As soon as I stepped outside, it was like I was caught in a tornado. The whole side collapsed." His voice went low and solemn. "As the building fell, the rocks crushed some of the worshipers who'd made it outside. I should have made them move farther away." Fresh tears dripped from his lashes and rolled down his cheeks.

"And the Mage? Did you see her?"

"When I came outside, yes. She was standing on the right side of the building. She was so . . . normal. Really tall, but normal." His body trembled. He stared off into the distance but didn't focus. "Except for those eyes. There's no way I should have seen them clearly, as far away as I was. But I could see them, burning into my soul." The priest faced Loken again. "Do you know what attracted her to the temple?"

Loken paused for too long before answering, and that telltale muscle in his jaw ticked. "How many fatalities?"

"We don't have a full count from inside the building. We estimate around twenty-two dead outside."

My chest tightened. So many. All for being in the wrong place at the wrong time. Later, I'd have to grill Loken about what he knew and wasn't saying.

"What about after the collapse?" Loken asked. "How many did the Mage kill directly?"

"I can't say. She entered the temple through the collapsed side. We need to get inside to see."

"What about outside? How many did she kill outside after the collapse?"

"None. She went inside, and then took off."

Loken's brow furrowed. "How many people were on the lawn?"

The priest's eyes flitted about the space around them, as if trying to re-create the scene. "Thirty. Maybe forty."

"Thank you, Father." Loken pressed the man's hand to his head, a common gesture of respect to Solaris priests. The priest nodded and went back to his prayers.

The two Ra priests in red robes had finished their prayers. Loken waited for them to rise to their feet, and then pressed each of their right hands to his chest, one at time, as a gesture of respect to Ra. He motioned for me to do the same. I did.

Loken left one of the priests to me. I asked him the same questions Loken had asked the Solaris priest. I learned nothing new.

As we finished up, the rest of the group filed out from the doors of the temple. Elder Flooder led the group, his long legs quickly eating up the space between us. The vials of water attached to his belt clinked together as he joined me, Loken, and the others who'd stayed outside.

Rey caught my eye, jerked his head toward Loken, and mouthed, *You okay?*

I ignored him.

"Let's get out of here," said Elder Flooder, already moving toward his transport. "The Mage is gone. There's nothing to learn here, and nothing we can do."

"Don't we want to talk about what attracted her?" I called after the elder.

He slipped into his transport and didn't offer a response. I looked around the group, silently pleading for someone to offer a logical explanation. The Flooders followed their leader back to their transport. With an apologetic shrug, Rey trailed after them.

My gaze landed on Mauryn, who seemed to know everything. He'd have an answer for me.

"That's clear enough," said Mauryn. "The Mage was attracted to the practitioners. Too many gathered in one place."

"Why does it matter how many were together?"

"Mauryn." Loken's voice was tinged with warning.

Mauryn didn't seem to notice, and forged ahead. "Practitioners attract Mages. More practitioners means greater attraction. That's why the Council encourages all practitioners to notify them of any gatherings."

Loken's gaze was landing everywhere except on me.

"Loken?" I said.

That muscle in his jaw twitched. "We should head back to the Council."

"Loken?" When he still didn't answer, I directed my next question at Mauryn. "So each of us is a Mage magnet?"

"Pretty much, yes."

CHAPTER 14

Questions swam through the cloud inside my head as our transport sped back to the Council. What Mauryn had just told me made so much sense. I should have seen it sooner.

The Mage who killed Pace had been after *me*. I'd attracted him, and then I'd been too weak to defend my brother. What if I hadn't brought Pace to the garden that day? What if I'd known all along that I had practitioner blood? And what if I'd been properly trained to manage the consequences of that?

I tried to block those thoughts from my head, and focused on other issues. Two days ago, Elder Kohler had told us that Mages were approaching Vallara, but he hadn't told us why. Had I even wondered why, or had I been too busy panicking?

"Mauryn." I tapped him on the shoulder. "If the Mages are coming to Vallara because of the practitioners, why don't we all just leave? Or why don't we spread out?"

"Because," Loken cut in before Mauryn could answer, "what if the Mages aren't the problem that's going to end everything? What if we send everyone away, and we're unable to stop something else that's coming, and unable to perform another rewind? Or what if the Mages keep coming, and there are no practitioners here to meet them? What if—"

"Stop!" Jin shouted, jumping out of his seat. His head banged against the ceiling, but still, he leaned forward and grabbed Yashor's shoulder. "Stop!"

The world slowed down outside my window.

"Okay. Why?" Yashor asked.

"Let's head east. There's a Believer village not far from here."

"There is?" Loken's brow furrowed. "The Council isn't aware of any village east of here."

"That's because not everyone feels the need to notify you people when we shower, brush our teeth, or pee."

Loken glared but said nothing.

"There could be practitioners there who didn't respond to your call for registration," said Jin.

"You think the Mage might have detoured into the village to find them?" Loken asked.

"It's worth a shot. What do we have to lose by checking?"

"Time," said Elis. I flinched at the sound of his voice; it had begun to grate on my nerves. "We have *time* to lose, and not much of it left." He made a show of staring at the countdown clock ticking down on his comm. He jabbed his finger toward the glowing red numbers in the sky—they were red in the daytime—as if we could possibly miss them.

"Could you just shut your mouth for a second and let the grown folks talk?" Krin said. I liked her so much.

I itched to look up in the sky where Elis had pointed, to check the time remaining. But that would do nothing except raise my stress level, which was already so high that I couldn't help my foot from tap-tapping on the floor of the vehicle.

"It's just a thought," Jin said. "We'll be quick. We'll ask if they've seen any activity. If not, we'll get back on our way with only ten minutes lost."

Elis crossed his arms over his chest and stared out the window, his expression set in a grimace.

"Let's do it," said Loken.

"Yashor," said Jin. "Turn due east here, and we'll run right into it."

A minute later, we climbed out of the transport at the edge of the Believer village. Jin had insisted that we not drive inside the village. Loken had agreed to this restriction only because Jin refused to help him gather information inside otherwise. Elis looked up at the clock in the sky repeatedly as we walked. Each time he did, my shoulders tensed more.

I hung back from the rest of the group, casting wary looks at the Believers staring at us as we passed. Unlike the people who'd been picketing outside the Council, these were not dressed in ceremonial red-and-yellow robes. Mostly, their garb consisted of earth tones; browns and greens, with the expected sprinklings of red and yellow in their accessories—bracelets, earrings, and wristbands.

We followed Jin, who walked a confident path through the town, never pausing to figure out where he was going. Though constructed of wood, like our homes, the ones in this village had larger yards. Water pumps and small fire pits occupied space on almost every front lawn. As we passed a doorway, I peered inside at the row of beds pushed against the back wall. I guessed these people spent even more time outside than we did.

Jin turned down the walkway of a house. A dark-skinned woman stood from her chair on the lawn. Although she looked about a decade younger than Jin, her glossy dark hair and unblemished skin mirrored his.

She jogged over to us and wrapped Jin in a tight hug. When she pulled away, she slapped him across the face. I cringed at the sharp sound of the impact.

Jin didn't even flinch. "It's good to see you too." He hugged her again, longer this time.

I let my gaze wander away, embarrassed to watch their show of affection.

"What are you doing?" The woman shoved Jin back toward the road. "Get out of here. I don't want the villagers to lock you up. They keep going on about how you betrayed us."

He turned to face all of us. "This is my sister, Naja. Naja, these are Loken, Mauryn, Krin, Elis, Ashara, and Yashor." He pointed at us one by one as he said our names.

"Nice to meet all of you." Naja nodded to us and turned back to Jin, planting her hands on her hips. Her lips pursed. "Are you going to tell me what you're doing here?"

"Don't worry," Jin said. "No one's going to cause any trouble for me. I came with backup."

Naja eyed all of us. Her gaze stayed on Loken longest. Her face relaxed. I guessed she'd decided that we could all handle ourselves. "Come sit down." She led us deeper onto her lawn and sat down on the grass, motioning for us to join her. When we were all seated in circle, she continued, "So what brings you here?"

"We thought a Mage might have come this way," said Loken.

Naja shook her head.

Jin dropped his head into his hands, elbows propped on his knees.

"What's going on here?" Naja's gaze darted back and forth between her brother, with his downcast expression, and Loken, whose fists clenched at his sides.

"I may have helped three Mages escape from the Council," Jin mumbled into his hands.

"No," I cut in. "It wasn't your fault, Jin."

Mauryn waved a dismissive hand. "The fault doesn't matter. What matters is that we find them."

"And they're clearly not *here*," Elis muttered, his voice barely loud enough to hear. Krin shot him a glare.

"So now what?" I asked.

Jin dragged himself to his feet and dusted the grass from his clothing. "Now we go back to the Council, I suppose."

The air shifted. From the looks on the others' faces, they felt it too—like a low hum vibrating through the air. A thrum of power, close by. A shout erupted back the way we'd come. I jumped to my feet and whirled in that direction.

Standing at the edge of the lawn was the female Mage. Her blond hair tossed in the wind, her expression eerily flat.

Loken leapt up and drew his sword.

The Mage darted toward us. I tried to run and, at the same time, tried to turn around. My feet tripped over each other, and I collapsed to the ground. I fell hard on my tailbone. My teeth clattered together. Pain rocketed up my back. Loken rushed forward to stand in front of me, blocking most of my view of the pale Mage and her billowing blond tresses.

All my muscles locked. I willed them to move, but they refused. I stared, open-mouthed. The Mage sped toward us. She moved so quickly that she seemed to blink into and out of existence. She darted to the side, disappearing and then reappearing closer. I became dizzy just watching her move. When she got close enough, Loken swept his sword to the left. She dodged to the side and disappeared.

She appeared again, twenty feet away. Her eyes locked on mine. I drowned in them, lost in their inky depths. I couldn't move. I couldn't scream, though my mouth hung open in silence. My pulse hammered against my ears.

She raced toward us again. Her shoulder rammed into Loken, who stumbled to the side. She bent over me, her fingers curled to tear me open. The wind whipped her blond locks into my face, bringing with them the scent of rot and decay.

I'm going to die now. I squeezed my eyes shut and hoped it wouldn't hurt much. I hoped I'd see Pace on the other side. I hoped Talin would console Mom and Sona.

A shriek ripped from the Mage's throat. My eyes flew open. The metal tip of Loken's sword tore through her abdomen. Warm blood sprayed across my face.

I scrambled backward out of her reach and climbed to my feet. Loken withdrew the sword and stabbed again. The Mage's screams echoed from every surface. They surrounded me, filled my head. Terror tightened my chest, cutting off my breath.

I didn't care about killing Mages. I didn't care about the end of the world. More than anything, right now, I just didn't want to die. Tears blurred the world around me as I ran. Loken's and Krin's voices followed behind me. They shouted my name, but I couldn't stop. My legs moved like they were possessed. I had to keep moving, or that Mage's clawed fingers would rip out my heart.

I ran until the dirt road curved, and then I kept running. I didn't hear anyone following me, but I abandoned the road, cut across the yards, and zigzagged between houses. With each second that passed, I imagined the Mage's breath hotter on my neck. I ran harder.

I tripped over a large rock and sprawled in the grass. My knees stung where small pebbles tore into them. I scrambled to the side of the nearest house, out of view of the main road.

My ears strained for any sound. But all was quiet. No footsteps pounded against the road. No nearby breathing except my own, unsteady but present.

A touch on my shoulder pulled a scream from my chest.

"Hey. Hey, sweetie." Krin's voice. "It's okay. It's just me."

I turned so I could look at her. Her manicured eyebrows pinched together as she examined my scraped knees and tear-streaked face.

"It's just me," she said again.

"Oh, gods." I pulled her down to the ground with me and crushed her in a hug, letting the tears stream down my face.

"Shh, shh." She rubbed circles around my back as I wept into her shoulder. "Shh, shh," she whispered again and again until my tears finally subsided.

With Krin being so sweet, patting my back and cooing at me, the truth of what had just happened hit me hard. I'd run. I'd panicked. I'd abandoned my team.

"I . . . I . . ." I inhaled steadying breaths, trying to make my mouth form words. "I'm sorry." I wiped my eyes and concentrated on keeping my voice from trembling.

"For what?" Krin brushed aside the loose strands that had escaped my ponytail.

"I ran."

"Don't be sorry. I would have run too."

"No." I shook my head. "No, you wouldn't have. You would have stayed and fought with Loken . . . Loken! Oh, gods, is he okay?"

"He had a handle on things when I left. Loken can take care of himself."

I leaned back against the house that hid us from the road and sighed loudly. "That's no excuse for leaving him alone." I slapped my fists against my head, furious with myself. "All the times I've whined at him for bailing on our relationship. And what I do? I leave him to die as soon as I feel the first hint of fear for my own life."

"I don't blame you. The way that Mage went after you—and with as little experience as you have handling your ability—I would have run too!"

"Well apparently, she's not the smartest Mage. She's supposed to find the greatest energy source, right? The rest of you have so much more power than I have."

Krin raised a brow.

"She should have gone after Loken, or Mauryn!" I flushed when I realized what I'd just said. "I didn't mean that like it sounded. I don't want either of them hurt."

I opened my mouth to speak again, but Krin held up a hand to stop me. "I heard something." She stuck her face around the side of the house and darted back. She paled. "She's out there. On the road."

I tried to scramble to my feet to run again, but Krin yanked me back down. "She's a Breather. Are you going to outrun her?"

Suddenly, I missed Rey a lot. He would be slower than the lady Mage, especially while dragging Krin and me along with him. But having him whisk us away to safety was a nice fantasy nonetheless.

"Is she coming this way?" I asked.

"You want me to check?"

"No, wait." I grabbed her arm. What if the Mage saw her and it got us both killed? Of course, the other option was to sit behind this house for who knew how long.

We sat in silence for a long time, staring at each other and counting the time that passed. I looked up at the sky and watched the minutes tick downward. I wanted so badly to look around the corner and see if the Mage was still out there. Instead, I sat on my hands to keep myself from moving.

Twenty minutes passed in utter quiet, except for the sounds of our breathing.

"You think it's safe to go?" Krin whispered.

Before I could answer, a boy I didn't know flopped down beside me. I started to squeal, but he slapped his palm over my mouth.

Krin's hand shot out and grabbed his wrist. A soft blue light emanated from her grip.

"Ow!" The boy yanked his arm back and scrambled away across the ground, out of Krin's reach. "I'm trying to help you," he hissed. He rubbed the reddened skin on his wrist where Krin had shocked him.

I searched his face, trying to get a read on him. Deep brown skin. Hair twisted into dreadlocks just past shoulder length. Broad shoulders and thick, muscular arms, but a baby face that could mean he was anywhere from his early teens to his early twenties. Despite his size, he had kind eyes. He didn't look too threatening.

I moved toward him. Krin grabbed my arm to keep me still, shaking her head hard.

"It's either me or the Mage," the guy whispered. "I can hide you."

I peeked around the corner, and my breath caught. The Mage stood in the center of the dirt road, facing the opposite direction, her blond hair billowing in the breeze.

I nodded toward the boy.

He stood and we followed him. He crept along the backs of houses until we reached one with a hole tunneled underneath it. He pointed at Krin and me, then jabbed a finger down toward the hole.

"I am not getting in there," Krin whispered. "I don't know what kind of creatures are down there."

I bent down and tried to peer under the house, but all I could see was darkness. I couldn't even tell how big it was or how steep the trip down would be.

The boy shoved me aside and propelled himself downward into the gaping hole. I strained to hear down there, but it was silent. No sounds of his screaming in pain. So it was probably safe. I crouched on the ground and prepared to follow him.

"Wait." Krin gestured down toward the darkness. "You don't know what's in there."

"No. But I'll bet there are no Mages."

I slid along the dirt for several feet before dropping into an opening. Inside, I pressed my hands along the edge of the space. It was a small cave under the house. There would be no way out other than the way we'd entered. I huddled next to the boy, who took up about half the small space, to make room for Krin.

"She's not far. Be quiet," the boy hissed after Krin joined us.

I unclipped my comm from my waistband and activated the display light. Krin followed suit. I raised my light higher and examined the wall nearest me. Bugs crawled in and out of tiny holes in the packed dirt wall. "Ugh." I inched away from the wall and toward the center of the cramped space. Imagining they were crawling all over me, I brushed nonexistent bugs from my shoulder.

Now that I had a chance to examine the boy in the dim light, he looked like a younger version of Jin. I guessed he was in his early teens.

The boy tucked his arms behind his head and shut his eyes. I shot a questioning glance at Krin. She just shrugged.

After a few minutes, his chest rose and fell in the steady rhythm of sleep.

I checked the time on my comm. Over half an hour had passed since we'd entered the village. I hated that Loken would think I'd not only abandoned him, but had also stayed away long enough that he would worry. But there was nothing I could do about that right now, with the Mage lurking just outside.

CHAPTER 15

"What!" I shouted as I jerked awake. The boy who looked like Jin had gripped me by both shoulders and was shaking me.

Krin shoved him away. "Get off her!"

"Hey." He threw his hands up in surrender. "I was just trying to wake her. I didn't save your life just to bring you to my cave and murder you."

Krin crossed her arms over her chest, her face still drawn with suspicion.

"I'm okay, Krin," I said. "And if he tries to kill us, you can kick him."

"Promise?" she asked.

"Promise. But he did save us out there, so he's probably not trying to kill us."

"So no kicking?" Her face fell.

"Sorry, no."

"Great." He peeked over the small ledge that led upward to the outside world. "Now that we've settled that, let's get out of here."

He climbed out of the cave easily enough, as did Krin. Being shorter than both of them, I dug my fingers into the dirt and scrambled my way out, kicking my legs for momentum.

I sucked in the fresh air as we emerged on the outside. Ra had already set, and Solaris was well on its way, which meant we'd been in the cave for hours.

The boy turned toward Naja's house.

"Hey." I reached for his arm. "Thanks for hiding us."

"No problem. I was headed for that little cave anyway." He held out a hand for me to shake. His face broke into a smile, displaying a pair of dimples. "I'm Hael."

"Ashara," I said. We shook hands. "And that's Krin. Are you Jin's brother?"

"Uh-huh. I saw you at the house earlier. Let's get back before Naja and your people start to worry."

My right knee throbbed as I dragged my feet back to Naja's house. I overcompensated by putting most of my weight on my left. Still, I wasn't moving as quickly as Krin and Hael.

"Did you hurt yourself?" Krin asked.

"I think so. Maybe when I fell."

I stumbled, but Hael caught me before I hit the ground. He scooped me up into his arms. My comm unit came dislodged from the belt loop of my shorts and clattered to the ground. Hael held out his hand, palm facing downward.

It zoomed up into his hand like he'd jerked it toward him.

My mouth dropped open. "How did you just do that?"

He winked at me. "I come from a long line of Ethereals. We understand it better than you Nonbelievers do."

"I've never seen Jin do anything like that."

"Jin is more like you guys than like us."

"Can you teach us?" Krin asked.

Hael's gaze traveled up and down Krin, determining her worthiness. "I don't know. It's kind of forbidden for us to encourage Nonbelievers to practice. You guys tend to . . . screw things up."

Krin's eyes narrowed. I could imagine the wheels spinning in her head. She wasn't one to hold her tongue. The fact that she was doing it now meant that she wanted information from Hael as much as I did. She said sweetly, "Well, show us how *not* to screw things up."

He shook his head. "It's no good. It's a religious difference. Your energy comes from the gods. If you don't believe that, it would be like trying to teach a blind man how to see better."

He was hopeless. I didn't need him to teach me—or carry me.

"Will you put me down please? I can walk."

Hael set my feet carefully on the ground, but kept one of my arms around his shoulders. My knee had loosened up by then, and I could have walked on my own but Hael's grip was firm. I leaned against him for the rest of the way.

Naja's house came into view. Jin and Naja sat in the front yard. Loken paced back and forth across the lawn, his eyes darting all over the place, searching. When he locked onto me, he broke out of his pacing and raced toward me. Hael dropped my arm and stepped aside.

I flinched as Loken stopped right in front of me. I expected foul words to rush from his lips. I clamped my jaws tight and braced myself for the tongue-lashing I deserved.

Instead, Loken cupped my face in his hands and turned it from side to side, examining it.

"What?" My voice trembled.

"You're bleeding. Are you hurt?" His hands explored my body, moving downward to my neck and shoulders. They swept over my breasts, my back, my abdomen. He patted down my hips and legs. When he was done, he released a slow stream of breath. "You're not injured." Relief was evident in his voice. "Whose blood is that on your face?" He glanced behind me to Krin and Hael, neither of whom had any blood on them.

"I-I think it's the Mage's." I was still waiting for the shitstorm that was sure to come for my running off in the middle of a Mage fight.

Loken enveloped me in a hug. My face pressed against his chest. My nose filled with his sweet scent. I collapsed into him and wrapped my arms around his neck.

He pushed me away and held me at arm's length. "Where the hell were you?" He gripped my upper arms, and his fingers pressed into my skin. I cringed under the pressure of his fingertips.

"I'm sorry. I'm sorry." Unshed tears stung my eyes, but I didn't let them fall. I'd shown too much weakness already today. "I should have stayed and fought. I shouldn't have left you like that. I'm awful. I'm so sorry."

"Who the hell are you?" he spun toward Hael.

"Hael." He stuck out a hand to shake.

"This is Jin's little brother," I said. "He hid Krin and me from the Mage. That's why we took so long getting back."

"Why were you leaning on him just now? You're not bleeding. Do you need assistance?" Loken turned to Hael and raised a single eyebrow.

"No, sir. Just trying to be a gentleman." Hael's hand still hung between them, waiting for Loken to join it in a handshake.

Finally, Loken clasped it. He clutched Hael's hand until his knuckles turned white. "I'm Loken—senior practitioner and head of the Ethereal task force."

Hael yanked his hand from Loken's grasp.

Loken took a step closer to Hael. I didn't know where that confrontation was going, and I wasn't going to stand around to find out. I turned the ill attention back to me, where it belonged. "Loken, I'm really sorry for running. It won't happen again."

He turned back to me, and his expression softened. "Don't worry," he said, his voice a soft caress. "This is all new to you.

The Council had no business putting you in this position." Anger danced behind his gray eyes, like a storm rolling in. "I told them you shouldn't be on the team. This is too dangerous and you aren't trained."

He was right, of course. I wanted to see those Mages burned and bloodied and cut into teeny-tiny little pieces. But it was time to face that maybe I wasn't the one to do that.

I had no business putting anyone else in danger. As soon as I got back to the Council, I'd convince Elder Kohler to take me off the team. I'd bow out with as much dignity as I could muster—little as that was after today's events.

Loken stared down at his feet. "I'm so sorry. We'll go to Kohler and ask him to get you some protection until all this over. We'll—"

"*You're* sorry?" I cut in, willing myself not to shout or cry. "*You're* sorry? I left you, remember? Just left you to die! How can you even stand to look at me? I'm a horrible, awful person. You should . . ." I couldn't think of something sufficiently awful that he could do to punish me. "You should—"

His mouth was on mine before I could come up with anything. His arms wrapped around my waist and lifted me up against him. My arms snaked around his neck.

It was so familiar and, at the same time, so refreshing. I'd missed the taste of him over the past months. Everything had fallen apart when the Vision came down. And then Pace had died, and I'd refused to even talk to Loken about it. So many things between us.

Now there was nothing except him and me.

With Loken's solid body pressed against mine, I could never believe the world was coming to an end. My senses filled with him; his scent, his strength holding me up. His heartbeat pounded steady and strong against my chest. My fingers tangled in his hair, and the world fell out from under us.

His lips were soft against mine, devouring me. I sucked the lower one into my mouth as we kissed, wanting more, taking more.

He pulled away just enough to speak. “Don’t ever scare me like that again,” he whispered into the tiny space between our mouths.

Instead of answering, I pressed my lips against his again.

“You are the most frustrating woman to ever walk the planet. You know that?” he mumbled against my lips.

“I know.”

CHAPTER 16

Despite the doom that hung in the air, everyone at the table was laughing or smiling. The crowd was larger than usual, so Sona sat on Talin's lap, shoveling forkfuls of his dinner into her mouth. Talin watched her with an adoring smile. Mom walked around the table with the serving trays, ignoring everyone's refusals for more food.

I'd invited Loken to join us, but he and his mother already had dinner plans with some close friends of hers.

Krin and Rey sat across from me. Rey had finished eating and had somehow managed to snake an arm around Krin's waist. She stole occasional glances at him from underneath her thick eyelashes. He soaked up the attention like a horny sponge.

Both sets of their parents were here too, on the opposite end of the table, having understandably insisted on joining their children for dinner. Rey's little brother sat next to Talin and Sona, playing in his food.

When I finished eating, I leaned back in my seat and soaked in the joy. If I died in eight days, I wanted memories like this to be the ones I carried into the afterlife—if there was an afterlife. And if there wasn't, I wanted moments like this to be on my mind when I blinked out of existence.

"Are you finished eating yet, little one?" I asked Sona, trying to hide a smile behind my hand.

Sona paused, a forkful of food raised in front of her, and shot a glance around the table. Everyone else's eating utensils lay across their plates. Most of us had pushed our plates away and moved on to conversation. A few rubbed our stomachs contentedly.

Sona stuck the fork in her mouth and chewed. Her eyes locked on mine as she took her time gnashing and then swallowing the bite. She set the fork down on the plate. "*Now*, I'm done," she proclaimed, pushing the plate away from her.

"Great!" Rey leapt from his seat, snatched Sona from Talin's lap, and gestured for Krin and his little brother to follow him. He lifted Sona into his arms and spun her in a circle. Her squeals of delight were soon joined by Rey's own laughter.

Talin, Krin's parents, and Rey's mother retired to the sitting area on the other side of the yard. Talin settled into his rocking chair. The others sat on small stools that Mom had set out earlier in honor of the gathering.

It was the first time I'd had my mother alone since all of this started. "Mind if I help you clean up?" I asked.

"Not at all. I could use a hand."

She piled a stack of serving dishes in her arms and hurried into the house. I gathered a collection of dirty plates and silverware from the table and followed.

After I placed the dishes in the sink, I asked her, "Will you tell me about my father?" I assumed I inherited my elemental ability from him, since no one in my Mom's ancestry that I'd ever heard of was a practitioner.

Mom's mouth made an O-shape. I shifted from foot to foot as I awaited her response. I knew little about my father other than his name and that he and Mom hadn't known each other for long.

She sat in one of the old, wooden living-room chairs and motioned for me to sit across from her. I did.

"I'm sorry I haven't initiated this conversation on my own," she said. "It's just that . . . I never really made my peace with how your father died. And I didn't want it to bother you too. I'll tell you whatever you want to know."

"I have some specific questions, but I'd rather start at the beginning. How did you meet? How did he die? I want to know everything."

Mom took in a deep breath and settled back into her chair. "Your father and I had a short but passionate relationship." Pink tinged her fair cheeks. She twisted a lock of chestnut-brown hair around her finger.

I held up a hand to stop her. "Okay, I take back what I said. I want to know *almost* everything about him, excluding your *passion*. Please don't ever use that word around me again. Thank you in advance."

"No passion. Got it." She chuckled, emphasizing the fine lines around her eyes and mouth, which had been worn into her skin over a lifetime of smiling and laughing. Not even Pace's death could take those lines away. It was nice to see them again. "Reesa and I met him at a Ratem festival, about a year before you were born."

The Ratem festival, celebrating the first day of the season in which only Ra was in the sky, was probably the only annual event that Believers and Nonbelievers celebrated together. For the Believers, it was a religious celebration dedicated to the god Ra. For us, it was just a reason to celebrate.

Mom continued, "As a Council member, he was at the festival to see and be seen. To help with the preparations."

"Wait." I held up my hand again. "My dad was on the Council."

She nodded.

My brow furrowed. "But you hate them."

"I didn't always. I'll get to that, but let me finish this part of the story first."

"Okay," I said, even though I wanted to jump ahead to my birth father's relationship with the Council. "What did he look like?"

She smiled. Her eyes swept over my face. "Like you. His skin was darker, and his hair much curlier. His ancestry was Earth-One African. But he had the same eyes and mouth as you."

I wished I had a mirror in front of me, so I could examine my eyes and imagine what my birth father looked like. I'd do that later. "How did you meet?"

"Nole was such a flirt!" She giggled then, girlish. I could imagine her nineteen years ago, giggling and flirting with a handsome boy who looked like me. "He wore the Seer robe. You know, with the hood." She mimed flipping a hood over her head. "So I knew he was a Seer. He told me he could see my future." Her eyes went distant for a moment. A wistful smile played across her face.

"He was a Seer?" I leaned forward in my chair. I should have been annoyed that I'd never known that. But at the moment, I was more interested in hearing my parents' story than I was in scolding my mom for something we couldn't change.

"Yes. He said he could see my future, and in it, he saw us together! I liked him right away. We spent the next five months together. Since he worked at the Council, I spent a good amount of time there."

"What was it like?" I asked. "At the Council, I mean."

"It was fine." She shrugged. "I was only allowed inside after hours, and no one ever discussed business in my presence. Most people were always kind to me. Nole was best friends with Elder Kohler—who wasn't an elder back then. Kohler and I never got along. But other than that, the Council was a pleasant place to be. We sometimes watched movies in the basement. Mostly old ones from Earth-One."

Sadness chased the smile from her face.

"How did he die?" I asked.

"Nole didn't show up for our date one day. He was always punctual. Like clockwork. I called him on his comm that night and all the next day. After two days, I showed up at the Council and demanded that Kohler tell me where he was. I—"

"What was Elder Kohler like back then?" I cut in.

"Same as he is now, as far as I can tell. Cold. Calculating. Indecipherable. He was friendly when Nole was around, but his smile never lasted for more than a second after your father left the room. I once caught him suggesting Nole should find a nice practitioner to date."

"So what happened when you went to see Kohler?"

Mom looked down at her hands for a moment, and then back up at me. "I assumed Nole had stood me up on purpose. I demanded a proper face-to-face breakup. I wanted him to come to the door and ask me to leave personally. I called your father a coward and a fool and . . . all kinds of names I'm not willing to repeat in front of my daughter." Her mouth opened to continue, but no more words came out.

"I'm sorry, Mom. I don't mean to upset you."

"I know. I'm actually surprised it took you so long to ask." She patted my hand. "Kohler had a bandage around his neck. He was so hoarse I had to put my ear right up next to his mouth to hear him. He told me that Nole had died. I assumed it had something to do with whatever happened to his neck, and that Nole had died at the same time that injury occurred. But he wouldn't tell me what happened, then or later. I bothered him about it for months after I found out I was pregnant."

"And then you had me."

"Yes. And I wouldn't go back and change any of it. I loved my time with him, and you are like him in so many ways."

"Like how?"

"Besides your eyes and your mouth, there's your determination. His Sight was important to him, and so was learning from it. Some days, he came home exhausted after trying to convince those stubborn Council members of something he'd seen."

Mom's brow furrowed. "I think he was working on an experiment to transfer his consciousness to one of the elders. So they could see what he saw. He was desperate to convince them of something. It wore on him, but he never gave up. And he always set it aside long enough to show me that I was loved. Just like you, and how you've been with Sona through all this." Her eyes narrowed as she spoke those last words.

"You're still upset about my assignment."

"Of course I'm upset." Her lips pursed. "I've already lost one child to those *things*."

I took her hands in mine. "Loken is watching over me. I'll be fine." When she didn't look convinced, I added, "Plus, apparently, I'm powerful. My first ether shield was stronger than normal. That's why I was assigned to the group without having been trained. So you don't have to worry."

She raised a skeptical eyebrow.

"Really. You can ask Loken," I said, hoping she didn't know that practitioners were Mage-magnets.

"I still don't like your being around those people. You can't trust the Council."

"Why do you hate them so much?" I asked.

She sighed a pushed a lock of brown hair from her face. "Kohler wasn't honest with me about what happened to Nole. As far as I'm concerned, he and the rest of the Council are the reason you spent the first five years of your life without a father."

"Well, you won't have to worry much longer. Loken wants me off the task force." Even though it had been my idea to have me yanked from the team, I couldn't help feeling a little deflated—a *lot*, actually.

"He would have asked Elder Kohler this evening to have me removed," I continued, "but Kohler was out doing super-secret elder stuff and couldn't be disturbed." I made my voice sound cheery. "But first thing tomorrow, I'm back to being a regular person!" I plastered a smile on my face.

Mom tilted her head to the side, like she always did when she knew I wasn't being entirely honest. "You're not happy about this."

"Doesn't matter. It's the best thing for everyone." And it was what Loken wanted.

CHAPTER 17
COUNTDOWN: 7 DAYS

My comm unit beeped me awake a full hour before our scheduled meet-up in the morning. This time I was better prepared than yesterday. I'd convinced Yashor to pick me up at the cluster entrance.

Today was a big day. My last day on the Ethereal task force meant it might be my last day with access to the Council building. I wanted to make the most of it.

I jumped into the steam shower for a few minutes, yanked most of the tangles from my hair, and kissed Sona goodbye for the day. She burrowed deeper under the covers. After locating a pen and paper in a kitchen drawer, I scribbled Mom and Talin a quick note telling them I loved them and I'd see them later.

Yashor was pulling up just as I raced from my home cluster.

"Good morning!" I slid into the vehicle. "Any trouble getting the transport?"

He shook his head. "No problem at all. All Breathers have full access to the transports. I guess they trust us." He chuckled to himself and turned the vehicle south toward the Council.

I averted my eyes from the front window, where trees flew past us. "How can you stand to stare out the window when we're moving this quickly?"

"I'd prefer that we not crash," he said with a hint of mocking in his voice.

"But doesn't it make you ill?"

"Not at all. I'm meant to move like this. I can even distinguish different objects as they fly past us, like you can do at speeds that are normal for you."

"That's amazing," I said. I wished I could move like that.

"Are you kidding? Your ability trumps anything I can do by far."

A loud guffaw slipped from my throat. "So far, all I've done is create a shield—which caused me a bloody nose. Oh, and I ran away from a Mage in a panic." Some big bad Ethereal I turned out to be.

"You'll be fine. Think of it this way: everything any of us can do, you can defend. And your power source is everywhere."

"So is yours."

"Yes, but yours can be manipulated more precisely. I can't form the wind into a shield, for example. And I can throw a ball of air at you, but it won't do much damage when I'm battling something bigger than I am."

"That's all good in theory. But I can't do any of the cool stuff I'm supposed to be able to do."

"At least you have a shot at greatness. At best, I'm just good for transportation. Speaking of which, we're here."

"Thanks!" I hopped out of the vehicle and hurried to the front door of the building.

The day's duties wouldn't begin until the suns rose, so the Council building was mostly empty now. A few older Council members were chatting in the foyer. Probably longtime members instead of new recruits, since they were here before the meeting times.

For their benefit, I strode straight to the back of the building toward the briefing room. *"Please stay calm. Remain calm,*" the female voice droned from the walls of the hallway. Not likely.

With a peek over my shoulder, I veered down a hallway and up two flights on the back steps. The third floor was the only place I hadn't been in this building. I figured all these Council stiffs had to go *somewhere* while we were occupying their main level and basements.

Sure enough, the stairs led to a hallway with doors lining each of the two walls. Thankfully, that annoying remain-calm message didn't play up here. I guessed it was only for the benefit of the new recruits, who weren't supposed to be up here.

All the doors were closed. I had no idea which one might have a Seer behind it, preferably an older Seer—someone who would know something about my father and what the hell was going on here. There was a reason the elders had added me to the task force despite my lack of experience and their apparent dislike of me. I intended to find out.

Tiptoeing down the hall, I peeked into the small window set in each door. In the first office, a woman sat scribbling behind a desk. A large bin filled with what looked like dirt sat in the center of the room. A Mover's office.

I ducked away from the window before she could see me. My pulse sped. I'd have to make this quick before someone came into the hallway and caught me. I didn't have an excuse for being up here, and "I got lost" wasn't going to work when none of the new recruits had been invited to this floor.

I wondered what they'd do if they found me up here. Scold me? Send me home? It wouldn't matter much after Loken spoke with Elder Kohler about yesterday.

I peeked into another window. The room was empty. I almost moved on to the next door, but stopped when I recognized the familiar scrawl of Loken's handwriting on a display board. My eyes darted around the room, searching for

Loken. Definitely empty. I turned the knob and pushed the door open. This wasn't why I'd come upstairs, but curiosity got the better of me.

Immediately, my senses filled with Loken. His sweet metallic scent. An array of metal weapons hanging on the far wall. His handwriting on papers neatly stacked throughout the room.

I couldn't help myself. Before I knew it, I was sitting in his office chair with my feet propped on the desk. I tapped a button on the computer. The screen flashed on, asking for a password. The chair was adjusted too low, since Loken was much taller than I was, so I moved the keyboard to my lap.

First I tried his mother's name. *Madriel.* No, that wasn't it.

My name? *Ashara.* I held my breath. But no, that was wrong too. I scowled at the screen.

I tried is birth date, his mother's birth date, my birth date, and the day we met. At that last one, a new screen flashed up. "Fingerprint entry," it said. A set of four fingerprint-sized ovals appeared on the screen.

Damn.

I canceled the login process and turned off the screen, redirecting my attention to the rest of the desk. Neat stacks of paper were arranged on my right. I grabbed one and slid it toward me. The top page had a single word across its center, with a question mark: "Traitor?" I set it aside and looked at the papers underneath. They held names—pages and pages of them. Some were underlined. Some were crossed out.

The top of the second page read, "Breather Task Force," followed by what I assumed was a list of Breather names. I flipped to the last page, which was labeled, "Ethereal Task Force." Under the heading, each of our names was listed: Elis, Jin, Krin, Mauryn, and me. Loken had scratched out my name. Jin's name was underlined twice and followed by a giant question mark.

Typical Loken. Always considering every angle.

I put the papers back the way I found them and glanced around the room.

A spare weapons belt hung from a hook on the far wall. I pushed away from the desk, strode over to it, and grabbed it off the hook. I attached it around my waist and pulled the strap to tighten the fit. Turning a circle, I admired the look and feel of the belt.

I touched a fingertip to the hilt of the sword, imagining myself pulling it free of its sheath and stabbing a Mage through the gut. The hilt was pure metal, not leather-wrapped like swords of non-Benders.

I unsheathed it and rotated my hand to examine the smooth metal. I'd seen a few swords in the past, and all of them had nicks and scratches. This blade was the exception, with not an imperfection in sight. Right now, it was the standard length for Vallaran swords, eighteen inches. I rapped on the silver metal with my knuckles, mesmerized by how solid it was when not bending to Loken's will.

I blinked. And when I opened my eyes again, the sword looked different somehow.

Squinting, trying to determine what had changed, I placed the blade against my left palm. Its cool metal was still solid. Still smooth. Still reflecting the lights overhead.

I must have imagined it.

I sheathed the sword. The point hit the bottom of the sheath, and the sword would go no farther. But part of the blade still showed between the hilt and the sheath. The sheath had fit the blade perfectly a moment ago, and now it was too short. Or maybe it had never fit, and I just hadn't noticed before.

The sword couldn't have changed. I was an Ethereal, not a Bender. That had been established on video, allegedly, as well as by the shield I'd created a couple days ago. Ethereals did not manipulate metal. They just didn't.

I made my way around the rest of the room. An archaic cork board hung on the wall opposite the desk. Numerous sheets of paper holding Loken's familiar scrawl stuck to the board. Long, heavy strokes scratched out most of the words on the papers. Some of the scratches had ripped the pages where he'd pressed too hard.

A large map, approximately ten feet wide, hung in the middle of the board. A map of Vallara and its surrounding regions, with multicolored pushpins strewn across the board.

I moved closer to the map. The push-pins appeared to be color-coded, with blue pins connected together in a sequence by blue thread, green pins connected by green thread, and so forth for numerous color variations—at least fifty.

Together, the threads and drawn lines looked like a firework centered on Vallara, like Vallara had exploded and spawned these lines going in every direction.

No. That's not right.

The lines weren't going outward from Vallara. They were going inward *toward* Vallara.

My gaze moved to just above the map, where Loken had scrawled on a piece of paper, "Why now?"

I stared at the page. Loken was tracking the movements of the Mages, and they were all coming here. Over fifty of them. But Loken was focused on why they were coming here *now*. Now, as opposed to the earlier timelines? What was different about this one?

This was insanity. I'd seen a hundred—maybe two hundred—people at our opening meeting a few days ago. That meant four people per Mage. If we were talking about four trained Council members against one Mage, I'd like those odds. But with the vast majority of the practitioners being untrained in Mage combat . . . An icy shiver crept up my spine. Seeing it on paper like this just made it all too real. These odds were not in our favor.

I had to talk to Krin or Rey before I reached complete panic level. My fingertips were already on the door by the time I remembered the weapons belt. I wrestled with the strap, unclasped it, and tossed it back onto the hook where I'd found it.

I threw the door open and barreled toward the stairs, colliding with a thick body already in the hallway. The man I'd run into clasped the top of my arm and held me upright. A hooded black robe cast most of his face in shadow even in the bright hallway. A Seer.

"What are you doing up here?" He continued to grip my arm and shifted me toward the stairs. "Recruits are confined to the lower levels."

My mind raced with all the questions I could ask him. About the Mages? No, I wanted to talk to Krin and Rey about that before babbling nonsensically to some guy I didn't know. So I asked what I'd come here to find out; it was now or never.

I shook my arm free from his grasp. "I'm looking for information about my father. He was a Seer."

The man's eyes narrowed, giving him an ominous appearance in the shadow of the hood. I shuffled away from him a couple feet. I shifted to the balls of my feet, ready to make for the stairway if I needed a quick escape.

"What's his name?"

"Nole. And he's dead."

The man's expression softened. "I'm sorry, child. May the gods watch over him."

"I don't believe in the gods."

He waved a dismissive hand. "Yes, yes, most of us here at the Council do not—except us Seers. We see them. I'm sure your father saw them too."

I was beginning to regret my plan. This man knew nothing about my father. And I wasn't in the mood for a lecture about the gods. "Forget it." I turned to go. I'd find Elder Kohler later and demand information.

"Wait." He placed his hands on my shoulders to stop me from bolting. I expected him to say more. Instead, he flipped back his hood and peered into my eyes. His pupils contracted to pinpoints, expanding the brown of his irises.

In the back of my mind, a small voice urged me to pull away. But curiosity won out. For minutes, we stood in the hallway, his hands pressing on my shoulders as he stared into my soul. "You are an odd puzzle, New One," he said.

"New One?"

He nodded. "Most of us—our bodies are worn, old, spent. But yours is not. You are new . . . somehow."

I inched backward toward the stairs, but his fingers pressed deeper into my shoulders.

After a moment, he released me and then nodded. "You will be the end." He tilted his head to the side, as if considering. "Or our salvation, perhaps."

I inched backward. "What does that mean?"

"That is all I can see."

I spun on my heel and ran down the stairs. I didn't stop until I hit the front lawn.

CHAPTER 18

It was way too soon for another field trip. But I didn't have many other options, since Elder Kohler hadn't yet officially booted me from the team.

Unlike yesterday, the task forces had split up today. Our team included me, Loken, Mauryn, and four people I didn't know. Again, Yashor piloted our vehicle, and Rey—grinning like a giddy fool—slipped into the driver's seat of the other, which would stay with us for this mission. We'd gotten word that the female Mage had been spotted just north of Vallara.

"You know, I don't have to go with you guys," I whispered to Loken. His arm brushed against mine in the transport, sending delightful tingles through my body every time one of us moved.

His forehead creased. "Why wouldn't you come with us?"

"Because you want me off the team."

He leaned his head back against the headrest as the vehicle rocked into motion. "No. I don't. I was just upset."

"Because I left you." My voice barely reached a whisper. I chewed the inside of my cheek but said nothing else. Conflicting emotions warred in my chest. I deserved some kind of punishment.

Loken stared up at the ceiling. "You abandoned your team." My heart dropped into the pit of my stomach. "But it was an unfair position for you to be in. And anyway, that's not why I was upset."

Our transport shot upward through the opening in the ceiling, and then sped north. I was getting used to the world rushing past me. I didn't even avert my eyes downward this time.

"I thought you were dead," Loken whispered.

I turned from the window to find him staring at me, his gray eyes silvery, reflecting the sunlight. I wanted to reach for his hand. But I didn't want to create an awkward scene around the other practitioners in the transport, especially since I knew only two people in here other than the driver. I hadn't made the best impression on the Ethereal task force. I wanted to start squarely within the good graces of these other practitioners.

I clasped my hands in my lap. "I'm fine."

"Thank the gods."

"You believe in the gods?"

"I'm working on it. It's a new development."

"Since when?"

One side of his mouth quirked up. "Since yesterday, when you went missing." He chuckled. Then his face became serious again. "I'm not going to lose you."

My fingers tingled with the need to touch him. I resisted. "Well then, I guess I'll just have to work harder on my ability, so I can protect myself and not drive you crazy."

"Thanks." He grinned widely, showing off a set of straight white teeth.

Mauryn's voice broke into our conversation. "Are any of us concerned that this Mage is clearly close enough to Vallara to go after all the practitioners at the Council, yet she's hanging out on the outskirts of the city?"

"Why should we be concerned about that?" I asked.

"If a Mage is drawn to something, he—or she, in this case—usually just goes for it," Mauryn said. "Why not this time? It's like she's waiting for something. Stalling. It's like she has a plan."

"Mages aren't capable of planning," said a blonde woman I didn't know. She tossed a haughty glance Mauryn's way.

"On what is that hypothesis based?" asked Mauryn.

"On the fact that they're nothing more than unintelligent energy-eating machines," she said. "Barely sentient."

Based on my limited exposure, I had to agree with Mauryn. "Well, that's clearly not true," I said. "How do you explain that the Council's captive Mages never attempted escape until their cage was damaged? If they operated on instinct only, they would have tried to escape before. They would have hurled every element they had at the glass and the door. Instead, they bided their time until they had a true opportunity."

No one spoke for a moment. Everyone stared at me—Loken, Mauryn, and four people I didn't know. A hint of annoyance clawed at me. Was it so shocking that I had something worthwhile to say?

"What? I'm smart," I grumbled.

"It's an interesting theory," Loken said. "They've never shown any ability to plan in the past. But that doesn't mean they're not capable of it. Maybe they didn't have the proper motivation. Animals in the wild are mostly instinctual, but even they stalk their prey when the situation calls for it."

"So we're prey?" I asked.

Loken shrugged. "Sorry."

"But this is more than planning by individual Mages," said Mauryn, scratching the dark stubble on his chin. "This is coordination. We've got numerous Mages coming in this direction. That's no accident."

"So what do they want now that requires"—I shot a glance at Loken—"*stalking*?"

We all looked at one another, dumbly silent. The blonde who'd originally objected to the idea now chewed her lower lip, looking less confident about her position.

The trees and the rest of the world outside had slowed their motions past the windows.

"Why are we slowing down?" Loken called up to Yashor.

"Look outside," he said. His voice was tight, struggling to climb from his throat.

A man sitting across from me—a Flooder, based on the vial of water attached to his belt—stared out the window behind my head. His mouth hung open. Dread tightened my chest as I twisted in my seat. I gaped at the ground outside the vehicle.

Strewn outside was a line of bodies, each one spaced twenty or so yards from the last one. The bodies stretched out in front of us. There must have been twenty or thirty of them, broken, bloody, their limbs twisted at odd angles. They lay face up and in a straight line.

"Yeah, that doesn't at all look like planning." My voice dripped sarcasm. I shot the blonde lady a pointed look.

The transport had slowed to a crawl now. Six of us pressed our faces against the large window on my side of the transport, squished together so we could all stare horror-struck at the scene. Only the blonde woman remained on the other side, her chest puffed up with now-false confidence. Her widened eyes said she felt the same horror we did, and she didn't need the close-up.

The end of the line of bodies came into view as we crested a hill. I moved to the back window and stared out along the route we'd traveled, along the path of bodies extending behind us into the distance.

The transport floated to a stop and settled to the ground next to the last corpse.

"Why do you think the Mage stopped here?" I asked.

Loken threw the door open and jumped out of the vehicle. "Because *she's* here."

My fingers curled around the armrest. That was the part of me that begged to stay in the transport, to stay away from the energy-sucking animal we now suspected was smart enough to stalk us—to plan a trap for us even.

But I would not be a liability to anyone anymore. And staying in this vehicle meant one less Ethereal was out there to destroy that Mage. I yanked my arm from the armrest and followed Loken outside.

"Remember your training, people," Loken shouted to the group.

Rey and another group of practitioners I didn't know stepped from the vehicle that had trailed us here. They trudged toward us from their transport, their eyes pinned on the corpses. One of them, a tall man with a shock of red hair, froze at the end of the line of bodies, staring down at the last corpse. Rey clapped him on the shoulder and nudged him away.

"As your team leaders will have taught you by now," Loken said when the new group joined us, "the basic Mage-kill strategy is a Breather on either side, and a Bender makes the kill blow." He pointed to Rey and then Yashor. "I'll need you two up front with me." He looked around at the group of practitioners surrounding him. "The rest of you need to be ready to assist if something goes wrong. Don't do anything stupid. Don't be a hero."

We all nodded, our faces solemn. Yashor's already fair face paled further.

"What should I do?" asked a male practitioner who'd ridden in my transport.

"We don't know which direction she'll come from, but when she shows up, get behind Rey, Yashor, and me. Stay on your guard in case she gets past us. If she does, you guys will need to keep her stationery. She's a Breather, so I can't catch her if she runs."

Loken spun a circle, examining the space around us.

"While we're waiting, a quick quiz: What are the alternative kill strategies?" His eyes continued to dart around our surroundings.

"The Breathers can be replaced by any other practitioners who can keep the Mage relatively stationary," said a Burner I didn't know. She'd ridden in the other vehicle.

"Just about any practitioner can do the job of the Breathers with proper control," said Mauryn. "But it's most natural for Br—"

"Here she comes!" shouted Loken.

He stared in the direction we'd come from. Terror and anticipation warred in my gut.

Along with the rest of the group, I hustled to the get behind the three people who would be fighting this battle. My fingertips tingled with nervousness. I concentrated on feeling the air around me. Ether occupied that air; all I had to do was tap into it.

The female Mage slowed as she approached. Her black gaze swept across the members of the group. My eyes targeted Rey and Loken. I feared for them as much as for myself. I imagined them broken and bloody, added to that line of bodies that had led us here. The image steeled me against some of the terror.

My fists clenched and unclenched. I wouldn't have anyone else die while I did nothing. If anything went wrong, I'd be ready to step in.

Rey and Yashor stepped forward on opposite sides of the Mage. In coordination, both Breathers pushed air away from them toward each other, and toward the Mage standing between them. Wind whipped around them and around her.

The Mage's progress forward slowed to nearly a stop as the Breathers held her in place in the pressure of their wind. Her mouth opened in an angry wail, so loud and high-pitched that I flinched away from the sound. It filled the inside of my head, trying to block out all other thoughts. My hands flew to my ears, but I resisted the urge to cover them. I'd need all my senses intact.

She pushed back against Rey and Yashor. Wind gusted around the entire group. My ears filled with the sounds of her screams and the wind streaming past. A few of my companions toppled over and slid across the ground away from the rest. Their bodies tumbled end over end, until they struggled back to their feet. I bent my knees and leaned toward the swirling air to brace myself.

Loken moved slowly into the midst of the miniature tornado. His body pushed against the wind. His arms trembled as he raised the sword against the air pressure and readied for the kill.

Muscles strained in Yashor's neck. His whole body vibrated, and he stumbled backward. The wind dropped suddenly as he lost control. No longer locked in place, the Mage charged Yashor in a burst of speed. She slammed against him and tackled him to the ground.

Pinning him underneath her, the Mage rammed her palms into Yashor's chest. His face contorted, lips twisted, eyes bulged. He released a scream that reached down into my stomach and twisted it into knots.

The Mage's hands glowed white, and color faded from Yashor's face. Like white fire, the glow rolled from her hands up to her shoulders. She sucked energy from Yashor and into herself.

Loken had changed direction and now pushed his way through the ever-increasing wind toward Yashor. The Mage continued to propel air outward, keeping Loken and the rest of us away from her and her victim.

I shoved my fear aside and pushed toward them. But every time I raised a foot from the ground, the wind pushed me backward. With each step, I moved farther away from Yashor, whose screams had reached a pitch higher than I'd never heard from a man.

Where the glow from the Mage's hands rolled up her arms and met her shoulders, it disappeared into her chest. Each roll of white flames left Yashor paler. He skin went white, then gray, then darkened. His scream broke in a whimper, although his mouth still hung open in silent horror. His head lolled on his neck.

I locked my gaze on Rey, silently begging him to do something. He didn't spare me a glance. His mouth was set in a tight line. His arms extended in front of him, continuing to propel air toward the Mage, trying to shove her off of Yashor. His muscles bulged with the effort. Sweat trickled down his temple.

Yashor jerked in the Mage's arms, and then sagged. He stopped moving. His skin continued to darken. It flaked away like charred paper. The glowing fire between him and the Mage stopped abruptly. She dropped his lifeless body. Yashor's corpse shattered as it hit the ground, like black paper scattering in the wind.

The Mage shivered, as if from delight. She spun toward Rey.

A shout ripped up my throat. I whispered a quick prayer and rushed her, flinging strokes of ether from my hands. Three hit her square in the chest in rapid succession. Each blast pushed her backward. A deep-crimson burn covered her chest—a mass of twisted flesh where I'd opened her up.

With a shriek, she flew at me in a blur of motion. I switched direction and flung more ether bolts at her as I jogged backward. It took her no more than a few seconds to reach me, even with my attacks pushing her away. Each attack I threw felt weaker than the last. My energy was waning. My arms burned.

Out of the corner of my eye, I saw the blonde Mover from my transport run toward us. The ground broke beneath her feet. A crack split through the earth and raced toward the Mage, welcoming her into its depths. The Mage dropped into the chasm. The ground rushed back together at her waist and clamped her torso into place.

"Kill her now!" the Mover shouted. She dropped to her knees. Her hands pressed into the ground, and her shoulders shook violently. "I can't hold it for long. *Kill her*!"

Part of the Mage's hair stuck in the ground. With a screech of anger, she jerked her head forward, tearing a large clump of it from her head. She twisted and writhed in the earth, steadily dislodging herself. Her body moved so quickly as she struggled, like a pale blur vibrating against the ground.

Loken held a hand in front of him. Six metal spikes flew from his palm toward the Mage.

Four of them took her in the neck. Her throat shredded into strips of flesh. Her head hung to the side, resting on her shoulder by the remaining bits of flesh. Screams spilled from her bloody maw.

Loken ran toward her and drew his sword. The shortsword stretched into a long, thin blade. Before he was within range of her arms, Loken swung the adapted longblade and sheared the remainder of her neck.

Her shrieking ceased. Her head toppled from her shoulders. The long curtain of pale hair tangled around her face as the head hit the ground with a thump and rolled.

CHAPTER 19

"Stop. Stop the transport!" I shouted, just as we reached the edge of Vallara.

The vehicle came to an almost instant halt, and I stumbled out. I doubled over and lost my breakfast all over an array of pink talablossoms on the side of the road.

Rey was beside me in no time, pulling my frizzed ponytail out of my face. My throat burned as I expelled the contents of my stomach. When my belly was empty, I continued to heave even though my body had nothing left inside it to surrender. I thought I might spit out my insides along with my breakfast.

When I was finished, I stumbled several feet away from the mess and fell to my knees. A shaky hand wiped the sweat from my clammy forehead. I didn't cry, even though the devastation that had started in my stomach was now seeping outward to my extremities.

I'd barely known Yashor. But he'd been one of us. It could just have easily have been Rey who'd died. Or that blonde Mover. Or me. Or Loken. But I wouldn't cry. If I did, it would mean I was too weak for whatever came next. So I sucked in deep breaths until I made myself light-headed, until my head became too cloudy to focus on how much it hurt.

There were seven days left. We'd barely gotten started.

I glanced around the rest of the group, embarrassed that I'd lost it. Only a few stared back at me, mostly with empathy on their faces. A few cheeks were tear-wet. Loken stood several feet away, eying me nervously. I imagined he wasn't used to working with people who couldn't keep their emotions in check. I scowled at him. We couldn't all be robots.

"You knew some of us would die, Ash," came Rey's soft voice from over my shoulder.

I shook my head. My mouth opened and closed. I tried to form a sentence, but nothing came out. He was right, although I hated to admit it. Finally, I was able to summon words. "W-we're not trained for this."

Rey sank to his knees beside me and rubbed my shoulders. "Before three days ago, only about twelve people on the continent were trained for this. Twelve Council members who felt that Mage-combat was a useful skill for the rare times Mages appeared in public. What would you have them do? Twelve people can't save the world."

"And we can?"

"Maybe. Maybe not. But if we don't try . . ."

"How many of us have to die?" My voice came out in a rasp.

He didn't answer.

"How many?" I asked again.

"Maybe half of us. Maybe all of us. And if we all die—every one of us—to save everyone else, isn't that the most noble sacrifice?"

A wave of emptiness hit me. I felt the truth of his statement deep in my core. I had to make my peace with the fact that I might die, perhaps even before the countdown clock struck zero. And still, I had to go home to my family, and smile, and tell them I'd see them later. Because I sure as hell wasn't going to tell them I was dying.

No. I *wasn't* dying. There was still hope for us. I wasn't going to accept that my mother would lose another child. She couldn't survive it. And even in the heavens, I would miss my little Sona.

"No." I rose to my feet and tugged Rey to his. "We are not dying."

"I'm not sure that's entirely up to us, Ash. We don't have the liberty of choosing to live right now. We have to choose life for everyone else, even if that means sacrificing our own. And I, for one, am ready to make that sacrifice. We owe Yashor at least that. He can't have died for nothing."

I shook my head hard. "Let's go." I stalked back to the vehicle.

Rey followed. We were all squeezed into a single transport now—since we'd lost our other driver.

"You okay?" Loken asked as I climbed back inside. His concerned gray eyes peered at me under a furrowed brow.

"I'm fine," I said. "Let's go. We have Mages to kill."

The truth was that I was more than fine. My insides were twisted into knots about Yashor. But physically, my body thrummed with power. Tingles ripped across my skin, begging for more action. Pinpoints of white-blue light danced around me. I squinted at them, watched them float around.

Ether.

The vehicle shot forward. I continued to watch the dancing lights for the rest of the trip, letting them soothe the ache in my chest. We arrived at the Council in a matter of minutes. The white-blue lights blinked out, but I still felt them prickling against me like a second skin—one I could control.

Loken pulled me out of the vehicle and led me to the third floor of the building.

"Where are we going? I've never been up here." I was a poor liar. Sadly, that's what came of telling the truth entirely too often.

Loken didn't seem to notice. "We don't have an assignment at the moment, but I have some materials to study. I'd like your company."

I cut a glance at him out of the corner of my eye. If Loken wanted my company, then I was probably in trouble. I wondered what clues I might have left from my prior uninvited visit to this floor.

He pushed open the door to his office. I scanned the room, pretending the place was new to me. All the while, I was acutely aware of Loken's attention on my profile.

"So this is your office?" I cringed as the words came out. I needed a lot more practice at this lying thing.

"Desk, chairs, map. Not much to it."

I wandered over the map and pretended to examine it for the first time. "What's this?" My voice rang false in my ears, too high-pitched. Or maybe too low-pitched.

He settled into his chair. "*That* is something I shouldn't be showing you."

"So why am I up here?" I examined one of the pieces of paper posted on the corkboard next to the map. A series of dates and locations, with the words "Mage No. 24" at the top.

"I decided that I may have seven days to live." I opened my mouth to object to this line of conversation, but he held up a hand to stop me. "Let's just be realistic here. This could all be a big mistake. The Vision could be wrong, or we could save ourselves. Or it could be legitimate, and we could fail. Seven days from now, I don't know where we'll be—or even *whether* we'll be."

"What's your point?" I had no desire to dwell on the what-ifs. I'd gone down that road after Pace's death. It led to nothing except more misery and denial.

"I want to be with you."

Heat crept over my cheeks. I took a large step away from him. "I thought your duty always came first." It was what he'd told me when he'd cut our relationship short months earlier.

"That was a lousy thing for me to say." He gave me a sheepish grin. "I was only trying to protect you, and protect everyone else at the same time. I couldn't live with myself if I put my needs above everyone else's. But I can do both."

"You mean, be with me and save the world? Isn't that a conflict of interest? Shouldn't you be unbiased among your teammates?"

"In theory, I'd agree with that. But whether we're together or not, I'm going to be biased."

"So you choose me?" I inched closer to him, so that I stood only a couple feet from where he lounged in the chair.

He pulled me into his lap. "Yes."

"And what if I don't choose you?" I whispered into his ear. Maybe I wasn't ready to forgive him for the breakup just yet.

"Then why are you sitting on my lap?" His fingers played on my lower back, just above the waist of my pants. Shivers raced up my spine, disappearing into the nape of my neck.

I leapt off his lap—even though I liked it there—and made my way over to the map again. I might owe him when it came to the battleground; I'd left him with that Mage. But with respect to him and me, he had some amends to make. I'd let him suffer a little.

"So this map." I tapped a finger against the large paper. "It's for tracking Mage movements?"

"You're really not coming back over here?"

"No." I shook my head, stifling a laugh. "The map?"

With a sigh, he pushed himself up from the chair and joined me in front of the cork board. "We have some data about their movements from the last timelines. But the elders' memories are flawed, and they had too much to remember anyway, since theirs were the only consciousnesses brought back. Mostly, I'm trying to determine if the Mages are behaving differently from the last timeline, and why."

"And are they behaving differently?"

"In some ways. Last time around, they didn't head here until halfway through the ten-day cycle. They started right away this time. But their target is the same. They're definitely coming here."

"Doesn't the fact that the Mages weren't a problem initially mean that they aren't the ones who will end things? The Vision occurred in the original timeline. Doesn't it have to refer to something that would have happened even without the new timelines?"

"Not necessarily. The Vision could just as easily refer to something that only happens in this timeline. Seers look into the future. Technically, this timeline is a future of the original timeline."

His logic made my head hurt. "The Seers can see multiple timelines, but not how things will end?"

He shook his head.

"That's rather inconvenient," I muttered, glaring at the map.

Loken stepped closer to my back, as close as possible without touching me. His body cooled me as he reached over my shoulder and pointed to a few of the colored strings. His finger traced one of the strings. It made a straight line except for one pin, which stuck into the board just to the right of the main line. Loken pointed to another string that was the same, mostly straight but with one pin that was farther to the right than it should have been.

"What do you see?" he asked.

"They went east for a bit and then returned to their main course. What does it mean?"

"A change in the pattern."

"They're not all headed here anymore?"

"No, they're still coming here . . ." His voice trailed off as he lost himself in the map.

"Then what's changed?"

"These pins." He pointed one by one to a bunch of pins and dots that were all farther east than they should have been. "They all represent yesterday. Many of the Mages went off course, temporarily."

"So what? I'm sure they get distracted by other energy sources along their routes."

"Yes, but they're usually straighter than this." He paused for a moment. Then he wrapped an arm around me and turned me to face him, leaving his arm hanging around my waist.

I leaned into him without meaning to, and then jerked away to put a few inches between us. Loken's mouth shifted into a cocky smile. I glared at him and pushed his arm from my waist.

"Of the over two hundred practitioners who work for the Council right now," he said, "only fourteen were east of here yesterday. Some were west of here, some north, some south. Some stayed at the Council. If the Mages were attracted to us as a group, we should have canceled each other out. They might have stopped moving, or continued en route to Vallara."

"But that didn't happen."

"No." Loken scrubbed a hand through his already disheveled hair. He'd worn it shorter and neater when we'd dated. It had grown almost down to his chin now. My hands ached to brush it off his forehead. I clenched them into fists and kept them at my sides.

"The Mages were following the practitioners who went east," I said.

"Yes."

"Who was east of here yesterday?"

"We were."

CHAPTER 20

"Yes, you were," came a familiar rasp from the doorway.

I shoved Loken in the chest, and we leapt apart. We both turned toward the doorway.

Filling the entry stood Elder Kohler and three other people who could be best described as his "muscle." Two men and a woman. Kohler beckoned his companions forward. They fanned out around us. The woman settled behind us, and one man took a place on either side.

The three of them towered over me, and stood even a couple inches than taller than Loken. They were silent, except the tallest of the men. A low hum vibrated from his chest like a growl. I inched away from him and toward the man on my other side.

"Loken," continued Kohler, in his low, gravelly tone. Without a microphone, his voice reached barely above a whisper. I strained to hear him. "I read your report from yesterday."

Loken didn't answer but stepped between Elder Kohler and me, as if to shield me from what was coming. I looked back and forth between Kohler and the other three, all of whom stared at me. Loken's muscular arms crossed over his chest. His posture straightened, pulling him up to his full height of a couple inches over six feet.

"Ah, I see you've already determined what this means," said Kohler. "That's good. It means we won't have to debate the matter."

Elder Kohler still blocked the doorway. He wasn't a large man, maybe five-ten. His thin arms were lean, not thick with muscle. I wondered if I could knock him down by throwing myself into him. I hoped it wouldn't come to that.

"Ashara," Elder Kohler said in an official-sounding voice. "I have a warrant for your arrest."

The largest of the three guards, a bald man with sweat beaded on his forehead, reached for my arm. Loken shoved him away and placed a hand on the hilt of his sword. "On what charge?" he asked.

"There's no charge," said Elder Kohler. "In these times, the only cause we need is the greater good. We have reason to believe the Mages are coming here for Ashara."

My hands trembled at my side. "Just because a few Mages veered off course yesterday?"

"And the fact that they started toward here in the last timeline—immediately after your ability manifested for the first time."

My jaw dropped open. I snapped it back together, but not before Elder Kohler had time to register my shock.

"So you understand," he said. "Good." His gaze shifted to Loken, although he continued to address me. "We're taking you into custody now."

Loken drew his sword and let it hang at his side.

"You don't want to do this, Loken," Kohler said.

"Where will you take her?" Loken asked. He pulled me closer to him. His gaze jumped between Elder Kohler and the two other men, while his arm shielded me from the woman behind us.

"To a safe place."

"You'll lock her up?"

Elder Kohler nodded. “She’ll be surrounded by Council members. Safe from the Mages.”

“And what happens if you decide we’re all better off if she’s dead?”

My muscles tensed at his words. Loken stroked my waist with his fingertips, trying—unsuccessfully—to keep me calm.

Instead of answering, Kohler shot back another question. “You think we’d be better off if she were dead?”

“That’s not what I said.” Loken squeezed out the words through gritted teeth.

Elder Kohler grinned, a wide smile with no joy. “But you asked that question for a reason. Because you know what Ashara is only beginning to understand—that her potential for power is the reason the Mages are targeting Vallara.”

“No,” I whispered. I hadn’t planned to speak, but words spilled out before I could stop them. “No. I . . . I hardly know what I’m doing. My ability just manifested. If I were powerful, it would have . . . a long time ago.” I shook my head back and forth, back and forth.

I stared up at Loken, who refused to meet my eyes.

“Loken?”

His jaw twitched. My heart stampeded against my chest.

“If Loken resists,” Elder Kohler said, “we’ll have to contain him as well—which would be detrimental to everything we’re trying to accomplish here.”

He was right, of course. Regardless of my alleged potential, Loken was the one with the experience. He was an integral part of the team, and the Ethereal task force would likely fall apart without him. I tugged on Loken’s shirt, silently urging him to step aside so I could give myself up.

I studied Elder Kohler’s three companions. They stood ready for action, arms tensed, legs spaced apart. If Loken was going to fight, I was going to fight with him.

Still feeling the prickle of ether against my skin, I summoned it to my palms. The effort knocked the breath out of me. I gasped. My head spun for a few seconds, and then righted. A small ball of light whirled around each of my hands, visible to everyone in the room.

Elder Kohler made the first move. He shot a stream of fire from his hands at Loken's sword. Smoke curled from it, and Loken dropped the sword with a shout. He barreled toward Kohler. The two of them went down. Loken's knees pinned Kohler's arms to the floor.

The man on the right rushed toward me. I raised my arms and shot a series of ether balls. The white-blue light streamed toward him. He lunged to the side to avoid it. His large body slammed into the wall. Some of Loken's pages of notes scattered to the ground. I shot another ether ball at my attacker, but willed this one to expand. When it hit him, it morphed into a shimmering blue cage, trapping him against the wall.

The woman slammed into me, tackling me to the ground. She pinned my wrists above my head and sneered. Her lips pulled back, baring her teeth. I thrashed against her grip, but she pressed my wrists harder into the floor.

With the help of one of her male companions, the woman flipped me over and cuffed my hands behind my back She yanked my arms upward to drag me to my feet. I cried out as pain ripped through my shoulders.

Loken lay on the ground with both arms up in surrender. His right arm was covered in patches of welted red skin. Kohler stood over him, his arms pointed toward me. Fire swirled around his hands. Loken lay obediently still.

"Is he going to be okay?" I inclined my head toward Loken.

Elder Kohler waved a fiery hand in Loken's direction. "He'll be fine. His punishment for insubordination will have to wait until this crisis ends." His soft voice dropped to a lower pitch. "But it *will* be harsh."

With a backward glance at Loken's prone form, I followed Kohler's muscle out of the office. We walked in a diamond formation, with Elder Kohler taking up the rear. The woman led the group. The two brutes locked me in on either side.

When we reached the main floor, the many practitioners there stared as we passed. I kept my head held high.

Elder Kohler led us to the metal door to the basement. Below was the glass cage that had secured the three captive Mages. My footsteps slowed as we approached. "You're putting me in the cage?" My voice squeaked.

Elder Kohler nodded and pressed his hand against the security panel next to the door. The door slid open with a deep whirring sound, revealing the empty, dimly lit basement.

"Why?" I asked, hopefully. "If the Mages are all attracted to me, wouldn't it make more sense to send me away?"

He beckoned for me to follow him down the stairs. "If they really are following you, then they'll continue to do so. We don't know what they'll do when they find you. Maybe it's what they'll do that will end us. Maybe it's what *you'll* do. Either way, it's best if you remain where we can keep an eye on you."

Our footsteps clanked on the stairs as we entered the dim basement. I dragged my feet toward the glass. No Mages stood behind it today. Still, I didn't relish the idea of being trapped in there for the next seven days—until the end of time.

Another metal door led into the glassed-in area. Elder Kohler activated it with his hand, as before. He reached for my waist and removed my comm from my waistband.

"Hey!" I said. He ignored my protest and shoved me toward the open doorway.

I took a final glance at each of my four captors, trying to determine whether I could escape. I was still handcuffed, and I didn't know how to use my ability without channeling it through my hands. Plus, I really wasn't in the mood to be burnt to a crisp. I trudged through the door.

Elder Kohler pressed something on the security panel, and the door slid almost closed. Six inches of space remained between the edge of the door and its frame.

"Face away from me and stick your hands through the crack, if you want me to remove your handcuffs," he said.

I obeyed, and he removed the cuffs. The door slid closed the rest of the way, issuing a metallic clank as it trapped me inside.

CHAPTER 21
COUNTDOWN: 6 DAYS

I shivered and wrapped my arms around myself. Someone must have left the air conditioner blasting. I wondered if they'd done it on purpose, to make this place even less inviting. As if the faint ammonia smell and the lack of an exit didn't do that already.

Concrete blocks lined the back wall and sides of my cell. Glass and metal locked me in from the front. I didn't know how thick the concrete was or what lay on the other side. I figured the glass was the weakest point of my cage, although I doubted it was weak at all. The Mages hadn't escaped until the security panel was damaged. Just my luck, it had been replaced since then.

I wondered if I could damage the glass from the inside.

Ether is everywhere, Loken had said—which meant it was even in this dank cell. With my eyes closed, I stood still and felt the world around me. Air and ether prickled against my skin. I could feel the difference now. I isolated the ether and summoned it to my fingertips. I didn't strike right away. Instead, I summoned more.

When I opened my eyes, shimmering light surrounded me, emanating from my hands. I flung it at the glass. It hit with a loud clang, which echoed as the glass vibrated—but remained intact.

"Ra's saggy tits!" I shouted. My hand flew to my mouth to cover the words. I shrugged off the instinct. I could curse as much as I liked down here. I was alone. And if someone was watching me through a camera—well, they deserved to hear all the curses I could muster.

I made an unladylike hand gesture for the benefit of anyone who might be watching.

I squeezed my eyes shut again and prepared for another attack on the glass. When I opened them, the light of ether shone around me. It didn't seem as thick as it had been a moment before. This time, I kept the ether around me as a shield and, after sucking in a deep breath, ran at the glass at top speed.

Pain exploded in my shoulder at the impact. I fell to the ground. My teeth clattered as I hit the cement floor, sending more pain shooting up my back. I lay there for a few minutes, curled in a ball, gathering enough will to give it another shot.

Just as I'd decided to get up and try again, light streamed into the basement from the top of the stairs. I sank down onto the cot in the corner, closed my eyes, and made my chest rise and fall in a steady rhythm, like I was asleep.

After a minute, I heard the metal door to my left slide open and the clatter of something being dropped on the floor inside my cell.

I leapt to my feet and flung a bolt of ether at the man standing in the doorway. Not a particularly strong bolt, but enough to shock him. It hit him in the chest. He flew backward into the air, out of the cell. I shot toward the doorway. But even with the man on the ground, the door clanged shut. By the time I reached it, it was closed.

I pounded my fist against it and shouted, "Let me out! Let me out, you sons of . . ."

The man staggered half to his feet, stumbled, and then succeeded in pushing himself off the ground. Scowling, he reached for the security panel. An overhead intercom crackled on.

"The door was set to close automatically." The man pulled his hand away, and the intercom went off. He clutched his chest and sucked in two deep breaths.

I pointed at the intercom, urging him to turn it back on. He stared at me for a moment, and then complied.

"I'm sorry," I said. "I didn't mean to hurt you. I'm just scared. Are you okay?"

He glared but said nothing.

"Why am I down here instead of upstairs, working out a plan with the other practitioners? We're on the same side."

"No." The man shook his head. "You're not one of us. You're something else. More like them—like the Mages. No human could attract Mages from the other side of the continent." He shook his head again. "You're not one of us at all."

He paused, as if waiting for me to respond, but I could summon no words.

"If you behave when your next meal is delivered," he said, "your other jailer just might let you give him your trash. Otherwise, it's going to stink up your cell—because I'm not going back in there." He strode back to the stairs and up without a backward glance.

I'm not like them.

Sure, I was still a little uncontrolled, learning my way around my ability. But I was fully in my right mind. I was no monster. I wasn't a danger to anyone.

A tray with a plate of food sat to the side of the door. It held a sandwich and what looked like pasta salad. I scarfed down the sandwich in only a few bites and then turned my attention to the pasta. I lifted the plate from the tray, looking for a fork hiding under the plate's rim. No such luck.

I wondered what damage I could have done with a fork. It wouldn't have helped me dig through the concrete blocks or break through the glass. But I was denied one anyway. Perhaps I should have taken it as a compliment that I wasn't trusted with so much as an eating utensil. I ate the pasta one piece at a time, picking up the food with my fingers.

When I'd cleaned the plate, I rested my head back against the wall and scanned the room. I wasn't getting out of here by force. The Mages who had been in here before, all of whom were more experienced than I was, included two Breathers and an Ethereal. The Ethereal hadn't been able to escape until the cage had been damaged. If he couldn't do it, surely I couldn't either.

A Bender wouldn't have any trouble getting out. The door was metal, and glass was often composed partially of metallic alloy. I'd have given anything to have Loken here, comforting me—and getting me the hell out of here. Or a Mover could deal with those concrete blocks.

I inched my way along the edges of the cell, examining the walls with my fingertips. I wasn't sure what I was looking for. An imperfection perhaps. Any sign of weakness in my cage. After what must have been hours of searching—I couldn't be sure of the time without my comm—I found none. I lay down on the cot and stared at the ceiling.

I wondered what my friends were doing right now. Assuming Loken wasn't captive somewhere else, he would have told everyone I'd been arrested. Mom, Sona, and Talin would be worried. Mom would be driving Talin crazy, insisting they come here and demand my freedom. Rey and Krin were likely working on a breakout plan. I hoped it wouldn't get any of us killed ahead of schedule.

I wondered whether Loken had returned to his duties like a good little soldier, or if he had been serious about our being together. What would he do when his duty came into direct conflict with something else he wanted?

I even thought of Hael, though I'd met him only once. He'd left quite an impression. An image played in my head of Hael calling my comm unit into his hand. How had he done that? It seemed more like something a Breather would have done, by directing the wind to lift the device into his hand. Maybe if he were here, he could just move that metal door out of the way.

I glared at the door that separated me from the world I should be trying to save right now. I stood and approached it. I ran my palms along the door, sticking my fingertips into the crevices around its edges.

Ether floated around it, tiny blue flecks hovering in the air. Glaring at the blue light, I willed the ether to move the door for me.

Move.

Nothing.

Move, please?

Still nothing.

The cool air of the cell raised goosebumps on my arms. I lay back down on the cot and snuggled as deeply as I could into the cushion. Then I went back to staring at the ceiling.

CHAPTER 22
COUNTDOWN: 5 DAYS

"Mealtime." The sound of a man's voice woke me from one of my many naps. There was little else to occupy my time down here.

Just inside the cell sat a small tray of food. The metal door clanked back into place. My fifth meal since I'd been here, which meant I was well into the second full day of my captivity.

"Am I on a diet now?" I shouted.

My jailer activated the intercom. "Say again?" His voice crackled through the intercom.

"This is a salad."

He nodded, a single eyebrow raised.

"May I have some meat *please*?" I said that last word through gritted teeth.

"Sorry. That's what they sent." The guy shrugged and made his way out of the basement.

I lifted the bowl from the tray, looking for a fork. I found none. I grabbed a handful of lettuce and stuffed it into my mouth. Bland. What would a girl have to do for a steak?

CHAPTER 23
COUNTDOWN: 4 DAYS

The sound of the door slamming, and the delightful smell of meat, woke me from my sleep. Rey and Krin stood just inside my cell. Krin held a tray of food. I jumped up and snatched it from her. Before I sat back down, I squeezed her in a quick one-armed hug. Steak and cheese-covered potatoes. Warm saliva filled my mouth.

My gaze darted back and forth between the plate and my friends. I was unsure which I was more excited to see. Krin flopped down beside me. I wrapped my arms tightly around her in a more proper hug. Then I rose to my feet and jumped in Rey's arms. As we embraced, he ruffled my already disastrous head of curls. I sat back down and pulled Rey down next to me.

I turned my attention back to the food. The smell of cooked meat teased my nose. I couldn't resist any longer. I picked the steak up from the plate with my hand.

"Wait," said Krin.

I glared at her. "You know my last two meals have been salads? I'm starved!"

She reached into her pocket and withdrew a plastic-wrapped fork and knife. "I have to take these away when they come to fetch Rey and me in about ten minutes." I snatched them from her and ripped the plastic off.

"You're a goddess," I told her.

She shook her hair out of her face in mock narcissism. "I know. Feel free to worship me."

"Hey, what about me?" asked Rey.

"You weren't the one carrying my food."

He grinned. "But I was the one who insisted you get a steak."

My mouth packed with food, I bowed my head in his direction. "Then you, sir, are also a goddess."

"Good of you to notice," he said, flipping his dark ponytail over his shoulder in an imitation of Krin.

"So what's going on out there?" I talked around the food stuffed in my mouth.

Rey's lips pressed together into a thin line. "The Mages are closing in on Vallara. We've spent most of our time keeping them out of nearby cities."

Krin reached across me and flicked his shoulder. "We said we weren't going to worry her."

"No," said Rey, reaching across me and flicking her back. "*You* said we weren't going to worry her. Ash and I have been buddies since we were in diapers. If I lie to her, she'll know. And then I'll hear about it every day for the rest of my life."

"Twice a day," I promised.

"Well you could have just said nothing," Krin grumbled.

I cut into their argument. "Rey's not very good at saying nothing. I keep encouraging it, but he prefers to run his mouth regardless of whether he actually has anything worthwhile to talk about."

"Thanks, Ash. That's sweet," he said.

"No problem." I gave him a wide smile.

"We had some more casualties," Krin whispered. "Several more in Rey's task force, which was a lot bigger than ours to begin with. And . . . Elis died." Her eyes watered as tears threatened to spill. I set my empty plate aside and rubbed her shoulder. "I thought he was a pain," she continued, "but I didn't want him to die."

"I know."

"And he was kind of brave. A Mage had hold of Mauryn. Elis attacked the Mage's back until he let go of Mauryn and went after him instead."

"It was a good death," Rey said, his face solemn.

The three of us sat in silence, thinking about those who had given their lives for this cause.

When I couldn't stand the quiet any longer, I asked, "And Loken?"

"Is a mess!" said Krin. "He's irritable. He snaps at us all the time. He almost got himself killed trying to dispatch a Mage earlier today with sloppy sword-work. He hacked at that thing's neck three times before the head came off. When did Loken get so sloppy? He's the most graceful and effective fighter I've ever seen. Well, he *was*."

The sides of my mouth tugged downward. "Has he mentioned me?"

Rey raised an eyebrow. "You'd like to know if Loken has publicly discussed his feelings? Is that something he does in private much even?"

"I guess not. So when do I get out of here?" I glanced around at the cage where I'd spent the past two days.

"We could break you out." Krin looked at the time on her comm. "We still have five minutes before the guards come back to get Rey and me. We could be long gone by then."

I shook my head. "I think it's impossible for Breathers and Ethereals to get out of here."

"How do you figure?" asked Rey.

"The Mages who were here before. An Ethereal and two Breathers. If they couldn't escape, I doubt we can."

"Oh, I don't know about that." Rey stood and felt along the edge of the cell where the glass connected with the concrete sides. "They may be more powerful with respect to how much ether they can move around, but they're bound by their limited intelligence. All instinct. No finesse."

I let Rey and Krin satisfy themselves by searching the nooks and crevices of my cell. I'd had days to do that. Eventually, they flopped back on the floor.

"It's useless," Krin said.

I nodded. "Uh-huh." I grabbed Rey's comm from his belt and pressed the command button. "Contact Loken."

"Calls are currently blocked," said the robotic female voice.

I tossed the comm back to Rey. "It was worth a try."

Light streamed into the room from the basement door. My heart sank into my stomach. "I think it's time for you guys to go."

We exchanged hugs and said our goodbyes just as four jailers opened the door to escort Rey and Krin outside. They disappeared up the stairway. The light streaming into the basement went out.

I stared up the steps, longing to be away from this cell. This was the last place I wanted to be if the world ended.

Light filled the stairwell again. A familiar silhouette came into view. Loken's face became visible halfway down the stairs. I pressed my hands against the glass.

"Loken!" I shouted, even though I knew he couldn't hear me without the intercom.

He strode to the door and tinkered with the panel next to it. The door slid open.

His gaze swept over me, from my feet to the top of my head. I guessed my face was as dirty as my dust-covered hands, since I hadn't had a shower in the days I'd been locked in this dusty cell. I pushed my hair out of my face and tried to look like I wasn't a complete mess. I doubted I succeeded.

Loken wasn't much better. A thin layer of stubble covered his chin. His eyes were bloodshot like he hadn't slept. They were also duller than usual, more of a flat gray than the sparkling silver they turned when he smiled. Still, he was beautiful.

My eyes followed the line of his jaw and landed on his lips. I licked my own, wanting to press them against his. They'd been so soft when I'd kissed him. It was amazing how much I could miss a person after only a few days. My heart fluttered in my chest.

Loken reduced the space between us and wrapped me in a tight hug. We held each other, and I breathed deeply to take in his scent. I wanted to remember it when he left.

"What's going on?" I asked when we stepped apart. I brushed his hair out of his face. "Have you slept?"

His arms circled my waist. He pulled me down to the floor. "No," he mumbled. He nuzzled into my neck. "I've spent my days fighting Mages and my nights arguing with the elders."

"About me?" I tangled my fingers in his hair, which was coarser than usual.

"Mm-hmm," he mumbled, not lifting his face.

"Is that why you didn't visit earlier?" I poked him in the bicep. It didn't seem to bother him, but it hurt my finger.

"They wouldn't let me. Elder Kohler threatened to lock me up too, which I know he doesn't want to do. But if I defy him publicly, he'll have to follow through."

"So what's changed that you can visit me now?"

"I think he just got tired of me asking." Loken pulled his face away from my neck, so I could see him. One side of his mouth twitched with a private joke. "Plus, I reminded him that there are cameras all over this basement, and that I couldn't possibly help you escape with all his fine security in place."

"Is he going to let me out?"

"I don't think so."

My eyebrows shot upward. "I'm supposed to stay here for the rest of my life?"

The muscles in his jaw clenched and unclenched. "I think that's their plan, yes."

Panic wrenched my chest. It felt like the cell was shrinking around me, becoming more confined. I wriggled from his grasp and jumped to my feet.

"Let me out of here!" I shouted, banging my fist against the glass. "Let me out!" The glass remained as solid as it had been these past two days. My hand throbbed where I slammed into it.

"Hey, hey," Loken said softly. He grabbed my hips and turned me back around to face him. "That's not going to help."

"It helps me feel better," I grumbled.

Loken pulled me back down to the floor. He placed my head on his chest. His T-shirt smelled of sweat and metal and soap. That and the steady rhythm of his heart calmed me a bit. I concentrated on matching my breath to his, steady in and out. I needed to figure out exactly how to get out of here.

I hesitated to say what I was thinking because I didn't want him to get into more trouble. I knew how important his job was to him. But I didn't see any other options. I said it anyway. "You know the door is metal. And the glass is part metal. You could—"

Loken stopped my lips with a kiss. At first, I tensed. I didn't want to be distracted. I wanted to get out. But his soft lips worked mine until they were pliant, until they molded with his. His tongue invaded my mouth, exploring me. I sucked on it, drawing him deeper into me.

My fingers clutched at his shirt. I wanted so badly to rip it off him, to reveal the hard muscles of his chest that pressed against me as he rolled me onto my back. His hands explored my stomach and inched higher. Cloudiness filled my head. There was nothing else in the world. Nothing except me and Loken.

Something hard pressed against my hip, and I reached for it—Loken's comm unit. Fighting against my baser emotions, I nudged Loken off me, so I could get a better look at the time.

I shoved him fully away from me. "We have less than four days left!"

He raked his hair off of his forehead. "Yes."

"I need to get out of here. I can't die in here, and I want to help. Tell them I can help! You can get me out."

"I was planning on it." His smile brought out the dimple on his right cheek.

"Then why aren't we gone yet?" I shouted.

Guilt painted his features. He flashed me an embarrassed grin. "I got a little distracted."

"Well, get un-distracted!"

He nodded and pressed his hand against the biometric panel next to the door. "Let's go."

CHAPTER 24

As soon as I stepped through the doorway, red lights flashed all over the basement. A sound like an air horn split the air.

"Gods!" Loken yelled. He grabbed my hand and yanked me toward the stairs.

He slowed at the top of the steps. Instead of opening the door, Loken placed a palm flat against it. "Ready?" he asked.

I nodded.

In the span of less than a second, the door melted outward into the door frame, leaving three shocked guards standing open-mouthed on the other side. Loken grabbed one of them by his shirtfront and tossed him down the stairs before the others had even started moving.

I flinched as the first guard tumbled down the steps and crumpled at the bottom. I was pleased to hear him moan; it meant he was still alive.

Loken unsheathed his sword so quickly that I hadn't even seen him reach for it. He pointed it under the chin of one of the remaining two guards. "Don't move," he growled to other, "unless you want your friend here to start breathing through his neck."

Loken gripped my shoulder and pushed me up the last two steps and past the two men. While he had them disabled,

I took the opportunity to snatch the comm unit from the waistband of one of the guards. We circled them until we'd put them between us and the basement.

"Now run!" Loken shouted.

I took off and felt Loken close at my heels. We raced around the corner and skidded to a stop as Elder Kohler came into view. Despite his thin arms and mellow demeanor, I knew better than to underestimate him now. Loken's arms still held the red welts Kohler had left during our last bout.

I spun in place and took off in the opposite direction. I rushed around the corner too quickly and hit the wall in front of me.

Loken grasped me around the waist, shielding me as the sound of a roaring fire filled my ears. Pressed against me, his body suddenly became much hotter. Terror stirred in the pit of my stomach. I peeked over my shoulder, dreading what was happening to Loken, who was directly in Kohler's line of fire.

"Oh, gods, Loken," I whispered as my gaze met his face.

The metal tattoo on the side of his face melted and spread. More metal climbed upward from his neck. The shining silver crawled along his face, over his cheeks and forehead, until it covered him like a second skin. Gripping me around the waist, his hands hardened against my arms as they, too, became metal.

"Stay down," he said, through lips that shone like liquid steel.

Fire burned all around us. It filled the edges of my vision. Sweat prickled at my skin at first, then streamed down into my eyes and dripped off my chin. Loken's hands around my waist, and his chin pressed against the top of my head, felt heavier and hotter as each moment passed. I struggled in his grasp, desperate to move, terrified that his metal skin would melt. And so would he.

Over the roar of the flames, I could barely hear the droning female voice in the walls: *"Please stay calm. Remain calm."*

Finally the fire let up. Loken let me wriggle from his grasp. As I raced for the back door, I shot a peek over my shoulder. Elder Kohler had doubled over and was gasping for breath. He'd tired himself out trying to kill us.

My back tingled as we ran, anticipating a surprise attack. I expected any second to be burned by fire, or stabbed by a Bender joining the fight. I approached the glass back doors and reached for the handle.

"Don't slow down. Go through it!" Loken shouted.

I hesitated for a split second until I realized what he meant. I hoped I was heavy enough and moving quickly enough to break the glass. Ether swirled around the door. I picked up my speed again, barreling toward the exit, praying to the gods I hadn't believed in yesterday to help me break through it.

White-blue lights winked around the door, reflecting the sunlight streaming in from outside.

Gods, help us.

I squeezed my eyes shut and leapt toward the glass. It blew outward; I didn't even feel it touch me. The glass shattered onto the grassy lawn. Shouts sounded behind us, but I didn't look back. Loken's hurried footsteps beat against the ground behind me.

We were safe. We were fugitives.

My breath came in shallow pants by the time Loken let me stop to rest in one of the many copses of trees just off the side of the road.

"What . . . now?" I huffed, sucking in deep breaths between words.

He grabbed my new comm from my waist—the one I'd stolen from the guard—and cracked it against a nearby tree trunk.

"Hey! I need that." I snatched at it, but Loken held it out of my reach.

The comm split across the middle, and the top of the device popped off.

"Here. Hold this." He passed me the plastic top.

Loken peered into the lower half of the device, with all its internal circuitry visible. A thin needle appeared in his hand, which he used to pry up a small computer chip. Loken displayed the chip between his fingertips, then tossed it in the dirt. I handed the top back to him, and he snapped it into place.

"Now they can't track you," he said. "But we can't stay here. They're too smart not to check the trees all along this road.

"So then what?"

He gave me a half smile, flashing his dimple, as he pointed to the east.

"Oh!" I turned to run away from the transport that hovered toward us across the grassy hills.

"Wait." He grabbed my wrist. "It's Rey."

We stepped from the shadow of the trees, and the vehicle sped toward us. It stopped and the doors slid open.

Rey stuck his head from the driver-side window. "We've got a few minutes. I disconnected the power supplies from all the other transports. It's an easy fix, but it will take them a minute or two to figure out.

I pressed a sloppy kiss on his cheek. "You *are* a goddess."

He grinned. "I know. I know. Get in the transport."

Loken and I closed ourselves in the vehicle, and we took off.

"Where are we headed?" I asked.

"Believer village," said Rey, turning toward the front of the vehicle. "Jin's sister offered you safe harbor."

A sigh of relief blew past my lips. I settled back into the vehicle for the short ride.

After a minute of silence, Rey asked, "Are either of you hurt?"

"Are you?" I asked Loken.

I peered at him, examining his, once again, bronze skin. I lifted the bottom of his shirt and inspected his muscled abdomen, then shoved him around to examine his lower back. The metal tattoos swirled across his torso and back, motionless. I traced a finger along one that ran up and down his spine. Even through the tinted windows, the metal winked in the sunlight.

"Shall I take of my pants?" he asked.

"Not while I'm around," called Rey from the front seat. "And let's leave the sexual innuendo to the experts, shall we?"

Loken chuckled. As he did, his abdomen tightened under my hand. "Sorry, Rey. Didn't mean to step on your toes."

"Just don't let it happen again." Rey twisted around in his seat to give us a mock glare.

My hands jerked away from Loken. "Watch where we're going!" I shouted, pointing toward the front window.

"Okay, okay." Rey turned back toward the front.

Loken watched me through slightly closed lids. My heart raced as I remembered the feel of his hands on my body. I lifted his arms up, and Loken obediently held them out in front of him. I inspected the skin and metal on his arms as well. Everything appeared to be intact, no burns, no open wounds.

I brushed my palms over the soft skin of Loken's arms. Not only did he have no new injuries or burns, but the burns on his right arm from our previous run-in with Elder Kohler had disappeared. I gripped the arm just under the elbow and twisted it around in my hand. Definitely no burns. My gaze traveled back up to his face, which shone with a healthy glow and slight redness on his cheeks.

"So no one's hurt?" Rey asked again. "Or are you guys too busy making out to answer my question?"

"If you must know, Rey, I feel like Ra's calloused foot. But your buddy here looks like he's never been in a fight a day in his life." I whirled around to lock eyes with Loken. "What just happened?"

Loken shrugged but failed to hide his smile. "You have an ether shield; I have a metal shield."

"On the rare occasions when I can get my ether shield to work, it doesn't heal me."

"Maybe it would if you actually learned how to use it," Rey called.

"Just drive the vehicle and shush!" I said. Then to Loken, "That was incredible."

The edges of Loken's smile twitched downward. "I wasn't able to hold it as long as I used to. And I used to not need the tattoos at all. I could do it by drawing metal particles from the air."

Again, Rey turned his head around to look at us. I scowled at him. "I'm slower than I was before the new timelines started," he said. "So Elder Kohler was right about our abilities being affected."

"Looks like it," said Loken. His eyes narrowed at me. "I wonder how powerful you were before."

I didn't respond. If I'd known about my Ethereal ability before, I'd have a little brother right now. These were not the types of things I wanted to think about.

The transport slowed as we reached the edge of the village where Naja lived. The suns had set by then, and most of the villagers had turned in for the night. The few that remained stared at us as we coasted through town. Most cast us disapproving frowns. I sank deeper into my seat, trying to pull my face below the bottom of the windows without blatantly hiding.

"Can we just get out here and walk?" I asked.

"Absolutely not," Rey said. "They don't care that we disapprove when they come to the Council building in their fancy red-and-yellow robes, protesting our causes. So no, we're not going to respect their silly pro-nature customs. And who says this transport isn't natural anyway?"

"I think the fact that the Council members built it means it's not natural," I said.

"Council members are natural, and so is their work product."

Naja's house came into view. The closer we got, the clearer it became that Naja's face held a hard scowl.

I pointed at her. "I think she would disagree with your analysis."

When we stopped, I jumped from the transport and raced to the door, putting distance between me and the custom-disrespecting vehicle.

Naja gave me a quick hug and pushed me inside the house. "Would you help me with the dishes please? I had dinner guests, and the sink is overflowing."

As I stepped into the house, she hissed to Rey and Loken, "Time for you gentlemen to go, and take that *thing*"—the word dripped venom—"out of here."

The kitchen was smaller than any I'd seen before. Just a sink and a square of counter space. I guessed Naja did most of her cooking outside over her fire pit. I grabbed a damp dishrag and got to work on the pile of wooden dishes. Muffled voices floated to me from the doorway.

"Fine," Rey said after a whispered exchange.

He came into the house, trailed by Loken. Rey and I hugged and exchanged cheek-kisses.

I tilted my head upward as Loken reached for me. Our lips met. My body tingled in his arms. This wasn't the time or the place to indulge in that—not with Rey and Naja as audience, especially with Naja tapping her foot against the floor and darting exaggerated glances at the transport parked just outside her property.

Loken and I pulled apart. He brushed his fingertips across my lower lip before turning to leave. The men climbed into the transport and took off the way we'd come.

"So," Naja said as she sauntered back outside. She beckoned for me to follow. We sat on two wooden stools in her outdoor dining space.

"So?" I still had no idea why she was allowing me to stay with her. The serious set of her lips suggested she was about to tell me.

"Do you know why you're here?"

She wasn't going to tell me after all; we were going to play a guessing game. Withholding an annoyed sigh, I said, "The Council thinks I'm going to be responsible for whatever's about to happen." Naja nodded. I added, "But none of that explains why you're willing to have me here."

Her mouth crept into a smile, which somehow was not reassuring. "You and I are allies. You see, you may or may not have the power to end things. Most likely, the Vision is a fluke, and there's no end in sight. But either way, this is not something people were meant to interfere in. See—"

I cut her off. "I don't understand. Don't you guys care that everything we know may come to an end?"

"*Should* we care?" she asked, with one eyebrow quirked upward. "All things must end. Such is the cycle of nature. If the gods have decided that our time is over, then we should move on to the afterlives they have set for us. The end is not something to fear. It's something to be welcomed."

Six days ago, I might have laughed at that statement, at the seriousness with which she spoke of these alleged gods. The same gods who'd been on vacation when Pace was murdered. Now, I had my doubts. Something had happened back at the Council when I'd called on them to get me through the glass door. Or maybe I'd imagined it.

Still, I wasn't buying Naja's theory. And I certainly wasn't willing to bet my existence on it.

"So if we fight and survive," I asked, "does that mean there are no gods? No one up there preparing to end the world?"

"If your people fight and survive, they were always meant to survive, and the Vision is a fluke."

Neither of us spoke for a while. Our eyes narrowed at each other across the dining table.

Naja stood and brushed dust off the seat of her pants. "I can see we're not going to agree on this." A smile brightened her face. "But I think we *can* agree that you need a place to stay, and I am willing to give you one. You'll stay in Jin's room, but only for two nights. After that, the Council will figure out where you are from the change in the Mages' movements."

Before she turned and headed for the archway into the house, she added, "The other villagers and I will provide you safe harbor temporarily. But if you get in our way, we'll kill you."

CHAPTER 25
COUNTDOWN: 3 DAYS

"Wake up!" I pounded on Hael's bedroom door. "Up, up, up. Only three days to live. You can sleep when you're dead."

"Go away," came a muffled voice from inside the room.

"No way. Your gods are already up. It's time for you to join them outside."

A series of clunks sounded from beyond the door, and Hael yanked it open. His dark eyes peered at me under narrowed eyelids. His dreadlocks fell over his shoulders. He tossed a few out of his face. "You're bossy. You know that?"

"People keep telling me that, but I don't believe it." I turned and headed from the house, calling over my shoulder, "Outside in five minutes please!"

He mumbled something I didn't hear before slamming the door. I doubted it was complimentary.

When I stepped outside, the fresh air energized me. My skin tingled with excitement about the day ahead of me. I wouldn't be killing Mages—sadly. But if I had my way, I'd learn how to perform that task better. I bounced up and down on the grass, barely containing my energy.

The air smelled fresher here, like dirt and rain and sky. I breathed in deeply through my nose and felt a smile dance across my face. Tension drained from my muscles, replaced by renewed confidence.

With Ra barely in the sky and Solaris still at the horizon, the world had a reddish tint. Dew drops clinging to the grass sparkled red. Crimson glowed on the faces of Believers walking one way or the other along the dirt road. Although it was early, the day had already begun here. Unlike the inner city, which was occupied almost entirely by Nonbelievers, the Believer village hadn't shut down its normal operations in light of the Vision.

The exception was schooling, since many Believers attended the University. The University was unmatched in any field except religion, so they could find classes that didn't violate their belief system. But it was inside the city and shut down until who knew when.

Right now, that meant Hael was out of school and available.

After I'd been outside for seven minutes—I was just on my way back inside to drag him out—Hael strode from the house looking like he'd been awake for hours. He'd pulled his dreadlocks back into a thick ponytail. His brown eyes shone brightly in the sunlight, and his feet bounced over the grass as he approached.

As I'd been the first time I'd seen him, again I was surprised at how eerily he looked like Jin. The main difference between them, besides the age gap and the hair, was that Hael seemed to be constantly cheery.

"So why am I awake at this ungodly hour when school's been canceled until the end of time?" Hael asked.

"Will you teach me the thing with the comm unit?" I said.

He stared at my comm. His brow crinkled. "What thing?"

"Last time I saw you, the comm unit jumped right into your hand. How'd you do that?"

He pursed his lips. "I'd like to teach you that. Really, I would. But you wouldn't believe me if I explained it."

"Try me."

His voice was flat when he said, "The gods helped me."

"Come on. Be serious." I unhooked my comm, dropped it on the ground, and held my hand out over it. "Now what?"

Hael tilted his face toward Ra. "Now, you ask the gods to channel your power, so you can call the comm toward you."

I stared at him without speaking. If there were gods up there, they had no more to do with elemental practice than they did with any other science. And that's all we had to rely on right now: science. There was no evidence of gods. In fact, there was evidence to the contrary—with Pace dead and the countdown clock ticking downward. Since my father was a Seer, I had to assume he'd believed in them. And where was he now? Dead too.

Even if the gods existed, they'd released control of our fates long ago.

Hael chuckled. "I'm serious. Although since you're new at this, it might be better to wait until both suns are up. And it's best if one of them is at their high point in the sky."

"Elemental practice is a science—not a religion." I thought he might have flinched when the word *science* left my mouth. I contemplated calling this whole thing a mistake and suggesting he go back to bed.

We were silent for long enough that I found myself shifting my weight from foot to foot. I dug through my brain for something to say to break the awkwardness.

"So," I said, "Loken keeps telling me how my ability is the harnessing of my internal energy into something outward. I can feel myself doing that, even without help from your gods."

"You don't need them for basic practice, no. But to access your ability fully, you do. The gods don't belong to just the Believers, any more than the grass or the air does. We're just the ones who've recognized them." He gestured with his hands as he spoke. His motions became jerky, showing his aggravation.

"Then why don't I see Believers doing amazing things with their abilities all the time, if that's all it takes?" I knew I was pushing him further than I should, but his position made no sense. Elemental practice was a science, always had been.

"I didn't say that's *all* it takes. Faith is just a part of it. There's also knowledge, practice, and inherent ability." His face relaxed a touch. "Have you ever done something you didn't think you could when you were thinking about them?"

I imagined the glass back at the Council shattering outward. I could have sworn it happened a split second before I actually touched the glass—a theory that was supported by the fact that it hadn't cut me at all. In that desperate moment, when I'd been worried about Loken being burnt to a crisp, I'd called on Hael's gods. And it hadn't escaped me that I'd said a prayer just before attacking the lady Mage as well.

But those were just coincidences. I had nothing but coincidences in favor of his gods, but hard evidence—in the form of a dead brother—in favor of no gods.

"No," I said. "There have been times when I've thought of the gods, and then my ability exceeded my expectations. But those were also times when I was desperate. Desperation makes things happen, makes people stronger and more capable."

He raised a solo eyebrow.

This conversation was going nowhere. Time to change the subject. "For argument's sake, let's say I believe in your gods. Wh—"

"The *world's* gods."

"Right." I resisted the urge to roll my eyes. "The *world's* gods. Let's say I believe in them. What are the mechanics behind making the comm unit come toward me?"

"That depends. What do you see when you're accessing your ability?"

"I can see ether in the air," I said excitedly. My chest puffed with pride. "Like little blue specks around everything."

To my surprise, Hael did not look impressed. He frowned. "When you are ready to fully access your ability, you won't see the blue specks any more, unless you're actually looking for them."

I stared at him, waiting for him to explain.

He continued. "If you were learning to breathe for the first time, you'd think about your lungs, about the breathing rhythms that are most comfortable—the same way you probably did when you first learned to swim. But since breathing is second nature to you, you don't think about it. You don't have to think about the mechanics of it. But your lungs work just as well anyway—in fact, better than they would if you tried to *make* yourself breathe. It's easier when you let it come naturally."

"And that's how I want to be with ether—so comfortable that I don't notice the blue flecks at all?"

"Exactly."

"How do I get there?"

One side of Hael's mouth quivered, like he was trying to keep from laughing. "Faith."

"What's my second option?"

"Mediocrity."

I scowled at him. "Let's just work on the mechanics for now, and you can lecture me on ignoring the mechanics later."

"Okay." He laughed, showing off that very Jin-like smile. "It's pretty simple actually. You can control the ether around you. All those little blue specks."

"But I'm not touching them. I can only control ether that I'm touching."

He gave me a knowing smile. "Ah, but you *are* touching them—indirectly. You're touching everything. There is no space that's completely empty. There's air between you and the ether surrounding that comm unit." He pointed at my comm on the ground. "And more importantly, there's ether between you and that comm. Some of that ether is touching you. Some of it is touching more ether. And some of it is touching the comm."

"So it's like a chain of stuff from me to the comm."

"Mm-hmm." He nodded and reached his hand toward it. The comm shot upward into his palm.

I snatched the device from him and tossed it on the ground. Its smooth, black surface formed a small circle. The digital screen on its face was now blank, dark except for the countdown clock running backward in small red digits.

Blue specks snaked around it, and around my hand, and in the space between my hand and the comm. It sounded simple enough. I imagined the blue specks all being connected to me. After a deep breath, I willed the ether to pull the comm toward me.

Nothing happened. The comm lay just as still on the ground as it had ten seconds before. I dropped my hand back to my side and glared at it.

"I told you what you had to do." He crossed his arms over his chest.

I gritted my teeth and thought of his gods. *Help me move this comm,* I asked them. Still nothing.

Shaking his head, Hael walked back toward the house.

"Where are you going?" I asked.

"I'm not going anywhere." Hael sat in the grass and relaxed against the house's exterior. His eyes closed. He mumbled, "I'll be right here if you ever want to discuss how your ability really works."

"Hael!" I called.

No answer.

I swept the comm up from the ground—by hand—and stomped across the yard. I stood in front him, so my shadow fell over his face.

"Can you get out of my light please?" he muttered, without opening his eyes.

"I thought you were going to teach me."

"I'd be happy to teach you if you were willing to learn. Move the comm unit one inch. That's all. Then get back to me." He yawned and scooted to the right, finding his light again.

I stomped back to the other side of the yard, and tossed his comm on the ground again.

I spent the rest of the morning trying to call it into my hand, while Hael slept against the house. The bastard. For a few minutes, I even tried praying to the gods to help me. I didn't mean it though. There were no gods up there—just two balls of gas and fire.

When both of the suns had crested and started a path back toward the horizon, I was ready to give up. Hael had long since abandoned his nap and moved on to the rest of his day.

"What are you doing?" a familiar male voice said behind me. I spun around with a smile. Rey and Krin stood behind me.

"Hey!" I wrapped them in a three-person hug. Krin giggled and hugged me back.

Krin's face had more color than usual. Pink tinged her cheeks, and her lips were plumper than usual. Her tousled dark hair stuck away from her head in numerous directions. She and Rey stood disturbingly close, so close their shoulders brushed together. And a hair was out of place in his ponytail.

"Oh no! Please tell me you two weren't kissing."

She shrugged. "Rey's not so bad. A little full of himself, but he's got great hair."

"Let's not forget my infectious personality," he said.

"I just hope for your sake he doesn't have any other infections," I whispered, too quietly for Rey to hear.

"I heard that," he said.

I stuck my tongue out at him and then hugged him again. "I'm so happy to see you guys. Won't you get in trouble for not being at the Council right now?"

"Nah," Krin said. "Loken's covering for us."

"You're going to get him locked up! You have to go back." I shoved Rey in the direction of the road, where his transport idled.

"No, we're good," Krin said. "A bunch of us have patrol duty just north of the city, but no Mages are expected to show. No one will even notice."

"Is he in trouble for my escape?"

Rey shrugged. "I'm sure he is. I'm also pretty sure his punishment is postponed for now."

I hoped it wouldn't be too awful, whatever it was. "What's going on? I mean, of course I'm happy to see you guys, but why are you here? Is everything all right?"

"We could all use a little fun," Rey said. "Maybe we could hang out at the lake. I'd like to spend some of my last days enjoying myself. All my old friends are tied up with their assigned duties, so you guys will have to do."

"Thanks, Rey. I love you too," I said. "Can we pick up Sona before we go? She loves the floaties at the lake."

Rey shook his head. "We checked on Sona on our way here. There are Council guards watching her. Looking for you, most likely."

"Oh." I stared down at my feet, disappointed. "I don't think I can go to the lake without Sona. I'd just think about her the whole time, and feel guilty for trying to have fun without her." There was something else I wanted to do with Rey and Krin, but I wasn't sure I wanted to put them at risk.

"What are you thinking?" asked Rey. His eyes narrowed in suspicion.

"Nothing," I said.

"Liar."

I sighed. "Okay, I kind of want to go back to the Council and—"

"No way," Krin cut in. "Rey and Loken worked hard to get you out. And you just want to hand yourself in? No. Not going to happen."

I held up my hands to stop her. "Relax. I'm not going to turn myself in. It's just, my mom mentioned that Elder Kohler and my bio-dad were friends. Kohler knows all about me, he knew my father, and he doesn't like me at all. Something's off about why I was assigned to the Ethereals, and I think it has to do with my birth father. I want the truth."

"So you're going to stroll into the Council, have a conversation with Elder Kohler, and then stroll out—without getting set on fire?" asked Rey.

"Actually . . . we'll most likely have to tie him up before having that conversation. But that's the gist of my plan, yes."

Krin's mouth hung open. "She's kidding, right?"

"Sadly, I don't think so." Rey turned to me. "How serious are you about this?"

"Absolutely serious. So serious that I will do this by myself if you guys don't want to get involved." I grinned sheepishly and nodded toward Rey's transport. "But I'm going to need a ride to the Council either way."

"No way," Rey said. "I'm not turning down an opportunity to tie up that bastard Kohler and help you at the same time. I'm in!"

"What about you?" I asked Krin.

She smiled widely. "Definitely."

CHAPTER 26

Rey ran us piggyback to within a mile of the Council building; first Krin, then me. He didn't feel comfortable leaving either one of us by herself any closer than that. We walked together the rest of the way.

With each step forward, we moved closer to the people who had locked me up for over two days, who would have kept me captive until the end of time. I fisted my hands at my sides to try to contain my anger. I needed to stay rational if we planned to get in and out without getting captured.

We kept to the tree line, just in case some Council members or recruits happened along the road. But the journey was quiet. The three of us didn't speak as we walked, and no one else passed by us. Tension hung thickly in the air. I guessed Rey and Krin were just as nervous about this plan as I was.

When we were hidden among a copse of trees about two hundred feet from the Council, Krin stopped walking and said, "Do you guys think we should warn Loken about what we're doing?"

"No." I shook my head. "He'll try to stop us. He wants me as far away from these people as possible right now. Plus, we want him to be able to deny all knowledge of this."

Rey nodded. "Agreed. We don't tell Loken."

Now that we'd arrived, this was going to be harder than it had sounded back at the village. We couldn't very well just walk through the back door. I'd be rearrested—or burnt to an unattractive crisp—and my friends would be tossed in the cell with me.

While of course I didn't want any of us to be locked up, I also worried that the loss of three recruits as opposed to just one might be damaging to everything the Council was trying to accomplish. The Ethereal team, especially, was small already without losing Krin too. If we caught up with Elder Kohler inside, and if we weren't caught, we'd all have to go into hiding. Either way, my task force would suffer another loss.

"Krin." I turned toward her. "You don't have to come with us. Rey and I can handle this."

Her face fell. "You don't want me to come?"

"I don't want you to get kicked off the task force."

"And there's no need for all of us to get killed." Rey chuckled. "I'd rather have you safe."

I could see the wheels spinning in her head. "I can take care of myself," she snapped. "And we can help even if we're not with our task forces." She tapped her fingernails against her comm unit. "We know approximately when and where this is happening. In Vallara—probably right here in High City. In less than three days. We'll be back here at the right time, and we'll help any way we can. We don't need task forces for that."

"But—" I started.

"I'm coming." She stormed ahead of us toward the building.

"Okay," I said. "Any idea how we can get inside?"

Krin turned and stared at me wide-eyed. "We came all the way out here, and you don't have a plan?"

"I have a plan," I said, even though I had no plan. "We go inside, restrain Kohler, question him, and get the hell out of there."

"That's not a plan. That's a goal!" Krin threw up her hands.

"I can get us in." Rey unhooked his comm unit and showed it to us. "Elder Breather programmed our comms to control the trapdoor to the transport holding area. So we can move transports in and out."

"But we don't have a transport," I said.

"We don't need one." He pressed a couple buttons on the screen of his comm.

The ground vibrated beneath us. Less than fifty feet away, the ground opened up. Two sides of a door in the dirt slid away from each other, revealing the underground transport holding area.

After a quick look around to make sure no one was watching, I left the cover of the trees and jogged over to the opening. I peeked over the edge, and then took several large steps backward. The floor of the transport area lay twenty feet below, with no stairway down.

"That's a long way down," I said as Rey and Krin joined me at the edge.

"No problem." Rey grasped me around the waist and leapt into the hole.

A scream tried to rip its way up my throat, but Rey's hand clamped over my mouth. We floated to the floor, his arm supporting me through the air. Rey left me and leapt back up to ground level. I watched, open-mouthed. A few seconds later, he and Krin floated down to the floor next to me.

"That was amazing," I said.

"Being a Breather has its perks." He smoothed back the front of his ponytail. "Plus, I'm handsome."

I rolled my eyes at Krin, but she was too busy nodding to notice.

When we arrived at the elevator to the main level, Krin reached for the call button. I grabbed her wrist.

"Rey will go up first," I said, "run around, make sure the coast is clear." I turned toward Rey. "We have to go to the third floor, so check the stairs and the upstairs hallway."

Rey nodded. "If someone sees me, I'll run. So if I'm not back in three minutes, hide. I'll come get you as soon as I can."

He pressed the elevator call button. I held my breath as the doors slid open. I braced for the possibility that someone would be in the elevator and we'd have a fight even before we reached the main floor of the building. Lucky for us, the elevator was empty.

Rey stepped inside, and the doors shut him in. As we waited, Krin's foot tapped a rhythm against the floor. She stared at the doors, while I shifted my weight from foot to foot.

I counted the seconds in my head. Two full minutes had passed already. This was taking too long. I opened my mouth to insist that we follow Rey upstairs—when the elevator doors opened again.

"Let's go." Rey beckoned for us to join him inside. "Everyone's out on assignment. The place is nearly deserted."

Anticipation bounced around in my stomach during the short ride up one level. We stepped out into an empty hallway. I followed Rey, running on tiptoe to the end of the hall. He pressed his back against the wall and gestured for us to do the same. He peeked around the corner and then waved us forward.

Just as I turned onto the next hall, a woman entered through the back door, stepping into our path. Krin froze. I shoved her from behind, urging her to continue walking. The sound of my pulse roared in my ears. The woman glanced at us as she walked past toward the front of the building. She didn't look back.

My heart rate slowed to a semi-normal pace. We raced toward the steps and took them two at a time up both flights.

No one occupied the hall upstairs, and all the office doors were closed.

Krin and I took one side of the hallway, while Rey took the other, peering into the windows as we searched for Elder Kohler.

"Found him!" Rey hissed at the fourth door on the left.

We crowded around the door and ducked beneath the window.

"Now what?" Krin whispered.

"We go inside," Rey said. "I'll knock him out. We tie him up and wait for him to wake up."

I peeked through the window and then ducked back down. "He's facing the other way. Let's go."

Rey gripped the door handle and glanced at Krin, who nodded. He turned the handle and burst through the door.

Elder Kohler spun toward us, but Rey was faster. Rey rushed toward him, his elbow cocked backward. The elbow swung forward and clipped Elder Kohler in the head. He sank to the floor unconscious.

"Now what?" Krin asked.

We stared down at Elder Kohler's motionless form.

"We tie him up," I said.

Rey scratched his chin and spun a circle, examining the room. "Mm-hmm. With what?"

"I don't know," I hissed. "Tying him up was your idea."

"Well *your* idea was to barge in here with no plan at all," he countered.

None of us happened to be carrying around rope or handcuffs—although, in hindsight, that would have been a good idea. I scanned the room. I eventually landed on a weapons belt on a chair in the corner. I picked up the belt, removed the sheaths for the sword and dagger, and tossed the belt to Rey.

Rey caught it and turned the brown leather over in his hand. He pulled it taut. "This will do. Help me roll him over."

We put Elder Kohler face down. Rey pulled his wrists together, wrapped the belt around one wrist, then the other, and bound them together with the belt clip. Krin yanked on the binding and nodded her approval.

Then we waited.

After a few minutes, I started to worry. "He's still breathing, right?"

Rey rolled the man onto his back and held his hand under Kohler's nose. "Still breathing."

"How long does it take someone to wake up after being knocked unconscious?" Krin asked.

Rey shrugged. "It varies a lot, and Elder Kohler is not a young man. Let's give him a bit longer before we freak out."

I paced the floor, checking out the window into the hallway every time I passed the door. "How long have we been waiting?" I asked after too long.

Rey glanced at his comm. "Twelve minutes."

I was close to calling the whole thing off, alerting the medics, and making a run for it—when Elder Kohler finally stirred. He groaned and tugged at his bonds. His eyelids fluttered open.

At first, he seemed to stare at nothing. His eyes glazed over as they darted about the room. He shook his head hard, then focused on us. "Rey, Krin." His gaze landed on me and stayed. "Ashara. Is there something I can do for you three? Some reason that I'm tied up?"

His speech was eerily calm and just above a whisper. The rasp of his damaged voice grated on my already frayed nerves. I couldn't tell if his tone was threatening or entirely a result of his long-ago accident. I recalled the heat in that stream of fire he'd shot at Loken and me. A shiver crept its way up my back.

"I'm going to ask you some questions." I leaned in close to him. "About why you locked me up. And about my father."

"Before we begin, will you do an old man a favor and sit me upright in that chair?" Kohler jerked his head toward the chair behind his desk. "My back aches." He wriggled on the floor to make his point.

Rey and I hooked our hands under Kohler's arms and half-lifted, half-dragged him into the chair.

"Better?" I asked.

"Much. Now what are your questions?"

"Why was it so important to include me on the Ethereal task force?" I shoved my face right up to Kohler. Our noses almost touched. "You kept looking at me during the briefing. And you put my training above the other Ethereals when you assigned Loken to our task force."

"The reason is self-evident: you are an Ethereal. We need Ethereals to combat the Mages. As many as we can get." His eyes radiated calm logic. I didn't buy it.

"You don't need Ethereals to kill Mages. You need Benders and Breathers. I'm an *untrained* Ethereal, and you seemed to focus on me from day one. So why was I added to the task force?"

Rey stepped behind Elder Kohler and yanked his bonds downward. Kohler's teeth gritted.

"You think I'm going to give you information if you cause me pain?" He raised an eyebrow. "I have experienced plenty of pain in my life. I can endure a little more." He stretched his neck upward and angled his head to the side, giving me a better view of his scarred throat.

Up close, his neck was like a patchwork of pale-white skin. The flesh looked soft, vulnerable, like small squares of skin pasted together haphazardly. I pulled my gaze back up to his face, willing my insides not to squirm at what I'd just seen.

"How'd you do that?" I pointed at his neck but didn't glance at it again.

"A little accident in the lab. A poorly executed experiment." He gave an exaggerated frown. "I'd be happy to tell you about it, but I'm not sure you'd like how it ends . . . Is that the question you came here to ask me? You tied me up to ask about an old scar?"

"Why am I on the task force?"

"I'm going to answer your question," Elder Kohler said. "But not because your friend back there is pulling my arms out of their sockets. I'll answer because you should know how dangerous you are."

Dread knotted my stomach. I suddenly regretted all of this. My gaze slid toward the door. I wished I were on the other side of it right now.

"Over the objection of every other elder, I personally selected you for that task force after your ability manifested in the last timeline."

"Why?"

"I expected you to be stronger than everyone else. Given Mages' attraction to practitioners, I needed to keep my eye on you." He added, nonchalantly, "Elder Ethereal was particularly against it. Her vote was for killing you in your sleep."

"Why did you think I'd be stronger? And why did she want to . . . kill me?" I choked out the last two words.

Elder Kohler didn't answer right away. He looked up at the ceiling, as if trying to decide how to proceed. "What do you know about your father?"

My eyes narrowed. I'd wanted to have this conversation, but I hadn't expected Elder Kohler to prompt the subject. "Not much," I said. "Just that he died before I was born." I hesitated, and added, "How did he die?"

"An accident in the lab. Nothing of note."

"He was my father," I said through gritted teeth. "His entire life was of note."

Elder Kohler didn't respond.

"*How* did he die?" I clenched and unclenched my fists, then darted another glance at the door.

"You don't want me to describe the exact manner of your father's death. It won't be pretty. And I wouldn't want you to be sick all over my office floor."

Krin blanched.

"Tell me," I said.

He shrugged. "If you insist. Your father died attempting to transfer his consciousness to one of the elders. Fried his own brain. Almost fried mine too."

I had the sudden urge to run for the restroom and empty my stomach contents into the wastebasket. I fought to keep the feeling out of my expression. But by the way Elder Kohler's lips twisted into a smile, I knew I'd lost the fight.

Kohler continued, "But that's not relevant to what you really want to know."

"And what's that?"

His eyes narrowed. His voice was as clear as I'd ever heard it. "We have precious little time until the end, and you are taking too long to get to the right questions."

I folded my arms across my chest. "Which are?"

"If you know the truth, you'll think twice about making reckless decisions in the future."

"If she knows *what*?" asked Rey, who still stood behind Kohler. The muscles in his neck and shoulders tensed.

Elder Kohler's mouth turned upward into a sly—though not comforting—smirk. "Your father was the first one to foresee the end. Like the current Seers, he couldn't see what caused it, but he knew it was coming. And he knew we were out of time."

I shook my head, hard. That couldn't be right. That didn't even make sense. "My father has been dead for almost nineteen years."

"I'm well of aware of that," Kohler said. "Your father foresaw the end several months ago—in the original timeline."

My head continued to shake side to side. "No. My father died long before that. Nineteen years ago."

"Not in the original timeline, he didn't. The timeline that all of *you*"—he jerked his head toward each of us, one at a time—"thought was the first timeline was the second. We performed the first rewind ritual after your father's prophecy. The elders didn't believe him. So we tricked a bunch of other Council members into helping us, and we did it without the elders' approval. The only consciousnesses we were able to preserve in the rewind were mine and his."

A hundred questions raced through my head. Too many questions. Not enough time to ask them all.

"I was doubtful about the whole thing," Elder Kohler rambled on. "I went along with it because Nole felt strongly. We went back as far as we could. We thought that would be a year or two, plenty of time to avoid the end he'd predicted. Apparently, we were stronger than we thought—much stronger than the elders are now—because we took ourselves back over nineteen years." Elder Kohler paused to chuckle, bitterly. "Nole had admired your mother in the original timeline. Had a bit of a crush on her after meeting her at a Ratem festival. I guess he saw a second chance with her."

"Someone's coming!" shouted Krin from her spot by the door.

My whole body froze. We had no plan for getting caught in this office. We'd be trapped, with no other doors except the one leading into the hallway.

"No. Wait," she said. My nerves tingled, on edge. "False alarm. It was just someone going into her office. But hurry up!"

Elder Kohler jumped right back into his story. "We elders refer to each person in this timeline as an echo. Have you heard that term yet?"

I nodded.

"We call it an echo because we're all different than we were in our original timelines. We're attenuated. Less. Weaker. Yet still a remnant of what we once were. Some of our scientists say that the degree to which we are different from our original selves depends on how many repetitions we've experienced." His eyes locked on mine. "And how long it's been since we were originals."

The truth hit me suddenly like a brick in the chest. "Did I exist in your original timeline? Was I ever born?"

"Now you're asking the right questions." Elder Kohler's smile grew wider.

Krin tore her gaze from the door. Her eyes widened. "Asha's more powerful than everyone else because she's closer to being an original? She wasn't rewound by nineteen years the first time around. She didn't exist yet. So compared to everyone else, she . . . she'd attract every Mage on the continent!"

"So you're the smart one of the bunch." Elder Kohler leaned back in his chair. His face looked too relaxed.

I gripped the armrests on either side of Kohler's chair. I was tired of these games. "What does all of this mean?"

"The Mages started toward here in the middle of the last timeline, immediately after your ability manifested. They will continue to be drawn to you. When your uncontrolled powers collide with theirs, it will be the end of us."

"How do we stop it?"

"Kill yourself," Elder Kohler growled. His smile disappeared for the first time since we'd started this interrogation.

"It was a mistake for us to let you live after your ability manifested. I thought maybe you were the key to saving us. Now I believe Elder Ethereal was right all along. You're a menace."

"We have to go!" Rey grabbed my shirtsleeve and yanked.

"What?" Before the words had left my mouth, my nostrils filled with the scent of burning leather.

A stream of smoke floated upward from behind Elder Kohler's back. He was burning through the belt we'd used to bind his hands. He'd be out any second, and we'd be in flames.

Krin threw the door open. The three of us bolted from the room and down the stairs.

CHAPTER 27

My mind raced even faster than my feet pounded against the floor. When I hit the bottom of the stairs, a stream of fire shot over our heads at the level we'd just left. Red lights flashed around the hallway. An alarm shrilled against my eardrums.

I focused on Krin's back and stayed close to her heels. She spun to the right and headed for the back door. It was the smart move. We couldn't wait for the elevator to take us back downstairs to the transports. The glass doors were fixed from the last time I'd made a hasty escape that way. A gust of wind burst around me. The doors flung open and slammed back against the outside of the building.

"Go!" Rey shouted from behind me.

We bolted through the doorway and kept running. My quads and calves burned, begging me to stop, but I didn't until we'd lost sight of the Council.

"We can't . . . outrun them!" Krin shouted. The words came out between pants.

"I don't plan to. Hide." Rey pushed Krin and me toward a cluster of trees and took off back the way we'd come. He disappeared within a matter of seconds.

A ball of nervousness tightened in the pit of my stomach as we waited. After a few minutes, a transport came into view. I darted out toward the road and waved Rey toward us.

"Wait." Krin grabbed my arm and yanked me back between the trees. "The Council will be looking for us in transports too. We don't know that's Rey."

The vehicle shot toward us. It stopped ten feet away. Four guards piled out and fanned out around us. Krin clutched my arm. Their circle collapsed, and the guards came closer. Krin and I pressed our backs together, eying the group, knowing we were caught.

One of the men gripped me by my arms. He lifted me from the ground. "Look what I got," he said. His breath smelled of garlic and onions. I turned my face away.

Another transport flew into view. This one showed no signs of stopping. It barreled toward us at top speed. The group of guards fled from its path. The man holding me dropped me and threw himself to the side, out of the way. I collapsed into a heap on the ground. The transport sped toward me. I wouldn't be able to get out of the way fast enough.

It came to an abrupt stop within a foot of my face. Rey stuck his head from the driver-side window. "What are you two waiting for? Get in the gods-damned vehicle!"

The guards had recovered. One of them ran toward Krin, his large body moving remarkably fast. She froze, eyes wide. I ran toward her and tackled her to the ground. The guard slammed into the shimmering ether shield I threw up around us. He bounced off and slid to the ground. A groan rumbled from his chest.

I dragged Krin toward the vehicle, shoved her in, and jumped in after her. The guards scrambled back to their transport. Their vehicle took off after ours.

"They're chasing. They're chasing!" I shouted at Rey.

"Hurry up!" Krin yelled.

"Stop shouting!" Rey shouted.

The distance between us and the other transport increased. As it did, my stress level began to lessen. My lower back throbbed from the tension it held, and from hitting the ground when I'd tackled Krin. I rolled my shoulders in an attempt to relax. Deep breaths in and out. We were safe for now.

When the other transport was almost out of view, I lay back in my seat and said, "I think it's safe to say that we're all officially fugitives. Welcome to my world."

Rey didn't take us in a straight line back toward the Believer village. We traveled west, north, east, south, west again, and then north and east toward the village. We lost the vehicles that gave chase long before we arrived.

Naja, in the middle of a conversation on her lawn, glared at us when we stopped in front of her house. I stepped out of the transport with my head ducked low, embarrassed to have once again brought a forbidden vehicle into her village and then flaunted it on the edge of her property.

Naja held up a hand toward the man with whom she was speaking, to stop him mid-sentence. She turned to Rey. "Are you going to leave that thing there?" The sides of her mouth turned downward.

Rey's expression stayed blank. "What should I do with it?"

"For starters," said Naja, "you can move it away from my land. Then I suggest you remove it from the village before you start a riot." She inclined her head toward the other side of the road.

I looked in the direction she indicated and felt even more like burying myself in the dirt. A number of villagers stood nearby. Every one of them stared at the transport with varying expressions of anger, disapproval, shock, and fury. A brute of a man with shoulders twice as broad as Rey's stalked toward us. His fists clenched as he stomped across a lawn on the other side of the road.

"We'll move it," I said, loudly enough for the man to hear us. He stopped and glared at us from a distance.

"We can't take it back to the Council," Rey said. He turned toward Naja. "We *borrowed* this transport without permission."

"You stole it?" Naja's eyes brightened. She didn't seem too upset about the Council having one less resource.

"*Stole.* That's such an ugly word," Rey said.

"But accurate," Krin piped in.

Naja was smiling broadly now. "In that case, you can keep it here, but out of view. There should be enough room in the shed out back if you can get it through the door."

Rey climbed back into the vehicle and drove it around the side of the house.

I collapsed on the ground, exhausted from a day that had ended up being a lot more exciting than I'd expected—and it wasn't even evening yet. As soon as my butt hit the ground, the weight of everything Elder Kohler had said pushed down on my shoulders.

"How are you feeling?" asked Krin, rubbing my back.

I hung my head over my lap. "I feel . . . I don't quite know how I feel. Confused maybe. How am I supposed to feel about the fact that I was never supposed to exist?"

"Well I, for one, am glad you do!" she said.

"As am I," said Rey. He slumped on the ground beside us.

"Me too." I laughed, although the words tasted bitter on my tongue. "Except if I didn't we might not be dealing with this Vision-thing right now. No me would mean no Mages coming this way."

"I don't think that's entirely true," Rey said. "Practitioners are becoming more powerful with every generation. If you have anything to do with all this—and that's something I doubt, for the record—but if you do, I think you've just sped along the inevitable. Someday, there was going to be a person as powerful as you are. And we'd have this same problem."

"But it's not someday, and it's not someone! It's me. It's now."

"Well, killing yourself is definitely not an option." Krin fixed me with a stern glare. "What gives that pompous gasbag Kohler the right to suggest that? If he didn't have all that firepower, I'd . . ." She made a stabbing motion with her hand.

"There definitely won't be any killing yourself," Rey agreed.

"Of course not," I said. I made my mouth form the words, but I wasn't sure I believed them. Like Rey had said days ago, some of us had to die for the good of the world. That's what we'd signed on for.

But I couldn't be sure my death would solve the problem. The Mages might keep coming, and without me around, there might be no one strong enough to stop them. So the way I saw it, I either had to *get* strong enough, or get dead.

I'd promised Sona I would live, so that was my first priority—which meant I needed to work harder on my elemental ability. I had no intention of leaving her sibling-less, or leaving my mother and Talin with one less child.

"So our options are *what*?" I said.

I glanced at Rey for an answer. He stared at Krin, and she looked at me. None of us spoke.

"We fight," I said, after the silence had grown too loud. "When the Mages get here, we fight."

"What if you lose control of your power?" Krin asked.

"Then he'll kill me." I pointed at Rey.

"He *who*?" Rey pointed at himself and raised his eyebrows.

"Yes, you. Rey, you're my oldest friend. I trust you to do this in a way that's both humane and for the greater good. You will do this, or if I lose control, one of two things will happen in the alternative."

They stared at me expectantly.

"One." I held up a finger. "I will be the end of us. Two. The—"

"I don't believe that," Rey cut in. "Even if you're as powerful as the Council suspects, we're dealing with over fifty Mages. *They're* the real danger here, not you."

"That brings me to the second thing that could happen," I continued, holding up another finger. "The elders—who seem pretty sure I'll play a role in the end of things—will murder me. And you can bet it won't be quick and with my best interest at heart." I reached for Rey's hand and pulled it into my lap. "Promise me you'll do this."

"No!" Krin leapt to her feet. "I won't let you do it."

"It's not up to you," I whispered, my eyes still locked with Rey's.

"I can see that." Sarcasm tinged her voice. "I'm nothing but the girl who just risked her life to help someone I've known for all of seven days. And I didn't do it just so you could commit assisted suicide." She shot a glare at Rey. "I did it because we're friends. Maybe you haven't noticed, but I don't like most people very much. So no, I will not sit by while you plan to die."

She slapped Rey on the back of the head—hard enough that he had to shake his head to clear the glassiness from his eyes—then stalked off down the road.

I wanted to run after her. Even though I hadn't known her long, I felt a connection. She'd supported me before she even knew me, during my first day on the Ethereal task force. I would have risked my life for her just as she had for me.

But that wasn't the issue on the table. I clutched Rey's hand to my chest. "Promise me."

He leaned toward me until our foreheads touched. "I promise."

CHAPTER 28

Rey and I were still holding hands on Naja's front lawn when another transport hovered through town. We scrambled to our feet. My knees flexed as I prepared to run if needed. But I spied a familiar silhouette through the darkened windows of the vehicle.

When the transport stopped, Loken emerged from the backseat. His face was implacable. Light winked off the metal threads on the side of his face as his jaw clenched and unclenched.

"Hey, honey!" I gave him a cheery smile. I could assume he knew all about our escapades at the Council today. That didn't mean I'd give him the satisfaction of admitting I might have done something reckless.

Loken stomped toward us and locked eyes with Rey. "You broke into the Council building." It was more of a statement than a question.

"*Broke in* is such an ugly term," said Rey. "We didn't *break* anything. We simply walked in and then out again—quickly and with evasive maneuvers."

I lifted a hand to my mouth to muffle a giggle.

"And," continued Loken, "you stole a transport."

"*Stole* is such an ugly word," I said, imitating Rey.

Loken silenced me with a glare. I cowered, ducking my head to stare at my sandals. He turned toward Rey. "Can you give us a minute?"

Rey nodded and sauntered toward the house.

Loken turned back toward me. "You kidnapped Elder Kohler."

"That's not entirely true," I said. "We'd have to take him somewhere for it to be considered kidnapping. We left him in his office where we found him, so . . ." My explanation trailed off under Loken's stare.

"What did you think you could possibly accomplish?" he asked, his voice low.

"I thought," I said, folding my arms over my chest, "I could do something worthwhile instead of lying low until the end of time."

He opened his mouth to speak, but I rushed ahead. "I *thought* I could make decisions on my own. Funny how I'm supposed to save the world—or destroy it—but you think I'm so weak that I have to go into hiding."

Again he tried to speak. I cut him off before he could. "I *thought* I had a right to know why I'm in this ridiculous position." I stabbed my index finger at his chest. It hurt, but it got my point across. "And *you* weren't telling me what I needed to know. Plus, your computer was locked."

"You tried to break into my computer?" His face reddened.

I waved a dismissive hand. "*Break in*—such an ugly term. But that's not the point. How much did you know about my father and why I'm allegedly so powerful?"

Loken was silent for several seconds, then said, "I had my suspicions. Kohler wouldn't confirm anything for me." That telltale muscle in his jaw twitched.

"Exactly *what* did you suspect?" I stepped closer to him and tilted my chin upward, so he could see how serious I was.

His eyes darted to the left and then back to my face.

"Loken!"

He sighed and scrubbed his fingers through his hair. The lighter strands caught the sunlight. "I suspected Kohler had an ulterior motive for adding you to the task force. Since I knew he'd been friends with your father, and had no other connection to you, I figured your father had something to do with it."

"Gods dammit, Loken!" I shouted. I pointed a finger at his face. "You should have told me that as soon as you found out."

He shouted right back at me. "You shouldn't have gone back to the Council after I rescued you the first time! How thoughtless and reckless could you be?"

"You shouldn't have let them lock me up in the first place."

"You shouldn't have been snooping in my office," he growled, stepping closer to me. The coolness of his skin brushed against me.

My breath caught, and not because of anger. "You shouldn't . . . You shouldn't . . ." I'd run of things to shout at him about.

We glared at each other. Loken's chest rose and fell heavily. Mine did the same. He reached for me and locked his hands around my waist. I wanted to struggle, to continue yelling at him. He deserved it, after all.

But the feeling of his hands on me melted my rage. Despite the chill of his skin, warmth filled my body and tingled at my fingertips. He pressed his lips to mine. My will to fight drifted away with the softness of his mouth.

"I should get back to the Council before they wonder where I've gone," he said.

I nodded, incapable of speech when he was this close to me.

"Be safe," he said. He headed back to his transport.

I nodded, knowing it was a lie.

Rey was at my side again, and I hadn't even seen him approach.

I rested my head on his shoulder. This day had been too long. I had to find Krin and get her to understand. I didn't want her angry with me. And I had to keep her from saying anything to Loken, who was likely to hand me back over to the Council for further caging rather than let me die.

A rumble rolled through my stomach.

"Hungry?" Rey pulled away from me and patted my stomach.

"A bit. Let's head over to the community kitchen. Do you know where it is?"

"I think I smell food that way." He pointed.

Believers tended to be more community-oriented than we were, likely because they didn't use the same technologies we used. It was less convenient for them to be independent. Most large Believer villages included communal kitchens where the people could eat at most any daylight hour in return for regular food contributions or labor.

Rey and I strolled along the side of the road. I kicked large bits of rock that had come loose from the dirt. Rey whistled a melancholy tune. The day had cooled now that it was evening. Though my skin itched from sweating earlier, the cool breeze brushing against it felt like heaven.

After a few minutes, we passed the fellowship area, filled with rows of benches for village meetings. Soon after that, smells of cooked meat wafted to my nose as we approached the kitchen at the center of the village. I breathed in deeply. My stomach growled louder.

No one stood in line outside the door, likely because the yellow sun now glowed orange at the horizon. Ra had already set. The kitchen would close soon.

Little food remained in the serving trays, having been picked over all evening. We scraped the last of it onto wooden plates and settled across from each other on benches in the dining room. I groaned as the first bite of stew touched my tongue. My mouth watered around the tender meat.

After I'd eaten enough that my stomach no longer ached, I asked, "Where do you think Krin ran off to?"

Rey put down his fork. "I don't know."

"I'm sorry I chased her away." I shoved another bite of stew into my mouth.

"It's not your fault."

"Then whose fault is it?" I mumbled around the food.

He grinned, but the smile didn't reach his eyes. "Yeah, you're right. It's your fault."

The two other groups of people sitting in the dining room left their plates on their tables and exited. The suns had set. In the darkened room, the fireplaces cast long, flickering shadows across the table.

A call came from the front of the kitchen: "That's it for the night. We're closed."

Two small children grabbed my plate and Rey's. When I ate my forkful, one of them snatched the fork from my hand as well.

"I wasn't done!" I shouted. The kids moved on to other tables. They cleared the plates, cups, and forks, tossing them all onto large bins. "Hey!" I shouted, with no response.

With a sigh, I pushed my bench back from the table and stood. "I guess we should find Krin."

Rey brightened immediately and strode toward the door, walking fast. I hid a smile.

With the exception of light from generously spaced lamp-posts, darkness now blanketed the village. In silence, we walked back to Naja's place. The house was dark too, and quiet. I peered through the archway into the interior. No sounds or movement inside.

"Not here," I said. "Where else would she be?"

Rey motioned for me to follow him. We turned a corner between two houses. Not far away, firelight flickered and voices floated toward us. Because of the low light, I couldn't see what was going on until we crept closer. We hid at the side of a house, where we could peek around to the front to spy.

A gathering of about thirty people stood in a cluster on the front lawn of the house that hid us. Their voices carried. From their tones, I could tell they were having a heated debate.

"We should go now!" said a deep baritone. I inched to the edge of the house and peeked around the corner. That guy was *big*.

"Agreed," came a softer male voice attached to a leaner silhouette. "Even if their Vision is false, they defy the gods. It's our duty to stop it."

Approving murmurs trickled through the crowd.

"My brother is with them," said a familiar voice—Naja's voice. "I don't want him hurt."

I clutched Rey's shoulder and whispered, "What are they talking about?"

"Shh," he hissed.

"If he's with them," the big man growled, "then he's not with us. His safety's not our problem."

"It's my problem!" Naja's voice rose. "What if it was your family?"

A deep laugh vibrated from the man. A cruel laugh. "My family wouldn't choose them over us."

"We don't need to act," Naja said. "We can trust our man inside to do his job."

"We can't rely on that. He could be caught, or change his mind. We have to go now."

"A fellowship! I call for a fellowship. A vote of the villagers. This decision is too important to make at night, when half of you have alcohol on your breaths."

Again, there were murmurs of agreement, this time in Naja's favor.

"Fine. We'll wait until morning," said the softer male voice. "A fellowship. Just after sunrise." His voice dropped to a lower pitch. "And Jin be damned if the vote goes in our favor."

The group dispersed, but Naja stayed, as did the large man. She gestured wildly as they discussed something in hushed tones. Rey tugged my arm to the back of the house, and we left the area out of view of the main road.

When I was sure we'd escaped earshot of the villagers, I said, "What do you think that was about?" I had a sinking feeling in my gut. I hoped Rey had interpreted the situation differently.

"They're going to attack the Council," he said.

"I was afraid you'd say that." I kicked a rock from our path. I needed an outlet for all this nervous energy. "We have to tell Loken." I hesitated to say the next part, because I had nothing against these people. But it had to be said. It had to be done. "We have to go back and warn the Council."

Rey grimaced and shook his head. "We're fugitives. If we go back there, they'll lock us up before we can say three words."

"We can't just let these people die fighting each other. What makes the Believers think they can beat the Council anyway?"

"If I had to guess?"

I nodded.

"I'd guess," Rey continued, "the Believers can put up a damn good fight. A few of their practitioners can do amazing things that folks at the Council will tell you are impossible."

"But the Believers will still lose!" And in the process, they'd likely kill people I cared about—like Loken. Or people I'd recently grown quite fond of—like Jin and Mauryn.

"Maybe. But they'll weaken the Council, which might be good enough to stop them from changing the course of the future."

"Then we have to keep the two groups apart."

Rey nodded but didn't answer. He stared into space for the rest of our walk, his face devoid of any discernible expression.

I grabbed his arm just outside Naja's house and made him look at me. "What are you thinking?"

He finally faced me. "This isn't what I signed on for. I was supposed to be defending the world against some unknown *thing.* A science experiment gone wrong. A natural disaster. And then, this timeline, we're tasked to fight Mages—and that's fine too. I hardly feel empathy for energy-hungry killers. But this . . ." His voice trailed off.

He moved to enter the house. I grabbed his arm again. "We don't have to kill anyone. Just stop them from killing each other."

"Right." He eased his arm from my grasp, his expression skeptical. "That sounds simple."

I led him to the back room where I'd slept the night before. In the bedroom, a lamp glowed on the bedside table. Krin was lying on the floor wrapped in a blanket, her mouth hanging open.

Rey pulled his shirt over his head, revealing a tanned chest and abdomen, and lay down beside her. He wrapped an arm around Krin and pulled her close to him. I kissed the top of her head and then lay down on my back at her other side. Krin mumbled something I couldn't understand and snuggled closer to Rey.

I hoped she'd forgive me tomorrow. It seemed she'd already forgiven Rey, so I couldn't be too far behind. I hoped.

My eyes traced the wooden boards over my head. Tomorrow, I'd have to be in top form if I was to use my elemental ability to protect people. So far, all I'd done with it was perform uncontrolled acts of desperation. Tomorrow, I had to be in complete control.

I let my eyes flutter shut and, against my better judgment, said a quick prayer to Ra and Solaris.

CHAPTER 29
COUNTDOWN: 2 DAYS

"Good gods, Asha! You sleep like the dead," Krin shouted in my ear, yanking me from dreams I was happy to escape.

"Ugh," I mumbled. I slung an arm over my face to keep out the light streaming through the window. "Is it morning already?" I'd hoped the morning would never come—but not in an end-of-the-world sort of way.

Both Rey and Krin had done their morning routine already and were dressed in new sets of clothing.

"Forgot your hair brush?" I grinned at Rey, whose usually impeccable ponytail wasn't as smooth as usual. Stray strands escaped the hairband and stuck out at odd angles. I pushed myself up from the floor and pulled at one of the stray hairs. "Are you really planning to fight with your hair a mess?" I teased.

"It is the end of the world, you know." He winked at me and smoothed his ponytail back. "You have five minutes to get ready, or else we're going to eavesdrop on this fellowship without you. Naja took off minutes ago, so we're already going to miss the beginning."

Krin had brought me a change of clothes, which my parents had been happy to lend her. Before putting them on, I spent about thirty seconds in the shower. I cringed at the awful creaking noise that emanated from the old pipes. If Rey couldn't get his hair to look right, mine was hopeless. I grabbed a mass of it and tied it back as best I could.

"Let's go." I headed for the door, with Rey and Krin close at my back.

We jogged toward the village center. More accurately, Krin and I jogged. An impatient Rey zipped forward every twenty feet and then waited for us to catch up, with a tight-lipped expression on his face.

After a few minutes, he glared at us and took off toward the village center. In less than minute, he was back.

"No one's there." His voice held a note of barely controlled panic.

"What?" I broke into a sprint. Before I could move ten feet, Rey had lifted me into his arms. He raced me to the fellowship space, dropped me on my rear, and arrived with Krin as I was rising to my feet.

I scanned the rows of benches arranged stadium-style around a low platform. Not a single person besides us occupied the area. My chest felt suddenly empty. We were too late. The Council would be attacked, and we wouldn't have time to warn them.

Krin's mouth hung open. "They've left already."

"Let's get to the transport!" I shouted, breaking into a run back toward Naja's house.

My clothes whipped around me as Rey sped past. Before we'd made it a quarter of the way back to the house, Rey's transport pulled up next to us. The doors popped open, and Krin and I jumped in.

The transport sped to the Council building. Trees whipped past my window, but my stomach didn't feel a twinge a discomfort. My mind was already at our destination, running through the possibilities of what we'd find.

Unless the Believers had Breather transports—which I strongly doubted—they couldn't get to the Council before us. Despite this, I drummed my fingers against the door frame and strained my eyes to see as far in front of us as possible.

Images invaded my mind unbidden. Loken, Mauryn, and Jin lying dead in the training room, covered in their own blood. Loken as a burnt corpse. Loken asphyxiated and blue, murdered by a Breather. Loken sliced in pieces by another Bender, drowned by a Flooder, crushed by a Mover. Each time my head emptied, new gruesome images filled it again.

I held my breath as the Council came into view, zooming closer by the second. Our vehicle stopped. I scanned the building slowly, looking for any sign of battle.

This felt wrong. It was too quiet.

I stepped from the transport. The only sounds were the birds whistling as they flitted about the trees and the rustling of leaves in the soft breeze. The fence around the building stood closed and locked, as usual. No one occupied the lawn. Beyond the glass front door, no one moved in the foyer. No flashing red lights filled the windows, as they would if the alarm had been activated.

I pressed my hand to the biometric scanner next to the gate latch. I flinched at the prick on my palm as my blood was tested. The scanner rewarded me with a grating buzz. Across the top of the scanner scrolled the words NOT AUTHORIZED.

"You try." I shoved Rey forward.

"I stole a transport." he said. "There's no way I'm still authorized."

"Good point." I nudged Krin toward the scanner. "You have the best chance."

"None of us are going to have access," she said. But she obediently placed her hand on the scanner. Again, the buzzer blared in response to the handprint. Her brow furrowed.

"What's wrong?" I asked. "It was a long shot anyway."

She shook her head and pointed at the front door. "Aren't you concerned that two fugitives just identified themselves at the Council gate, and no one rushed out here to arrest us?"

Maybe Elder Kohler was right, and Krin really *was* the smart one.

A man moved in the foyer and pressed his face against the window. It was good to know someone was in there, alive and kicking. Still, catching us seemed less pressing than something else that was happening.

"Be right back." Rey scrambled up and over the gate before I could object. When he reached the door, the man inside stepped out. He and Rey whispered for a minute. Their mouths moved, but I couldn't hear them from where I stood. Rey's hand gestures became more and more animated with each moment that passed.

Rey turned as if to head back toward us, but then whipped around and caught the man's arms behind his back. Several inches shorter than Rey and less muscular, the other man struggled to escape the grip. Rey's mouth moved by the man's ear. The guy nodded, said words I couldn't hear, then began struggling again. Rey released him, ran toward us, and scrambled back over the gate.

"Get back in the transport!" he shouted.

We piled into the backseat. The transport took off even before I got the door closed all the way. Rey's posture was rigid as he drove.

"What's going on?" I asked.

"He says they received several distress calls about four Mages converging about twelve miles north and east of here. Almost every practitioner who wasn't on assignment already went to check it out. The building's nearly empty."

"Twelve miles north and east of here?" Panic rose in my chest. That would put them close to the Believer village we'd just left.

The horror behind Krin's eyes matched what I felt. Although we'd just taken this trip in the opposite direction, the ride back toward the Believer village seemed to take three times as long. My fingers twisted in my lap. My ears buzzed with the imagined sounds of fighting.

With my face pressed against the glass of the vehicle, I was facing the wrong direction. I heard the battle before I saw it. People shouting. Swords clashing. My gut clenched as I turned to view the scene.

I scanned the crowd of ripping, clawing, fighting people. I thought I spied a bit of Loken's golden hair, but the hair was attached to a woman I didn't know. We leapt from the vehicle. Without hesitating, Rey rushed into the midst of the fight.

"Rey!" I shouted. No answer. I lost the back of his head in the crowd.

The blue light of ether sparkled around me. I drew it into my hands, prepared to attack. But the battle was a mess, with no division down the middle to indicate who was fighting whom. Power pulsed through my body, but my hands froze in midair. I turned toward one person, poised to attack, and then another person.

I wasn't sure who was on what side. To top it off, I doubted my precision. What if I attacked the wrong people? What if I killed someone by accident?

I squinted into that crowd and thought I saw Loken holding his own, blocking blow after blow from an attacker with a red strip of cloth twisted about his wrist.

The colors. Some of the fighters wore some shock of red or yellow, colors most Nonbelievers avoided. I flung ether toward Loken's attacker. It hit the man square in the chest. He reeled off balance long enough for Loken to slam him in the head with the butt of his sword. The man sunk to the ground, unconscious but alive.

The Believers, on the other hand, appeared more than ready to take lives. I counted at least four bodies as I searched for another person to attack from afar.

I dove to the ground as a powerful jet of water flew toward me. It collided with a giant tree. The trunk cracked at the impact and teetered to one side.

"Move!" I shouted to Krin, who stood in its shadow.

She stood frozen, her arms locked straight by her sides. The tree tilted toward her. She turned to stare, her mouth agape, her feet still frozen in place. It creaked as it fell, and crashed to the ground just to her right. She leapt into the air, clutching her chest in surprise.

I exhaled a loud breath. She was okay, for now. "Do something!" I shouted to her. I gestured at the battle. "Help someone."

She nodded and raced to the other side of the battle. As soon as she left my view, hidden by all the practitioners, regret stirred inside me. I should have stayed with her. Three people I loved were lost in this fight. They could be dead already for all I knew.

I raced into the fight in the general direction of where I'd seen Loken. Bending and dodging blows, I weaved my way through the crowd. A sword swung toward me. I leapt to the side. The blade rang through the air as it breezed past me. The sound of my pulse grew louder.

A thin man in a yellow shirt caught my attention. Fire engulfed his hands as he moved toward a familiar back. I recognized Mauryn's head as the man's target. I shot a bolt of ether at the man. After a stunned second, he fell to his knees. I cocked my arm back and, using my running speed as momentum, slammed an elbow into his head.

The man fell but stirred on the ground, groggy. Gritting my teeth and hating every second of it, I kicked his head twice until he stopped moving.

Another man's large back collided with me. I stumbled to the side. My hands clutched at the air and flailed out. The ground rushed up toward me as I teetered, but rough hands grabbed me under my arms and righted me. I turned to see who had helped me and thought I recognized Jin moving on to fight someone several feet away.

A body fell to the ground in my peripheral vision and stopped moving. My chest tightened. This fight wasn't ending. More people were falling, possibly dying. I shoved my way to the edge of the battle again. When I got there, I gazed up at the suns, asking them for guidance.

Ra, Solaris, help me.

There was no way we were all getting out of this without a little help.

The ether ball I'd used to attack Loken's opponent hadn't killed him, but it also hadn't rendered him unconscious. I filled each of my hands with just a bit more power than I'd used before. I wanted enough to knock people out.

After another quick prayer and a deep breath, I attacked everyone. I slung ether ball after ether ball into the battle without prejudice. Anyone standing was a target. There was no time to determine who was a Believer and who was a Nonbeliever. It didn't matter anyway. The goal was to stop this madness.

One by one, fighters fell to the ground and stopped moving as my attacks hit. Most didn't see it coming. I hit them in the head or the chest. They dropped to the ground and stayed there.

I downed about fifteen people before the remaining fighters got wise to what was going on. Some turned toward me. Their faces twisted into angry scowls as they rushed me. I hurled more ether, increasing my throwing pace. My shoulders burned as I flung attack after attack, felling the fighters before they reached me. Their unconscious bodies littered the ground.

I turned my attention back to the few remaining people battling one another. I spotted Rey's sleek ponytail. Krin lay at his feet, her eyes open but her right arm twisted at an odd angle. Rey swooped Krin up from the ground and turned to run toward me.

He froze in place. The color washed from his face. Trembling arms dropped Krin back to the ground.

My eyes locked on Rey's and then traveled downward—to the sword tip protruding from his chest. He slumped to the ground, revealing the man behind him holding an elongated blade. The sword shrank back to normal size. The man wielding it looked up at me. His mouth twisted into a cheerless grin. He turned toward Krin, who lay just a few feet away from him.

She scooted backward away from him across the ground. Tears streamed down her face. Her eyes darted back and forth between the man holding the sword and Rey's motionless body.

Leaping over bodies, I ran toward them. Screaming filled my ears, and it took me a moment to realize it came from my own throat. I skidded to a stop in front of Krin and faced the man who'd murdered my best friend. His sword swung toward me. I felt its approach. Ether pulsed around it, around me. The tip pricked my chest, and the blade exploded outward like a thousand shards of broken glass.

I reeled my arm back and slammed my palm upward into his chin, putting into the blow all the ether energy I could muster. His head snapped back, and he stumbled a few steps. He recovered, dropped the remains of his broken sword, and wrapped his thick arms around me. His grip pinned my arms to my sides.

He crushed me to his chest. My lungs burned. My mouth gasped for air that it couldn't catch. I pushed ether outward.

At the same time, I shoved outward with my arms. The man's hold burst open. Fresh air screamed through my tired lungs.

The hilt of his broken sword lay on the ground where he'd dropped it. Only a small piece of the blade remained. I swept up the hilt. With a quickly whispered prayer, I jabbed the broken sword at the man's neck.

As it moved, the blade reformed—not of metal, but of shimmering blue light so bright that I squinted against it. I jammed the blue blade through the man's neck. Blood sputtered from his lips as he fell.

Around me, the few conscious Believers and Nonbelievers stood still. Their weapons hung at their sides. With so many of them unconscious, and with the remainder staring at me, the fight was at a standstill.

CHAPTER 30

The world moved in slow motion. I was in it, but not a part of it. People moved past me. Colors. Shapes. All blended together. Rough hands grabbed me, pulled my arms behind my back, and cuffed my wrists together. Someone shoved me into a transport. The vehicle traveled somewhere. It didn't matter where.

Rey.

Mom and Rey's mother had been thrilled when they'd ended up pregnant two months apart. If I didn't know better, I might have thought Rey and I were twins. He'd always been there. Sharing a crib with me. Playing in the park with me. Forcing me to make friends on the first day of school. He was the other half of my spirit. Now, I felt empty. Like half of my heart had been ripped out—and stabbed.

The Council building loomed before me as the vehicle stopped. Someone yanked me from the transport and led me back to my cell in the basement. I slumped to the floor and closed my eyes. Tears dripped from under my eyelids. I tried to sleep. Maybe that would make the pain stop.

It didn't.

I sat up, sure it had all been a horrid dream. But I was still in this cell. Krin sat on the other side of the room. Her body shook with sobs. So all of it was real. Back to sleep. Any dream would be a welcome escape.

I awoke again. I didn't want to be awake. I clenched my eyes shut and tried to empty my mind. Nothing existed outside of me. Nothing existed outside of the hard floor beneath me and the chill on my skin. My world had not just been destroyed.

Still, my head filled with images of Rey. Rey with a sword through his chest. Rey staring at me, knowing he was dying. Rey's lifeless body crumpled on the ground.

I don't know what I'd been thinking by attacking everyone at the battle. I should have focused on my friends. I should have been with Rey, should have fought back-to-back with him. I should have—

Soft sobbing floated to my ears. At first I thought it was my own. Although tears still clung to my eyelashes, the sobbing came from the other side of the cell. I dreaded facing the world, but I opened my eyes anyway. Krin huddled in the corner across from the metal door. Her right arm hung in a sling supported by her shoulder.

"Krin," I whispered, so quietly I wasn't sure she heard me. She didn't look up or respond. Her body continued to shake with sobs. "Krin," I said, louder this time.

"Leave me alone." Her voice cracked. I flinched at the sound.

I wiped a hand across my eyes and dried my tear-wet fingers on my shirt. I stared at Krin, debating how to proceed. I yearned to hug her. We could mourn our friend together. I didn't want to lose her too.

My chest ached. It wasn't supposed to have a hole in it like that.

I pushed myself up off the floor and moved to her side of the cell.

She lifted her head from her arms and stared at me through narrowed, red-rimmed eyes. "I didn't say you could come over here," she spat.

"I know." I sat down beside her.

She glared at me, eyes narrowed. When it became clear I wasn't moving, she dropped her head back to her arms. I slung an arm over her shoulders and squeezed. She stiffened and then relaxed into my side.

She mumbled something into her arms.

"I can't hear you," I whispered.

Louder, she said, "I could have loved him. I mean, I know you've known him forever, and it's probably like losing a brother." A new wave of pain crushed my insides. That made two brothers I'd lost despite being less than twenty feet away from them at the time. Krin continued, "But I could have loved him. We had . . . *something.* You know?"

I fought my urge to lash out at her. She couldn't possibly feel this loss like I did. In the names of the gods, she'd known Rey for eight days! Eighteen years, I'd known him. But I held my tongue against the harsh words threatening to spill. Instead, I rubbed her back and lay my head on her shoulder. I didn't have the will to fight with her.

Her tears subsided. We sat in silence, leaning against each other.

"You're so powerful," she muttered. "The way you stopped all those people, and killed the man who murdered Rey. It was like swatting a fly. Why didn't you save him?"

"I . . . I . . ." I had no words. Shame crawled up my stomach and spread over my cheeks in a hot flush. I'd had that power all along. Hael had tried to teach me how to tap into it, but I'd mocked him. If I'd believed what Hael had told me, I might have taken the fight into my own hands earlier. I'd *let* Rey be murdered.

Krin's body tensed beside me. "Why didn't you save him?" She shoved me away from her.

I shrugged, unable to summon an answer. My chest burned where my heart had been torn loose. And then stabbed. I'd felt this way once before. The pain would only dull; it would never go away. I'd never get that piece of me back.

I filled that empty part of my chest with new determination. I'd make sure Krin and Loken lived. Let the world end if it must. I would not live to see any more of my friends die.

"What kind of friend are you?" she shrieked. Her face flushed red. She scrambled to her feet. "What were you doing while I was fighting by Rey's side anyway?"

"Trying to stop the it." My voice was quiet. I knew it was not an answer that would satisfy.

"I see." Her voice dripped bitterness. "While you were protecting complete *strangers*, you let your friend get stabbed."

Tears stung my eyes, threatening to spill over. I blinked them back. She was right; I should have been at Rey's side. Or at Loken's side. I should have prioritized my efforts instead of trying to save everyone. It had been a silly goal—one I'd failed to achieve.

"You're right," I whispered. My voice rose. "It's my fault!" I shouted, before I even realized my lips were shaping the words. But they rang true. I'd failed Rey. I was the worst friend and the worst sister. On every level, I had failed.

I scrambled to my feet and clawed at my chest. I wished I could rip this Ethereal power out of me. The most powerful practitioner on the planet, possibly even more powerful than Mages, and I couldn't save anyone who mattered to me.

A shrill scream ripped up my throat. I slammed my fist against the metal door. The metal dented under the impact. I leaned my forehead against the dent. Finally, I let my tears fall without restraint. They slid down my face and pooled above my top lip. My chest clenched with each gasp for breath between sobs. I sucked in, but my lungs refused to be satisfied, wanting more. Needing more.

Nothing was enough. It would never be enough.

If Rey could be here with me, he'd wrap me in his arms and tell me it would all be okay. He'd do it with an inappropriate joke. A vision of his lopsided grin floated behind my eyes. I reached for it. I tried to draw it out into the real world.

The vision blurred and disappeared. I couldn't call it back. Instead, I saw him run into battle. His corpse lay bloody on the ground.

Tears continued to roll down my cheeks. My chest and abdomen ached from gasping between my cries.

I pounded at the door again. The dent grew larger. I pulled my bloody fist from the metal and stared at it. Red dripped down my knuckles. It felt a little better to have other pain to focus on. I could almost pretend it was just my hand that burned, and not my heart.

I banged on the door again. Each impact increased my desire to smash the door into a crumpled ball of metal. I pounded until my blood spotted the dented door. My shoulders and knuckles screamed for mercy.

"Asha!" Krin grabbed my shoulder. She tried to pull me away from the door.

I hit it again, relishing the way it creaked and bent under my fist. I liked the sound. It drowned out my sobs. I liked the hurt.

"Ashara!" Krin clutched my arm.

I shook her off. She landed on the floor with a thump and a loud groan. I raised my fist for another blow. The door opened, creaking along its track now that it was misshapen. Four men rushed in. I turned toward one of them, ready to slam my fist into his face and damn the consequences. But a sharp sting in my rear caught my attention.

The world went out of focus. My arms fell limply to my sides. I staggered around to stare at the man standing there with an empty syringe. I took a shaky step toward him.

Blackness inched inward from the edges of my vision. The room spun, and I slumped to the floor.

CHAPTER 31
COUNTDOWN: 1 DAY

Chatter floated toward me from the other side of the cell. My ears perked up. Not just Krin's voice, but also Jin's and Mauryn's. My eyes flew open when Loken's voice joined theirs.

"You're awake." Loken knelt beside me.

My head pounded behind my eyeballs. I suspected my eyelids were red and puffy. I urged my aching muscles into a sitting position and accepted Loken's hug. I pressed my face into his neck and inhaled deeply.

I looked toward the others. Even though I'd heard their voices, I was relieved to see all their faces and to confirm that they all still lived. For the most part, they looked okay. Red rimmed Mauryn's bloodshot eyes. He looked like he might keel over and fall asleep at any moment.

Jin looked the worst in terms of injuries. Bandages wrapped one of his thighs. He stretched that leg straight in front of him as if to avoid bending it. A jagged cut stretched from his ear to the bottom of his chin, marring his even brown skin. Stitches crisscrossed the cut. But his posture was straight. In that respect, he looked better than he had last time I'd seen him.

"Hey, guys." I waved and mustered a small smile for their sakes. It felt wrong, like a lie. The smiles I received in return looked just as false. "What's going on?" I turned to Jin for an answer because, despite his injuries, he looked the most whole of the group.

"We wanted to see you two." He squeezed Krin's hand. "Our group is so small to begin with. We had a task force meeting, and it felt wrong not to have you there."

Krin stared straight ahead and said nothing.

"What are we meeting about?" I asked, more cheerily than I felt. My voice sounded hollow in my ears. All eyes except Krin's turned toward Loken.

He exhaled loudly and said, in a rush of words, "We have no more assignments as a task force."

For a few seconds, we were all quiet. Then everyone spoke at once.

"No more assignments?"

"Why?"

"What about the Mages?"

"Are we giving up?" I asked.

Loken held up a hand and waited for silence. "The elders have decided this timeline is a failure. They're putting all their efforts toward preparing for another rewind ritual." His jaw twitched. "The practitioners are being split into three groups for patrolling the edges of the city. Each group will be too small to fight off the Mages on their own, but they'll slow them down. At this point, I don't think the elders could care less about protecting anyone except those who are meant to take part in the ritual."

"So we'll get another shot at this?" A twinge of hope jumped inside me. If the ritual happened, we'd get a fresh start. I'd get Rey back.

Loken nodded. "But, Asha, with everything that's happened this timeline, I strongly doubt you're going to be in this task force next time around."

"What? Why?"

Without access to the Council, I'd have no way to protect Rey, or Loken or Krin for that matter. If the Believers attacked, Rey would die again. I wouldn't even get a second chance at saving him. Without me there, who else would die with him? And that female Mage. I'd played a role in dispatching her. There was no telling how bad things could get if I wasn't assigned to this task force.

Loken spoke slowly, as if speaking to a small child who refused to see the obvious. "They believe you're the one drawing the Mages here. Most likely, they will keep you in a strategically chosen location for the whole of the repetition."

I scowled. "You mean they're going to lock me up the whole time."

"Can you blame them?" asked Mauryn. "We know you don't intend to bring the Mages here. But they have to use their knowledge of your power in a way that keeps the general population in mind."

"So what you're saying is," I said, "I'm a danger to everyone around me."

"That about sums it up, yes," Krin muttered, the first words I'd heard from her since I'd awaked.

My lips itched to snap out an angry response, but she was only saying what I was thinking—which was why it hurt so much.

Mauryn asked, "So what are we going to do for the remainder of the timeline?"

Loken pointed at Jin. "You'll attend a briefing first thing in the morning, where you'll be assigned a location to guard." He looked back at Mauryn. "Elder Kohler is impressed with your intelligence and drive. He'd like you to stand as backup for the ritual."

Mauryn's posture straightened. "What's backup?"

"Report to the briefing room now. They'll spend tonight training you. You'll step in to take someone's place if any of those assigned to perform it die before—or during—the ritual."

"*During*?" I asked. "People die *during* the ritual?"

Loken nodded. "It's not expected and would only happen if a person gives up all his energy to the rewinding. You have to hold onto a little to keep your heart pumping and your neurons firing."

"That makes sense," said Mauryn. His gaze left Loken's face and travelled to the ceiling. "So they'll teach me everything I need to know?"

"That's right," Loken said. "The elders consider this an honor. You should be proud."

Mauryn continued to stare upward, as if deep in thought. "I'll learn about the timing, and everyone's role, and how to perform my part?"

"Yes, of course. You'll be fully prepared to step in if you need to."

Mauryn nodded, but his lips drew into a taut line.

Loken patted him on the shoulder. "Don't worry. It'll work out fine."

A voice sounded over the intercom. "Time," it said. The cell door slid open.

Loken glanced down at his comm, then said to Jin and Mauryn, "The group's time here is up. You guys should go before they send guards down to drag you out."

I grabbed his arm before he could leave. "What about us?" I gestured between Krin and me.

After a pause, Loken said, "You'll stay here until further notice."

"What does that mean? *Until further notice*?"

Krin continued to stare straight forward. "It means," she said bitterly, "we're stuck here until the new timeline starts—or until we die."

"Actually." Loken's gaze dropped to the floor. "It's just Asha who has to stay. Krin, you can go." Krin didn't move, but her eyes shifted toward him. "You can go," he said again. "There's little damage you can do at this point, and the elders are at least a little compassionate."

Loken pulled Krin to her feet and pushed her gently toward the door. I hugged Jin goodbye. Mauryn had already left the cell. I waved at him through the glass, but his gaze was pinned on his feet. He shuffled toward the basement steps. I moved toward Krin to hug her too. Her arms hung at her sides, but she let me squeeze her tightly before she followed Jin out the door.

The door slid shut behind her, leaving Loken and me inside. They trod up the stairs and out of the basement.

My stomach did a little back flip when I looked around and realized we were alone. I ran into Loken's arms and buried my face in his shirt. As usual, his skin was cool to the touch, but his arms warmed me anyway. He held me, gripping one hand around my waist. I shut my eyes and tried to lose myself in the feel of him, in his muscled arms and tender touch.

Loken pulled me to the floor and sat cross-legged across from me. "I brought you something. It's chilly down here." He inclined his head toward a jacket lying on the cot. "How are you?" he asked.

I chuckled, but there was no joy in it. "My best friend is dead." I choked on the words. "I'm stuck in a cage until I die, so . . . I could be better." I raised an eyebrow. "Unless you're going to break me out again."

"It wouldn't work this time." He pointed to the stairs. "There are six guards outside the door upstairs, and they'll be there until tomorrow morning's briefing begins. Every one of them expects us to make a break for it."

I'd known he would refuse, but it was worth a shot. Plus, I liked teasing Loken. It was better than dwelling on . . . other things.

"Well, what good are you?" I smiled, the first genuine smile I'd mustered since Rey died. As soon as I realized what I was doing, the expression fell.

"So," he asked again, "how are you really?"

"As well as could be expected." I didn't want to talk about that right now. I wanted to talk about absolutely anything else. "What are you hiding?"

His eyes widened into a look way too innocent to be anything but a lie.

"That look is not fooling me," I said. "When the group was here, your jaw did that twitchy thing it does when you're omitting something important. So what's the bad news?"

He said nothing. His lips pressed more tightly together.

"Out with it."

He stared up at the ceiling. His shoulders slumped with the weight of all the responsibilities that had been heaped on him. "This will be the last rewind ritual."

"The elders know how to stop this thing in the next time-line? That's great news!"

"No." Loken shook his head. "Some of the elders are likely to die performing the ritual this time."

My eyebrows shot upward. My mouth opened, but no words emerged.

He continued, "They're too weak in this timeline. They're confident they can perform this last ritual, but most of them will die in the process. That means little or no guidance next time around." He face took on a pained look. "And I don't think we can do this without them."

"So the next timeline," I said, "it does nothing but delay the inevitable for another ten days."

His eyes dropped from the ceiling and met mine. He gave one sharp nod.

The hope I'd had a few minutes before—when Loken had told me about the upcoming rewind—drifted away. I'd get

Rey back, but only with enough time to say goodbye. My eyes stung with tears I refused to release.

Less than a day from now, Loken and I would be estranged again, and we'd all be on our way to our deaths. But at least for now, I could try to enjoy the time I had. I would make the best of these last few hours.

I pasted a smile on my face. "Tell me what you'll do with your last day."

Loken returned my smile with one I suspected was just as false. "I don't have much free time actually. Tomorrow morning, I'll help set up the ritual. Then I'll guard the Council before and during to make sure no Mages or Believers stop it from happening. It shouldn't be that tough. The Council building is very safe when all security measures are activated."

"That's it?" I frowned. It would be tough to live vicariously through Loken if he was going to be working.

"There's one more thing." He pulled me into his lap and squeezed my waist. "Tonight I get to stay with you." He whispered into my ear, his voice low, "And they promised to turn the cameras off." The words and his breath on my neck sent a hot flush racing through my body.

I wanted to be with him completely, to clear my mind. I couldn't help the way my body molded with his, wanting to become one with his. I opened my mouth to respond. Whatever I was going to say, the words caught in my throat.

Loken's fingertips tickled up the back of my neck and gripped my hair. I tilted my head back, leaning into his touch. Tingles shot up and down my spine.

His lips curved upward against my earlobe. "I think it's safe to say that Rey would approve of this activity."

Tension rushed out of my shoulders. My heart hammered in my chest. I wondered if he could feel its rhythm; we were so close. I pressed my lips into his, softly at first. I would savor every moment of this night with Loken. This could be our last night alive. Our last night with these memories.

I tangled my fingers in his thick hair and pressed his face closer to mine. I drank in his sweet metallic scent. My mouth opened, and his tongue invaded it. I explored his lips and tongue and let him explore mine.

With a groan, he rolled to the floor and pinned me underneath. Cool hands searched my body. I ran my fingers over every inch of his muscle as he clutched me to his chest.

CHAPTER 32
COUNTDOWN: 0 DAYS

I knew it was morning. Not because light shone through the windows—the cell had no windows. I knew because I could feel the presence of the sun gods outside these walls. I knew because the ball of dread and grief that sat in the pit of my stomach for the last ten days had grown so large that it filled me entirely.

Loken stirred as I rolled over to face him. Still mostly asleep, he pulled me closer to his body. I brushed the fair hair off of his forehead and kissed him. My lips traced the metal threads at his temple. My eyes swept down along his body. Even covered by a blanket, the tight curves of muscle urged me to wake him for a repeat performance. But there was no time for that.

I shook him gently and whispered, "When do you have to go?"

"When my comm tells me the suns are up," he mumbled into my neck, and then traced tiny kisses up my earlobe.

I tensed. If he took this further, I'd need a good excuse for turning him down. And I was a horrible liar. I breathed a sigh of relief when the kisses stopped.

"Loken," I whispered.

No response. He'd gone back to sleep.

I counted sixty seconds before moving again. The suns had risen already, so his comm could alert him any second. My plan wouldn't work nearly as well if I had to incapacitate him, so I had to move fast.

After a full minute, I tested Loken by squirming in his grasp. No reaction. I wriggled away from him and pulled the blanket up to his shoulders. That way, he wouldn't notice my body wasn't warming him anymore.

I dressed in yesterday's clothing, which lay in a pile along with Loken's clothes in the corner. I patted through the pile until I located something solid—Loken's comm. I detached the device from his pants and clipped it to the waistband of my shorts. From the pile, I also withdrew the hooded jacket Loken had brought for me. The hood might come in handy.

As an afterthought, I grabbed Loken's weapons belt and clasped it around my waist.

I pressed my hands to the door and slid them along the now-dented surface. Ether pulsed inside it. I felt it so completely that it nearly spoke to me. The door wasn't metal all the way through. Two large slabs of steel enclosed a concrete center. I understood how to unmake it. And more importantly, because of the concrete, it would hold Loken inside. Next, I tested the glass wall of the cell, and was pleased to find that it contained no metal alloy.

The biometric pad for the door included a metal plate with some sort of etched design, and a digital readout running horizontally above it. I sucked in a deep breath, held it, and slammed my fist into the plate with all the ether force I could muster. The device crushed into the wall. The digital display blinked and went out.

At the noise, Loken shot upright into a sitting position. "What!"

I didn't wait around to explain. I pressed myself against the metal door and willed the ether to pull me into and through the metal and concrete. I melted through the door before Loken had scrambled to his feet.

On the other side, I watched Loken through the glass. His mouth moved as he ran forward. He pounded the glass with his fist and yelled something. Muscles strained in his neck. The cell was soundproof, but I was relatively sure he was pissed off. Those were not pretty words his mouth was forming.

He pressed his hand to what remained of the biometric sensor. I couldn't see the sensor from this side of the cell, but Loken's face flushed red after a few seconds. His lips twisted in anger, and he went back to pounding the glass. His mouth moved into more words that I imagined were not complimentary.

Of course, I regretted that Loken would be angry with me when life as I knew it was ending. But my top priority was to save us. I couldn't do that with Loken's protective instincts hanging over me.

I blew him a kiss and raced up the stairs.

Loken's comm unit read only twenty-eight minutes until the end of life as I knew it. The way I saw it, I had few options. I could find a place to hide and let the trained men and women of the Council do their sworn duty to protect us all. But if their idea of protecting us was to perform another rewind ritual—one that would leave us without their guidance in the next timeline, and without the ability to perform another ritual—then they had already failed.

Alternatively, I could release Loken and spend these last moments with him. But as soon as I let him go, he'd go running off to help the elders do absolutely nothing useful.

So it was up to me. Unfortunately, I needed information from the Council before I could do anything. I needed to know exactly where the Mages would show.

At the main level of the building, I raced up the stairs to the Council member offices. I was acutely aware of my unguarded back. If Elder Kohler saw me before I saw him, my back would be on fire and I'd be dead. But if I saw him first, I could defend myself. I was confident. My power thrummed inside my body, vibrating through the air around me.

The empty hallway stretched before me as I crested the stairs to the third floor. I hurried down the hall, peeking through the window of each door on the right and, on my way back, peeking in the windows on the other side. Not a single soul occupied the rooms.

Gods be damned! I froze as soon as the thought played in my head, and followed it up with, *Um, sorry. Please let me keep my power.* I made a two-thumbs-up sign to the ceiling.

My footsteps clanked against the steps on my way back down. At the bottom, I hesitated, unsure of where to try next. The briefing room. Loken had said there was a morning meeting.

I raced back to the main level and toward the briefing room. As I ran, the female voice in the wall droned, *"Please stay calm. Remain calm. Please stay calm."*

Not a chance.

With no window in it, the briefing room door gave me no hint as to what lay on the other side. I pushed it open an inch or two and peered in. As soon as I saw a full room of people, I let the door swing shut again. I'd found them!

Sucking in a deep breath, I cracked the door open enough to squeeze through. It closed behind me with a soft click. Luckily, the man closest to me towered above most of the others. I slipped behind him, where I hoped no one who'd recognize me would notice.

"If you see this girl," came Elder Kohler's voice from the front of the room, "incapacitate her—even it means killing her. We need to perform the ritual, not save lives that we'll have back as soon as the next timeline begins."

I peeked around the side of the big man who blocked me to see the front wall, where a humongous image of my face displayed. I gasped and shrank backward. I flipped the hood of Loken's jacket over my head and tugged the top down to shadow my face.

"Time to get to it," said Elder Kohler. "I hope to see you all in a few hours, enthusiastic to start this process over again." Nervous laughter trickled through the group. "Take your places. Dismissed."

Almost everyone in the room turned my way and began to push toward the exit. I ducked my head lower in the hood and joined the exiting crowd. At a hallway intersection, I pressed myself against the wall of the adjoining corridor and waited.

As expected, most people hurried through the hall toward their destinations. Some paused only briefly to exchange hugs or handshakes. Tension thickened the air with the unspoken goodbyes that no one was willing to admit might be final. Most appeared to be heading downstairs to the transport holding bay, either by way of the elevator or the stairwell next to it.

I recognized Elder Kohler's gray-haired head just after he passed the hallway intersection. I waited until three more people passed between us before stepping back into the main hall. Kohler slipped out the back door, as did another elder nearby. Mauryn's familiar figure went that way as well.

So the elders were performing their ritual out back. I didn't care about the ritual right now, but I was relieved to know exactly where Elder Kohler was. I was relieved that he wouldn't be setting me on fire without my seeing it coming.

I followed the other practitioners down to the transport holding bay in the basement. I took the stairwell, not wanting to stand still on an elevator. Anyone in the elevator car with me could recognize me, and I'd be caught.

At the bottom of the stairs, I kept my head down and followed the two people in front of me into the nearest transport. I took the last empty seat and closed the door behind me. We took off across the room and up the vertical exit. Outside, the transports shooting up from the holding bay split off into three groups. Our vehicle stayed with one of them. The other two groups of transports zipped off in opposite directions.

The seats inside were positioned in two rows across from each other. The man who sat opposite me eyed me, his expression implacable. I dropped my gaze to my lap and hoped the hood covered just enough of my face to hide my features, but not enough to make it look like I was hiding.

My already high stress level skyrocketed the longer he stared. I clutched my hands together in my lap to avoid drumming them against the armrest nervously. I debated whether I had enough control over my ether to protect myself if I ripped the door open and flung myself out of the vehicle. Just as my fingers inched toward the door handle, the man turned to look out the window. I released the breath I'd been holding.

We slowed at the top of a hill. When we stopped, I leapt for the door and jumped out before anyone could recognize me. Other transports stopped all around us. Practitioners spilled out.

The group of about sixty practitioners thinned out into a line, side by side facing north. Many of them checked their comms as they waited. Others glanced up at the ever-present countdown clock in the sky. I glanced up too.

Eighteen minutes.

CHAPTER 33

My foot tapped nervously against the ground. I shoved my fists deeper into the pockets of Loken's jacket.

I jumped in surprise as a series of beeps issued from Loken's comm at my waistband. The numbers on the main screen blinked red, no longer a solid readout. The time counted down from fifteen minutes. My stomach lurched, and I fought hard to keep my breathing steady.

It was clear to me now how Ethereals were the most powerful practitioners. I didn't need to manipulate any other element. I could open up the ground and crush any Mage who attacked, just like that blonde Mover had done when we'd killed the female Mage. The ground was made as much from ether as it was from dirt. The same went for water, fire, and the other elements too. I could kill every one of these Mages, and I wouldn't even break a sweat.

I'd do it for Rey. It would mean never seeing him again if I succeeded and the rewind got called off. But that was a sacrifice Rey would have happily made. In fact, he *had* made that sacrifice.

Lined up facing north, the practitioners segmented in groups, each staying near its transport. My gaze darted to one group as they all piled back into their vehicle, zipped out of sight, and returned a minute later.

Then another group of practitioners did the same thing. Followed by another. Each time a group of practitioners arrived back in the area and exited their vehicle, they grew more and more restless, pacing and glaring at one another.

My eyes narrowed as I watched this process. *What are they doing?*

The people near me moved toward our transport. I rushed to join them, since I had to look like I knew as much as they did. I couldn't bring attention to myself.

We zipped in a wide circle around the Council building. Everyone's face pressed to a window. When we arrived back, we piled out and took our positions back on the hill. The cluster of practitioners to our right moved toward their own vehicle for their turn.

That's when it hit me: *They don't know if or where the Mages will show.*

This was just one of their best guesses. Loken had said the practitioners would be split into three groups. The other two clusters of transports must have stopped elsewhere, in case the Mages reached their positions first. The practitioners in my group waited here, while scouts—the ones who took turns circling—searched the area just in case the Mages managed a different route to the Council.

I grew more restless as each minute passed. My gaze darted across the horizon, first to the east, then to the west. I turned a circle and examined the southern horizon as well. As each transport returned from its trip around the Council building, my stress level rose. To get my mind off the anxiety, for just a moment, I imagined the way Loken had looked this morning, his solid body naked and resting on the cot.

Forgive me, I asked silently. *If we get through this.*

I wondered what he'd say if he were here with me, as I waited to put myself on the front lines. That was easy; he wouldn't say anything. He'd toss me over his shoulder and march me back to my cell or somewhere else that he deemed safe. But if he didn't do that . . . he'd remind me of all the information on Mages that he'd taught me. Remove the head, or permanently incapacitate. Distract. Run.

At the end of the day, a Mage will always be attracted to the most powerful thing in the area, Loken had said.

A smile tugged at my cheeks.

While all these people were worried about where the Mages would show up, and whether they'd be able to stop them from getting to the Council before the ritual was complete, I knew for certain that the Mages would come straight to us. I was a Mage-magnet. All I had to do was wait.

They'd come to me.

I blinked.

When I opened my eyes again, four Mages had rushed the west side of our line. Breathers—moving so quickly they looked like a blur of skin colors. The other, non-Breather Mages wouldn't be far behind. I was positioned closer to the east side of the line. Before I could react, two practitioners dropped to the ground. One jumped back up into a fighting stance. The other lay still.

The Mages stayed in almost constant motion, blurring in one direction and then the other, stopping every couple seconds to strike blows. The practitioners, with their swords and their elemental talents, fought back. But they took damages in the process. Another practitioner fell and stopped moving.

Bloody wounds opened up on the limbs of those still standing to the west side of the line. My ears roared with the sounds of fire and flood, which slowed the Breather Mages in their progress—in their progress toward *me.*

My eyes followed the largest Mage, who weaved through the other practitioners in a blur. He was older, more focused. The other practitioners didn't distract him.

I drew the sword from Loken's weapons belt and held it in front of me. Each time the Mage stopped moving for an instant, his black eyes bored into me. He flashed over to my right. I twisted around to face him. Before I'd planted my feet, he stood on my left again. He moved closer every time he blurred into motion. Holding the sword, my hand itched to strike.

The big Mage appeared directly in front of me. My first thought was recognition; he was the largest one from the basement. My second thought was pain.

His arm struck outward, and an impact cracked into my chest. I rose into the air and flew backward. My grip on the sword released. My teeth clacked together as my body slammed into something solid. Pain bit into my back. I slumped against the trunk of the tree I'd hit. Colored spots danced in my vision.

My hood fell away from my face, but I couldn't be bothered to cover up again. I struggled to keep my eyes open. If I passed out for even a second, this Mage would tear me to pieces. A second would be too long.

I scrambled to my feet, clenching my teeth as my back scraped against the tree trunk. He appeared in front of me again, trapping me between himself and the tree. His hand shot out and gripped my shoulder. His thumb pressed into the soft nook above my collarbone. A shriek tore up my throat.

I slammed the palm of my hand upward into the lower part of his arm, trying to dislodge his grip, but his fingers pressed harder. The colored spots swam faster through my vision. I smashed both fists into the sides of his face. He didn't flinch. His soulless eyes glared. The eyelids drooped like he was almost bored. I slammed his head again.

I sensed the movement before it actually happened, and twisted myself toward his death grip on my shoulder. I cried out as my movement pressed his fingers deeper into my neck. But it was worth it. Where my head had been less than a second before, the Mage's other fist crashed into the tree trunk. Bark sprayed outward. A fleck of it stung my eye.

Gritting my teeth against the pain, I twisted further into his grip. The sound of fingers cracking popped in my ear, and his grip loosened. I ducked beneath his arms to escape the trap between him and the tree.

I spotted Loken's sword, just outside the main cluster of the battle, fifteen feet away. After only a few steps, I knew it was mistake to head toward it. I couldn't outrun a Breather.

Before I could develop another plan, my legs were swept from under me, and I tilted toward the ground. My hands shot out to catch me, but my elbow collapsed as I hit. My forehead bounced off the dirt. An ache bloomed and spread to the back of my skull.

The Mage twisted me around and pinned my arms at my sides with his knees. My head throbbed. I shouted, wriggling my body to try to free my arms. I refused to look into those black eyes staring down at me.

Why aren't I dead yet?

The Mage pressed his hand against my chest. A burn traveled from his palm through my body. My breath caught in my throat, and immediately, sweat flowed from my forehead.

"Gods, help me," I muttered. I didn't want to die like this. I wrenched one of my arms from under me. Guided by some unseen force, my hand floated upward to the Mage's chest. A still calm flooded through me. Quiet. Peace. Stop the pain. The Mage's body exploded into a million particles of blue dust. They scattered to the ground and floated away on the wind.

For a moment I lay still, wide-eyed, my hand still raised in the air to the place where I'd touched the Mage.

I jumped to my feet. The world tilted beneath me at first. I felt weaker after my tangle with him. I blinked a couple times, shook my head to clear it, and the world righted again. The pounding in my head cleared. The sword lay on the ground to my left. I swept it up.

More Mages had joined us by then. Bodies lay scattered on the ground, most having faces I recognized—dead practitioners. A few of the bodies, headless ones, were oversized. Black pools filled the eye sockets of separated heads—dead Mages.

More practitioner bodies littered the ground than Mage bodies, but the numbers of the living were now close to even on the two sides. Soon, more practitioners would die, and the remaining few would be overwhelmed by these Mages.

I ran to what looked like the center of the fight, swinging my sword at a Mage's head on my way. As I raced past, the head toppled to the ground. The body slumped next to it.

The Mages reeked of energy. It was easy to pinpoint them among the others. I threw ether balls into the battle around me. I spun in a circle, shooting ether as quickly as I could generate more energy at my hands. Each strike landed its mark. But my attacks were too weak. I didn't have enough time to recharge in between.

I had to do this right. I had to move quickly. There could be no more avoidable deaths. No one else's best friend would die today. Too many had died already.

Each ether ball did no more than push its Mage target back. But that would work for now, so I kept up the attacks. I hit them over and over, pushing them back.

As I struck, the Mages moved outward, toward the edge of the battle. They separated from the practitioners. They moved until they stood in a wide circle—and we were trapped in the center.

CHAPTER 34
MAURYN

Inching their way to the top of the sky, the suns bore down on the practitioners behind the Council building. A little farther, and the practitioners would be at full power. A little farther, and Mauryn could finally accomplish what he'd been born for. He could finally prove his worth.

In the backyard of the Council building, Mauryn and five others stood in a wide circle. At the center stood eight more practitioners—the elders. Elder Ethereal, Elder Kohler, and Elder Seer occupied the very center of their formation. The other five elders formed a small circle around them in the middle of Mauryn's circle.

According to the training Mauryn had received about the ritual, power over all six elements was needed to initiate the rewind, and to preserve the consciousnesses of the elders—who would all remember this timeline when the next one began.

The six elder elemental specialists would perform the bulk of the work for the ritual. Elder Kohler's and Elder Seer's participation would be minimal, but their consciousnesses would be preserved. The elemental specialists would draw power from every living being and thing on the planet. Each would draw energy related to his or her own element. Elder

Ethereal would tie all the elements together and kick-start the time shift.

In the off-chance that Elder Ethereal overexerted herself and died or passed out during the ritual, Mauryn was tasked to step in and perform that most important function. Mauryn wiped his damp palms against his pant legs.

His finger twitched to reach for his comm unit, to check the time *again*. Or he could just look up into the sky and see the time there. He gave in, tilted his head upward, and inhaled. Six minutes.

He wished they didn't have to wait until the last second. But waiting was their best chance, since practitioners were most powerful when the suns were at their highest. Ra would be cresting the sky in a few more minutes. If they started too soon, they could fail. It was tricky business—rolling back time.

Mauryn had positioned himself next to a Bender, whose name was Koulis. Now Mauryn almost regretted the choice. Koulis had been a last-minute replacement when Loken hadn't shown up for duty this morning. He looked almost as nervous as Mauryn.

Koulis's eyes shifted to the left and right every ten seconds or so. Likely, he expected the Mages to break through their first line of defense and attack at any minute.

That would be fine as far as Mauryn was concerned.

Although Mauryn might have preferred Loken's calm dignity over the stress-inducing Koulis, Koulis would put up less of a fight when Mauryn did what he had to.

In some ways, it was a shame. These people had accepted him in a way he'd never before experienced. Growing up in the Believer village, Mauryn had been an outcast even as a small child. Too interested in science to fit in, but too dedicated to the gods to go into exile. When he'd heard the call for practitioner registration, he'd seen a way to redeem himself.

He'd seen a way to finally gain the adoration he deserved for his quick mind *and* devotion to the gods.

Sadly, he'd stay his course and accomplish what he'd come here for. He regretted it had to end like this. He'd met some good people here—even met some who might have been lifelong friends if things had been different.

Mauryn checked the time again. Five minutes. Time to move.

He yanked the sword from the weapons belt around Koulis's waist and slammed the butt of it into his head. Koulis dropped to the ground, stunned.

"My apologies, friend," Mauryn said, before spinning to his other side and stabbing the Breather standing there through the heart.

The inner circle, too preoccupied with watching the suns' progress, didn't notice his activities right away. The outer circle reacted immediately, rushing toward him.

He raced toward the inner circle at a speed that only an expert Breather could match. With the gods helping him, he could displace air almost as efficiently as any Breather, since ether was an essential part of the air. Before any of the others could react, he'd reached the central circle.

Mauryn elbowed Elder Burner out of the way and aimed for his primary target, Elder Ethereal, the strongest among them. His momentum slowed as the sword met and sank into the flesh of her throat. Blood gurgled from her lips as she fell.

Elder Breather was the biggest threat; with his speed, he'd react first. Mauryn ripped the sword from Elder Ethereal's corpse. He pushed his energy into the bare metal handle and felt the sword lengthen. When Elder Breather lunged toward him, Mauryn jabbed. The sword slipped cleanly through the elder's rib cage. Blood spurted from the wound as Mauryn withdrew the sword.

The ground shook beneath his feet, preparing to crack and swallow him up. Mauryn stabbed Elder Mover through the heart, and the shaking stopped.

Fire and water shot at him from Elder Kohler, Elder Burner, and Elder Flooder. A sword swiped at him. Mauryn leapt backward out of the blade's reach and threw up an ether shield. The fire and water struck the shield, which held under the attack. Sparks and droplets collided with the barrier and sprayed outward.

Elder Bender slashed with his sword. Metal clanged against ether. The shield held.

Mauryn sat cross-legged on the ground. He'd taken out a Bender, a Mover, and—most importantly—two Breathers and the other Ethereal. With both the primary and backup Breathers for the ritual gone, and with no available Ethereals, the ritual could not be performed.

Fire, water, and metal slammed against his shield, but the barricade held strong—at least for the moment. It was the remaining Mover, from the outer circle, who would be the one to kill him. The ground would open up. Mauryn would be lost into the depths of the earth.

But he'd die having made his people proud. He'd stopped the ritual.

CHAPTER 35
LOKEN

Loken slammed his metal-covered fist into the glass *again.*

When he got out of here, he was going to . . . he was going to . . . probably shout at Asha until she lost her temper. And then kiss her until the world ended. Frustrating woman!

He slammed his fist against the glass again. This time a small crack appeared where he hit it. It teased him—just enough to tell him he had a shot of getting out of here, but not nearly enough to warrant celebration.

Sweat prickled at his forehead. He used to be able to hold metal all over his body for an hour straight. Now, twenty minutes with just his hand metal-clad, and his body begged to shut down.

He'd tried waving his arms and jumping up and down in view of the camera that hung from the basement ceiling. But his friend who'd reduced security for his night with Asha had done his job too well. Loken suspected the cameras remained off, and his friend had long since gone to wherever he'd chosen to spend his final minutes. Expecting anyone to come and let him out was not an option.

Loken slammed his fist into the glass again. This time, the crack spiderwebbed outward. His heart leapt. He redoubled his efforts, melding the metal threads of his skin across his other fist as well, and then slamming repeatedly, one fist at time into the glass. Each impact caused the crack to spread farther outward.

A grin stretched at his cheeks. Not even shatterproof, metal-less glass could hold him.

A small piece at the center of his impacts popped out of the glass wall and fell to the floor. With the next hit, more pieces tinkled to the floor. After a few more hits, he'd produced a hole the size of his head.

Loken closed his eyes and concentrated. He liquefied the metal threads weaved into his skin, letting the metal creep over his body until it encased him. He trembled violently with the effort.

He threw himself at the glass. It sprayed outward as he leapt through it. He was out! The metal receded from most of his skin, back into the tattooed pattern.

Loken shot up the stairs, authenticated himself to the security panel at the basement door, and raced through the hallway. Shouts assaulted his ears as he ran. The ground rumbled. It shook and rolled beneath Loken's feet, tossing him sideways. His shoulder slammed into the wall.

He stopped to steady himself, leaning next to the double glass doors that led to outside. The rumbling stopped. The volume of the shouts rose. Before he could take off again, Loken caught a glimpse of the back lawn through the door.

A crack had split the ground, running from the Council building to the back fence. At the edge of the broken earth lay three bodies, still and bloody. Another body lay farther away, near the fence. The closest corpse had taken a sword to the neck and had been nearly decapitated. A mere flap of flesh kept the body attached to the head—a head with a long blond braid.

Elder Ethereal?

Bile threatened to crawl up his throat. Loken swallowed it down.

Standing over her body, Elder Kohler glanced up and caught Loken's eye. Kohler waved Loken toward him. Loken shook his head and shuffled away from the door. He needed to be somewhere else right now. He'd already wasted too much time.

Kohler's mouth moved. But from this far away, and with his torn voice, Loken couldn't make out the words. Kohler tapped Elder Bender on the shoulder and gestured toward Loken.

"Three elders are dead." Elder Bender's deep voice drifted through the glass doors. "We can't perform the ritual. We need to devise a new plan."

Loken's mind raced. *They* did need a new plan. He had a plan already—one that had just become more urgent. If Asha died, he wouldn't get a second chance to save her. No rewind ritual meant no second chances.

Without a backward glance, Loken spun away from the door and tore down the hallway. He leaned on the elevator button to the transport holding bay until the doors opened. There had better be a Breather waiting down there for emergency travel.

Asha would have followed one of the three practitioner groups to their assigned waiting area. The Mages would come for Asha. There were three places she could be, and not enough time to check all of them.

CHAPTER 36

My hood had fallen from my head at some point. Whispers of my name skittered through the remaining practitioners. They clustered close to me, toward the middle of the circle I'd formed by pushing the Mages outward.

I erected my ether shield, wider than any one I'd used before. It stretched around us and protected us from the Mages, who stood on the outskirts. Their black eyes stared from expressionless faces, like dark pinpoints through the twinkling blue of my shield.

A sharp stab hit the back of my eyelids. It seemed to pull from behind me. I turned to find a Mage—a blond male—shoving his body into the white-blue hemisphere. I tensed and concentrated on holding the shield.

The other Mages joined his effort, shoving and pounding at it. I felt them as if they shoved and pounded directly at my skull. Their energies stabbed at me, like knives slicing into my skin. A scream tore at my eardrums. It took me several seconds before I realized it came from my own mouth.

My throat grew rawer with each passing second. I fell to my knees and fought against the impacts invading my head. I filled my vision with an image of the wall I'd erected, forcing the ether to obey me and stay in place.

I struggled to keep my eyes open, to stay conscious. Through the slits of my eyelids, I saw the practitioners around me stumbling. They clutched one another to stay upright. Their swords clattered to the ground as they fought for balance. The shaking inside my head wasn't just inside my head.

The ground rumbled and cracked. A split raced from just in front of me to the north, extending under the shield. The blond Mage who'd started the attack on my shield slipped through the crack and disappeared into the earth. But the pounding continued.

My head spun, and I fought to focus. Too few of us remained inside. The Mages would decimate us if I let them. Gray clouds darkened the sky. Thunder rolled, vibrating in concert with the earth beneath my feet. Despite the darkness, the suns shone brighter, streaking the sky with reds and yellows. I felt them in my chest—the suns and the clouds, the thunder and the lightning, the vibration of the earth.

I cleared my mind, shoving the pain away. The clouds dispersed. The ground stilled.

A sharp stab hit me in the gut as a Mage swung a weapon at the shield. Lightning struck behind my back, out of my field of view, but I felt it anyway. More lightning. The ground trembled in rhythm with renewed thunder.

A practitioner to my left leapt over a crevice in the earth to avoid being drawn into its depths. Another wasn't so lucky as lightning struck him. My nostrils stung with the stench of burnt flesh, and his corpse slumped to the ground.

I had to end this.

The ether wall shimmered like specks of twinkling lights in the growing darkness. I didn't know how long I could hold it. Maybe forever. Maybe only another minute. But I needed it to fall on my terms.

The shield pulsed all around me. I exploded it outward toward the Mages. It broke into large sharp pieces that sliced them limb from limb. My own extremities burned as I felt their pain. Tears sprang to my eyes and rolled down my cheeks.

I sucked in a deep gasp. With the shield gone, a weight lifted from my chest. I feasted on the air like I'd almost drowned. The cool air screamed its way down my lungs. A welcome burn, like pins and needles washing away the numbness. I inhaled again.

Energy continued to hum through the air. It buzzed. But not all around me—just behind me. I felt inhuman movement tied to the energy. I whirled around. One more Mage stood there, still alive. Nude, with thick veins pulsing over his muscles. He approached with slow, even steps.

At ten feet away, my head still had to tilt upward to see his face. His large frame was capped with a mass of tangled sable hair hanging past his shoulders. Above a thick waist, a muscular chest jutted out. He looked as solid as a building. My eyes watered as I tracked the Mage, rather than letting them drift shut and sleep.

I struggled to rise to my feet and attack. But my disobedient limbs hung lifelessly. I tried again, willing ether energy into my body. My muscles screamed as I climbed to my feet and took a leaden step forward. Thunder vibrated the air, a stark contrast to the perfect, sunny sky that had existed just minutes before. Another flash of lightning shot through the sky and struck the ground nearby. The sound of the strike rang in my ears.

The Mage lifted a hand. I flinched, but my arms moved too slowly to block. So tired. So very tired. I squeezed my eyes shut and prepared for the final blow. I cringed at his touch, though it was soft against my skin at first.

When the Mage gripped my upper arm, my body felt light—like I might blow away into the swirling wind. Sona's voice whispered in the back of my head to fight, but my limbs refused to obey. They twitched and then fell limp again.

The Mage's touch ripped my breath from me. My chest burned with a fire I couldn't see. Everything I'd felt a moment ago—the thunder and lightning, the practitioners screaming and running in all directions—it all became muted. My sensitivity to the world bled from me, from my skin into the Mage's.

I tried to call ether to my hands, but I couldn't sense it anywhere.

The Mage's skin glowed a reddish tint. It was the first time I'd ever seen a Mage smile. His lips stretched wide to reveal sharp teeth. Black eyes that I wouldn't have thought capable of joy danced with happiness. Laughter shook his thick chest. The vibration of it moved down his body and into the ground.

The ground rumbled more forcefully. I stumbled, but the Mage held me upright, dangling me by my arm. Weakly, I yanked away from him, but he held tight.

So this is death.

My brother's voice sang to me sweetly. My eyes fluttered, begging to close for a final time.

The world fell apart. The sky burned a fiery red even through the dark clouds. No bits of blue shone through the angry red and gray. Cracks splintered across the ground every few yards. Fire burst upward from the cracks, and water pounded down from the sky. Any minute, lightning would strike me, or fire would engulf me, or water would fill my lungs.

My head sagged to my chest.

A glint of silver caught my attention in my peripheral vision. *Beautiful.* My lips tugged into a smile.

A metal blade swung toward me, ringing as it cut through the air. Blood sprayed on my face. It stung my eyes and filled my mouth. Through the red drops in my vision, I watched the sable-haired head as it was severed from the Mage's shoulders and tumbled to the ground.

Without the Mage to support me, my body dropped. Cool hands gripped my arm and swooped up my legs. My nose filled with the familiar, comforting sweet scent of metal. I nuzzled into a lean chest.

"Loken," I mumbled.

"I've got you," he said.

CHAPTER 37

Loken and I leaned against the fence surrounding my home cluster, on the day after the world was supposed to end. The gray-blue sky stretched above as muted orange split across the horizon. Clouds still blanketed the sky, so thick and solid like they never planned to recede.

Ra would grace the sky in just a moment, followed by Solaris. I said a quick prayer to welcome them back. It couldn't hurt.

When Ra's tip peeked above the horizon, I exhaled the breath I'd been holding. I glanced down at my comm. Instead of the countdown clock, it showed the time of day. A new day.

"You know all of this was my fault, right?" I finally voiced the thing that had nagged at me since yesterday. "If I'd just killed myself like Elder Kohler had suggested—"

Loken shifted his weight to wrap an arm around me. What remained of my home cluster fence creaked when he moved. The earth had swallowed up over half of it. The wood now jutted upward from cracks in the ground at irregular intervals. We'd have some rebuilding to do, and not just here. As far as I could see in the distance, jagged chasms marred the earth.

"If you'd killed yourself," he said, "the Seers would have foreseen a new end to the world, caused by a different person entirely. It was inevitable that someday someone would be powerful enough to attract Mages from all over. We're lucky it was you. You helped us stop it."

"And when the next super-powerful person is born, then what?"

"We probably won't know about him until the Seers foresee another end. Then we'll deal with it when the time comes."

I mulled over this as Ra emerged fully over the horizon. I sneaked a glance at Loken's profile. His strong cheekbone and metal threads had a red cast in the morning light. He graced me with a smile. Glorious tingles raced through me.

"Have you heard from Krin?" I asked.

He shook his head. "I called her a couple times. She left me a message saying she knows I'm contacting her on your behalf. So she won't answer."

I frowned and stared down at my feet. "You think she'll ever forgive me?"

"Maybe. She just misses Rey."

Rey.

He'd left another hole in my heart, right next to the one for Pace. It was a wonder I had any heart left. I blinked back tears, and angled my face away so Loken couldn't see them.

"What about you?" I asked. "You're not going to break up with me again, are you?"

He grinned. "I didn't realize we were dating."

I shoved his shoulder, letting my face break into an honest smile. He caught my wrist and pulled me toward him. I let him fold me into his arms, feeling the pleasant chill of his skin through our shirts.

His gray eyes, silvery in the new sunlight, peered into mine. "I'm not going to break up with you, Asha. You're not getting rid of me that easily."

I leaned back against the broken fence, which creaked to accept my weight. "Will you go back to work at the Council?"

Loken stared toward the horizon for a long moment. His face went somber. "The Council has a perfect memory. They're not going to forget the practitioners they lost in the Believers' attack. I'm not going to forget either. If I go back, they're going to demote me. But I haven't decided one way or the other." I opened my mouth to object, and he added, "Besides, someone has to keep an eye on Elder Kohler. I don't think he'll be a problem for us anymore though."

"Now that I'm a powerless weakling, you mean?" I smiled so brightly my cheeks hurt.

My elemental ability hadn't come back to me when Loken had killed that last Mage. And that was just fine. I missed the power thrumming through my veins, but I'd had enough pressure about saving the world—or destroying it—to last a lifetime. I was happy to leave the next crisis to the professionals.

"On the bright side, you don't have to worry about any of the elders locking you in a basement." He smirked. "But I might lock you up. Depends how much you annoy me."

"I'm never annoying." I leaned against his shoulder, loving the feel of his cool skin against my cheek.

I inclined my head in respect as Solaris made its daily appearance, turning the red world brighter. Although the wall of clouds blocked most of the light, the yellow sun's warmth penetrated through. Squinting upward, for a moment, I thought white-blue lights winked in the air. I blinked, and they were gone before I could be sure.

"So what am I supposed to do with the rest of my life?" I asked.

Loken shrugged and wrapped his hand around mine. "We have time to figure it out."

ABOUT THE AUTHOR

Alicia Wright Brewster is a mild-mannered lady of average height and above average paranormal obsession. By day, she works in an office. At night, she's an author, an electronics junkie, and a secret superhero.

In her virtually non-existent free time, she loves to read, watch movies, and eat food. She is particularly fond of the food-eating and makes a point to perform this task at least three times per day, usually more.

www.aliciawb.com